Something Old, New, Borrowed & True

Something Old, New, Borrowed & True

A NOVEL

Pamela R. Jeffers

HARVEST TIME INNER-VATIONS

ISBN: 0-61529-486-3
EAN: 978-0-615-29486-5

Harvest Time Inner-vations LLC
Somerset, New Jersey USA
Email: harvesttimeinnv@gmail.com

Printed in the United States of America

Dedication

*To the three females in my life who have shaped me,
supported me and settled me:*

*My mother, Madeline Wiggins, thank you for your
unwavering support and your continuous belief in my
writing talent.*

*My daughters, Taylor Jenee and Darcel Joi, thank you
for being my blessings and for proving the goodness
and faithfulness of God each and everyday.*

In Loving Memory

*To My Sisters in the Spirit,
whose sunset came too soon:*

*Michelle "Missy" DeFense (1960 – 1989)
Dawn Valerie Morris (1960 – 1995)*

It is beyond words, how much you are missed.

From My Heart, I Give Thanks!

First and foremost, I must give honor and glory to my Lord and Savior, Jesus Christ. Thank you for calling me to salvation and a personal relationship with you. Thank you for blessing me with the gift of expressing myself through the written word. It is a true blessing to see what you have placed in my heart brought to fruition to bless others.

Special thanks to my husband, Rick, whose love and support encourages me daily to explore and cultivate my gifts. Thank you for being my financial benefactor for this book. I know full well that if you have a dollar, I have a dollar!

Thank you to those whose prayers kept the vision of this book alive in my heart; my brother Ronald Wiggins – Thank you for your phone calls that kept me moving forward and your promise to escort me on my Book Tour, Road Trip. My mother-in-law, Ondina Jeffers who took the time to edit and critique this story – Thank you so much for your gifted input. My youngest brother, Keith Wiggins – Thank you for always being impressed with my writing by asking, "You wrote that?" My good friend, Glynnis Woolridge – Thank you for your PR expertise, for telling others of my work and for being my last set of eyes on this project. My new friend and colleague, Doreen Wells-Ellis – Thank you for trusting me with *your* writing endeavor and for relaying to me the word from our pastor, Bishop Donald Hilliard, Jr., *"That God has not forgotten..."*

Something Old, New, Borrowed True

PROLOGUE

"I Am My Beloved's..."

"*G*url, you should take a look at yourself," Valerie announced as she put the finishing touches of my makeup on. She then turned my chair around to face me toward the mirror.

"Wow, is that me?" I marveled and we both laughed.

"I look rather good, if I must say so myself."

"You can't take all the credit. I am a whiz when it comes to makeup, you know," Valerie teased. "But seriously, Tvoya, you do make a beautiful bride."

"Thanks," I said as I took my headpiece and veil from her. I was placing it on my head when my mother walked into the room at our church that's reserved for the bride and bridal party.

"Oh, baby, you look beautiful," my mother remarked as she stopped mid stream to take in the vision. The vision being me, as I had been earlier referred as by Margo.

"Thank you, Mommy, I feel beautiful."

"And you should, you deserve this day," Valerie declared.

My mother smiled gently nodding her head. She was about to get all teary eyed, and I couldn't afford any of that; not with Valerie just completing my makeup. She would kill me if she had to do it all over again.

"Mommy, are the flowers here yet?" I asked. There! That should keep her focused. We all didn't need her getting all sentimental and circumspective on us now.

"Oh, yeah, Margo just got off the phone with them. They got lost but she set them straight, so they should be here within a few minutes."

I stood up and faced the full length mirror to get a better view of myself. Was this really real? Was I getting ready to walk down the aisle to become the wife of the man of my dreams and prayers? Thank you Lord, I whispered softly. Margo then rushed in with all the flowers that were missing.

"Thank goodness we used a different florist to decorate the church. Those flowers were delivered hours ago. Can you imagine, if they were to just get here? We would just be decorating the church now while the guest are sitting there," huffed Margo as she handed each of us our respective bouquets.

"Calm down, gurl, you're gonna make Tvoya nervous," my mother remarked to Margo as she positioned her corsage on her wrist.

"Mommy, I'm fine. I've never been more calm in my life," I answered.

"Ok, it's show time y'all!" Margo yelled. "Are you ready T?"

"Yes, I'm ready."

"Oh, I wish Elizabeth could have been here to witness this," Valerie proclaimed thinly.

"She's with us in spirit," my mother answered thoughtfully. Valerie smiled.

"Well, let's get this show on the road," Margo announced.

1

" I "

The lettering or wording on the wedding invitation had not changed in all of the dozen times I had read it. So, why was I now reading it yet again?

Ms. Tooya Harrington & Dr. Byron Munroe, Jr.
together with their parents,
Dr. and Mrs. Byron Munroe, Sr.,
Ms. Yvonne Grant-Harrington
&
Mr. Thomas Harrington
request the honor of your presence to witness the marriage of ...

I stopped at that point. Enough was enough. Getting these invitations printed was a nightmare I cared not to relive. It started with Byron's mother mentioning to him since that they were contributing monetarily to the wedding, their names should be on the invitation. Then, my mother and father felt theirs should go on as well since they were my parents and I, their only child. I know even Faye added her two cents to an already costly editing fiasco. But my father didn't bother to mention that. Maybe because my mother put her foot down when he stopped by her house to ask me if Faye could attend the final fitting for my dress.

"What did you just ask our daughter?" loudly voiced my mother. "Can Faye come to Tvoya's final fitting?" Answering her own question, she didn't wait for a response from my father.

"Oh, most definitely…, she cannot." There she goes again, I thought. She's having this conversation with herself. She didn't even give me a chance to voice my opinion. Even though I did stand in agreement with her, it was still my wedding we were talking about.

"Yvonne," my father tried to reason. "Let's look at it from Faye's point of view. She is Tvoya's stepmother."

"Oh, no he didn't just go there! Oh, no he didn't!" yelled my mother.

"Mommy, please!" I pleaded with my mother to stop yelling. This wedding was starting to stress us all out. I put my hand on her shoulder as I cut my eyes to look towards my father. He caught and understood my look as he dropped his head, casting his eyes downward. My mother slowly took a seat at the kitchen table. "Ok, baby, I'm calm." She silently sipped her coffee as her eyes looked up to reach my father.

As I began to speak, I intentionally made my words deliberate but calming. We could not afford for my mother to fly off the handle each and every time my father made a suggestion, especially when the suggestion involved Faye.

"I know the both of you love me very much, and since I am your only child this wedding is very important to you. But you have to remember, this is Byron's and my wedding. We will of course consider everyone's suggestions, but you two have gotsa chill," I reasoned, and looking towards my mother to get confirmation she was hearing me, I continued,

"Mommy, you have gotsa calm down." As I turned my head to look at my father, I could hear her sigh. Still addressing my mother but squarely looking into the eyes of my father, I wanted to get a point across to him that continuously eluded his comprehension, but needed to be reiterated again.

"We can't keep having this argument each time Daddy brings Faye's name up. It is what it is; Faye is Daddy's wife and I respect that. But..." now addressing my father directly.

"But, Daddy you and Faye have to respect the fact that in the tradition of a wedding the bride's mother is the only one besides the maid of honor who gets to go to the bride's fittings. I will let Faye know what she can do to be a part of this wedding. So please wait until then, ok?"

My father only nodded his head in agreement, admitting defeat. I wanted so much for this scenario to be different. Why did my parents have to be divorced and my father remarried? Why was my mother still without a mate, someone she could love and love her in return? It just didn't seem fair. I was getting married to a wonderful man and although my mother was happy for me, it was a another reminder that she was alone and those around her were moving on. My mother wasn't territorial, she just was very vulnerable to the fact that she and I were approaching a good place and it was now being threatened, as it had been at other times in our lives. Besides, my mother was a drama queen from the old school. She never missed an opportunity to exhibit her passionate side. And these days, Mommy was passionate about nearly everything. I wondered if maybe there was something more to all this.

My mother, Yvonne Grant-Harrington was a recovering alcoholic. She had only begun her one-day at a time journey just three years prior. Her dark excursion in this world with alcohol as a deceiving guide had been a lot longer. She had been drinking since she was a teenager, undercover for the first five to ten years. Discovered, but categorically in denial for many years after until the consequences of an out of control life began to cash in on all its wagers. She found herself divorced and at odds with most of her family members. With the help of God, our pastor Rev. Underwood, Mr. Strickland, and her best friend, Margo, she was able to come back. She was reacquainted with me, her only child and given an opportunity to own her own business. Essentially, she was given back her life, but the one thing that eluded her and where restoration was never realized, was her marriage. It was a certainty she never quite got over. While most of her days were spent in a fogged out reality, my father having had enough, met his present wife, Faye, who was a significant source of this relentless reminder to my mother. For my mother realized much too late that getting my father back was not an option. It was quite apparent Faye had an incredible hold on him. And she wasn't about to let my father go.

"I hope you're hearing her, Thomas," my mother added to my little speech. I watched my father specifically for the first time and recognized he was aging. His hair, now salted although still full, was now worn more closely cropped than the afro once sported back in the day. Chiseled lines bore deep into his cheeks, making his dimples more pronounced. He did however still have it going on. I smiled at the thought as he reached for his mirrored sunglasses, kissed my cheek and let himself out of the side door of my mother's place that led to the driveway. He never said another word or even acknowledged the comment made by her.

It was getting late. Margo would be here shortly to pick me up to meet Valerie and Charlene for their final fitting. I hated leaving my mother there sipping her coffee knowing in my heart she was still stewing over my father's request. But I had to go.

"Mommy, I'll talk to you later, ok?" was all I could get out without sounding patronizing and I knew she hated that.

"Ok, baby....Uh, look, T, I'm sorry about going off like that on your father. I'm trying, baby."

She was at that...trying and trying was showing on her as well. Mommy's pecan tan complexion in comparison to my father's darker pigmentation showed stress all the more. The luminous glow of her coloring lately showed visible signs of aging thought to be brought on by her abuse of alcohol. It was hard to admit, but my parents were getting older. And my wedding was helping to accelerate this process.

"I know, Mommy, but you have to stop worrying about whether or not Faye is going to take over your position in this wedding. It's not happening....so check the worrying, ok?" I said as I leaned over her to hug her neck and give her a kiss on her cheek.

"I'll call you tonight," I said over my shoulder as I walked out the same door my father just had.

2

"Take Thee"

*P*lanning this wedding was close to becoming impossible. Thank God for Margo Underwood, my wedding consultant. She was relieving me of so many of the major responsibilities and details of planning a wedding, while keeping me abreast of its accompanying minor trivialities. She had just pulled up into the driveway as I stepped out of the house.

"Gurl, you're gonna live a long time. Your timing is perfect," I said as I opened the door to her car.

"Oh yeah? I'm a little early. I was hoping to say hi to Yvonne," answered Margo as she shifted her car into reverse.

"If you had been any earlier you could have witnessed Mommy going off on Daddy. I'm glad you weren't there; she would have used you as ammunition. You would never believe what Daddy had the nerve to ask me, in the presence of Mommy at that."

"Gurl, are you gonna tell me or keep me in suspense?" Margo laughed, responding to my lengthy pause.

"Daddy asked if Faye could come to my fitting!"
Margo almost drove off the road as she screamed in laughter.

"I could hear my girl, Yvonne going off! I thought I felt the earth shake as I was driving over. But wait...wait!" Margo was still laughing hysterically, and I knew why.

"Your gown is done. Don't tell me you and Yvonne didn't even bother to tell him that. Oh my God, you just let that poor man leave thinking his wife was being kept out of something important, when it has already been done?" Margo continued to laugh as she shook her head. "That ain't right, that ain't even right!"

We laughed almost all the way to the bridal dress shop. I was so grateful to Margo for not only being my wedding consultant, but she was also my mother's best friend. And man could she laugh. When Margo laughed you just had to laugh too. Margo was cool. Real cool.

"After we're done with your girls' fittings, I'll go by Yvonne's to check on her." Examining the void of my response, Margo continued, "T, she'll be all right."

"Did you get a chance to look over the invitations? You know they have to go in the mail by tomorrow," Margo asked altering her voice to business mode.

"Oh, I have them right here," I said as I jostled my briefcase onto my lap to retrieve them. "I'm so glad to be turning them over to you, I don't think I can give them another look."

"I know what you mean, gurl. I'm sorry I couldn't keep the editing prices down to a minimum."

"Not a problem. I understand. It was Byron's and my family creating all the fuss anyway. I'm just glad to be getting this part over with. You were right when you schooled me on how families could be when planning a wedding. I had no idea. I just wish my mother and father would chill. They're driving me nuts."

I was exhausted from all the changes the two families were putting me through concerning these invitations and the rest of the planning for that matter. Needing a break, I plopped my head back on the headrest and closed my eyes.

"Yeah, go ahead gurl and take you a power nap," said Margo as she reached over to gently pat my hand.

Margo knew my concerns and our family history. She was part of it... my mother's cutting buddy. Back in the day, Margo also had her problems with alcohol. But while my mother was taking her drinking to another level, Margo was giving her life to the Lord. Margo had been through it all with my mother. I remember when I was a child, I would watch from the doorway of my bedroom while they would be getting inebriated in the living room. They would start out laughing and talking about who said what to whom and who did whom. Then what they did or did not like and love about their men...to crying all snot nose and blubbering about how they loved each other. And then they would finally pass out with the record player needle swimming 'round and 'round at the end of the record. This was after my father had finally had enough and moved out. Aunt Lulu would come in from working nights at Uncle Ray's restaurant to find them out cold. The scene would be the same each and every time. Aunt Lulu would wake them up by cussing, fussing and throwing things. Margo would stumble down the block to sleep off the rest of her high at her cousin Peaches' house. And my mother would just curl into a fetal position and cry. I would run to Mommy and cradle her head in my lap while yelling back at my Aunt Lulu for her to stop yelling at my mother. It was definitely crazy back then.

On one Thanksgiving it looked as if things between my mother and father were getting better. Although my father was no longer living with us, he came to have Thanksgiving dinner with Mom and me. My mother was happy and she had cooked a mean dinner. Since Dad had moved out we had been having our subsequent Thanksgiving dinners upstairs at Aunt Lulu's and Uncle Ray's. But Mommy announced to everyone this particular year that just her, Thomas and I would be having dinner alone. I overheard her and Aunt Lulu talking a few days before the event that she was going to do whatever it took to get my father back. When the day finally came, the apartment was clean from top to bottom and the food cooking in the kitchen smelled real good. My father came early, and to my surprise had even kissed my mother when he entered the house. We had fun playing all of my favorite board games. Even though it appeared she had everything under control, I detected she was growing more and more tense as the day went on. After our last game, I could tell she had not kept her promise to me of not drinking on this day. I didn't want my father to notice, so I offered to help her set the table and serve the food. I was afraid he would catch on and leave early. I was not ready to have my father leave. Dinner was now served and my father said the grace. He sat to my right and my mother sat directly in front of me. He was cracking his usual corny jokes and laughing at himself, when I noticed my mother had been staring at me for a very unusual length of time. I was puzzled my father had not even noticed. I kept my head looking downward into my plate trying hard not to meet my mother's weird stare. I tried hard to concentrate on my father's stories and laugh at the appropriate cues, but the pretense was too much to uphold. It became more and arduous even for Mommy to uphold the façade. I resolved to take a gamble and looked up at her just in enough time to see her eyes glaze over and her head fall right into her plate. She was out stone cold. Happy Thanksgiving. This episode also marked the beginning of my disappearing acts, whereas my best friend, Valerie, would stow me away at her house; sometimes for days at a time. Sometimes that would be about how long it would take for someone in my family to miss me, anyway. Aunt Lulu and Uncle Ray, too busy. Daddy too absent and Mom too drunk.

My thoughts were interrupted by Margo's announcement that up ahead she could see Valerie getting out of her car. I wondered where Charlene was since she was supposed to hitch a ride with Valerie.

"Looks like Valerie's on time as usual," Margo happily acknowledged.

"Yeah, but I wonder where Charlene is," I said as I got out the car.

Margo's face frowned at the mention of Charlene's name. She didn't say a word, but I knew what she was thinking. Margo had mentioned to me more than a few times that it seemed Charlene was trying to upstage me in my own wedding. I would always dismiss her comments and defend her by saying, "Charlene is just being Charlene."

Valerie approached us. We all did the hug of love thing and entered the bridal dress shop to finalize the bridesmaids gowns.

"Where's Charlene?" Valerie inquired once we went inside.

"I thought she was traveling with you," I said as I looked around for the saleswoman we had our appointment with. Margo was already on the case as she disappeared into the back of the store. She then emerged with her assistant, Thelma and our sales person trailing in tow behind her with the bridesmaids' dresses.

"Ok, ladies, let's do this," said Margo as she took the dresses and assigned Valerie to her dressing room.

As I waited for Valerie to change, I realized I had not heard from Byron all day. I took out my cell phone from my bag and dialed his number. It went right to his voicemail indicating he probably was with a patient or in surgery. I left a message and as I disconnected the call, Charlene walked

14

into the dress shop.

"Hello, my love." Charlene's kiss airbrushed my cheek.

"Charlene, you're late," snapped Margo.

"Sorry, Boss Lady," Charlene offered as she took her dress from Thelma and went into an available dressing room. My eyes met Margo's disapproving scowl.

First to emerge from their dressing room was Valerie. Her dress was a soft baby blue that accentuated her fair complexion well. It was evident with the many times her dress had to be let out that Valerie was continuously gaining some serious weight. But she didn't seem to mind. When questioned, she would say since having Poetry she still was carrying around baby weight. No one pointed out that Poetry was going on four years old and Valerie had lost that baby fat very soon after that. Margo and I felt this was something more. But for now the topic was left alone.

"You think I look all right?" Valerie asked as she tugged at the sides of the dress looking into the mirror behind her to see the rear view. Margo was first to give her kudos. The dress was finally right for Valerie. "Gurl, you look fantastic."

"Yeah, gurl, it's perfect. Lamar is going to be chasing you up and down that aisle at the wedding," I chimed in. I had always admired the way Lamar showed his appreciation of his wife. He was never ashamed of being affectionate toward her in public, or from what I heard from Valerie herself, in private either. Lamar loved himself some Valerie. And she loved him as well. I hoped and prayed Byron and I would have that same kind of marriage. Byron was more open in his affections in public than he was in private, but maybe it was because I had made a vow of celibacy when I accepted the Lord in my life and I wasn't giving it up until after the wedding; much to Byron's disapproval. But I promised him it would be well worth the wait. A wait both of us were most assuredly struggling with. Thus, the reason for our short courtship and engagement.

Byron and I met only a year ago at a mutual friend's house warming party. I didn't have a date and felt very uncomfortable about going alone. I figured these friends were married a long time and probably didn't have many single friends, so I asked Charlene to come along. But boy was I wrong. There were several eligibles, consequently affording Charlene and me a very good time. Charlene actually was introduced to Byron first, but much to my benefit, he asked her to introduce him to the friend she was with. At first, I believe Charlene was a little taken aback by Byron's request. But she soon cooled when she witnessed the chemistry Byron and I exhibited. Besides, she had the attention of two other fine gentlemen that vied for her attention all night.

Byron and I soon became inseparable. That is whenever he wasn't making his rounds at the hospital and I wasn't teaching my fifth grade class at school. Valerie always referred to our relationship as "whirlwind" since it was rather surprising and soon that he proposed. We had just left his parents home after my meeting them for the very first time when he stopped the car in the middle of the street, got out, pulled me out of the passenger side, got down on one knee and asked me to marry him. The scene was nuts. Cars were going around us with their horns honking, some were really irate until I said yes and Byron started yelling that I said yes, then other motorists realized they were a part of our love story and started cheering us on. It was crazy. After, we drove straight to his parent's jeweler and he told me to pick out my ring. I felt all woozy and exhilarated as my 4-carat solitaire emerald cut diamond engagement ring was fitted to my size five finger on the spot. We called his parents on his cell phone to tell them the news, as we made our way first to my mother's beauty salon. It was one of her late nights but thank God the place wasn't too packed. My mother was in the back doing inventory when we arrived. Byron was the first to begin. He stood in the middle of the shop and proclaimed we had an announcement to make.

We women are very perceptive, for Linda the shampoo girl went running to the back to get my mother, screaming and yelling that her baby just got engaged. Once she appeared, Byron let the cat out of the bag and bedlam let out right there in Locks and Whatknots, my mother's shop. She was beside herself; her child was marrying a doctor.

Then we had to go to see my best friend, Valerie. Valerie was putting Poetry down for the night when Lamar answered the door. He was surprised to see me since he knew I respected their marriage and never came over unannounced. But one look at our faces and he knew this was important and that our news was happy. Reading my mind he summoned Valerie to come into the living room. When she came in, all I had to do was run my index finger under my nose and Valerie let out a scream that woke Poetry. We yelled and screamed and cried and jumped up and down, all while holding on to each other as if for dear life. Lamar and Byron thought we had lost our ever lovin' minds. Valerie then pulled me into the kitchen as I proceeded to give her the blow by blow account of Byron's proposal, leaving Byron to help Lamar put Poetry back to sleep.

♥   ♥   ♥

"Walla!" announced Charlene as she came out of her

dressing room, looking equally fantastic. Her dress was a deeper blue, similar in style to Valerie's only flowing out fuller at the calf down to the floor. It was important to me that the matron of honor's dress be different than that of the bridesmaids'. Valerie was my best friend and my matron of honor. Her allegiance to me throughout our friendship was outstanding and I wanted to point that out. If it was a problem with the others in the wedding party, the compliant never reached my ears. I probably had Margo to thank for much of that.

Charlene strutted her stuff up and down as we taunted her on. I glanced at Margo to catch her rolling her eyes.

"You go, gurl!" Valerie said, being the good sport as she joined in and the two took to emulating two models on the cat walk. Well, I thought, at least it wasn't a cat fight. Somehow, I knew Charlene must have been listening from the dressing room to all the attention Valerie was getting about her dress. Charlene never could be out done. Thank God Valerie was secure with herself and her relationship with me. She knew Charlene didn't like her very much and it was partly because Valerie was my best friend. But Valerie was wonderful about keeping the peace. What concerned me though was that in about two weeks my cousin Priscilla was due in town from California, and she unquestionably did not like Charlene and did not care who knew it, especially if it was Charlene.

"Ok, ladies, the fashion show is over. We have a fitting to finish here," Margo reminded all of us.

"Valerie, I need you to step up here so we can put on the final touches," Thelma said as she passed the measuring tape to the shop's sales person.

I was glad this portion of planning was becoming finalized. What seemed to be ending on a good note did not begin that way. I originally wanted and had picked out *real* form fitting snug dresses, until after the first try on I saw this choice did not go well with Valerie's changing shape. She played it off and said it wasn't a big deal and if I wanted her to wear the snug dress then that's what she'd wear. I knew Valerie would wear a burlap sack in my wedding if that's what I wanted. But I couldn't allow my girl to be uncomfortable on the most important day of my life. It was important for me to know she would also look her most outstanding best. I could never understand how some brides would be looking like princesses and their girlfriends in the wedding party look more like chambermaids than bridesmaids. It wasn't happening in my wedding. The search was then on to find dresses everyone could be comfortable with. Valerie's would be a little different but within the same style. Everyone was fine with this decision except Charlene, who wanted to show off her slender frame in a snug dress. Even after I explained to her why, she still could not get it. But without exposing that Valerie could possibly be having problems, Margo set her straight and that was the last I heard of it. I never did find out what was said in that conversation.

Price never seemed to be a factor, but still in all I did not want to put anyone into a financial fix just to be in my wedding. I prided myself on being a considerate bride. Valerie would tell me that was something I should not concern myself with. Her reasoning was if the women I asked to be in the wedding consented to be in it, then they should go along with anything I wanted. She and Margo would tell me often that this was my day....a once in a life time experience. I guess I was having trouble with the "my" part. I felt if people were spending money, they should have a say on how it was spent. However, I know what they were trying to get across to me...that it was ok for me to be a little selfish. Both of them had seen over the years where my parents made decisions concerning my life that I had nothing to do with and they were letting me know I should not feel in any way guilty for my happiness now. I thanked the Lord every day for Valerie and Margo.

My cell phone rang as we were leaving the dress shop. I didn't recognize the number that appeared on the screen.

"Hello?"

I could hear Valerie say to Margo, it probably was "snookums" on the line. I waved my hand to shoo them and their comments.

"Hey, baby, it's me," said the cool voice on the other end. I knew immediately it was my future husband, Byron.

"Hey…," I paused just before I said, "snookums."

"Where are you?"

"I'm just leaving the dress shop with Margo, Charlene and Valerie."

"Meet me at Pastoria in two hours."

"In two hours?" my voice held the weight of wanting to ask why the demand, but in mixed company, the timing was inappropriate.

"Yeah, I'll see you there. I love you, baby." With that the connection was broken.

Puzzled and a little miffed, I put my cell phone back in my bag and went to join the rest of the gang at Valerie's car. Charlene had already left, which surprised me none. Valerie and I embraced. Margo and I silently watched as she drove off. Margo was the first to break the quietness. "What's going on with Valerie, T?"

"I don't know, really," was all I could say.

3

"To Be Mine"

Once Margo dropped me off at my place, I raced inside, kicked off my shoes and picked up the phone to dial my mother. She assured me that she was fine. When I told her that Margo was on her way over to see about her, she complained that we were both being silly, fussing over her like this, but she would welcome seeing Margo since they have been so busy with their businesses lately, they hardly had time anymore to shoot the "willie bobo" (breeze). I told her I loved her and as I placed the phone down, I shook my head at my mother's old school slang. My mother was definitely a trip.

Now what was I going to wear to Pastoria, I fretted as I looked in my closet. I was an educator; I hardly had the wardrobe for being a doctor's wife. Note to self; I had to do something about that. I settled on a cute little black dress that would be perfect, reached for my black open toe sling back pumps and raced for the shower. I had to talk to Byron about these last minute dates, I thought as I let the pulsating jets of hot water penetrate onto my aching muscles. I hadn't realized until then how much the stress was manifesting itself in my body. Having dinner out with Byron was what I actually needed. I smiled as I came to the conclusion that he probably had been thinking about this very thing…that taking me out to dinner tonight would be exactly what I needed. Goodness, what a man! I was so blessed.

♥   ♥   ♥

"You look beautiful, baby," said Byron as he stood to his feet to greet me with a kiss on my cheek. I had been escorted to the table by Symone, my favorite Maître d', and I hadn't noticed the two other people sitting with Byron until he turned to introduce them.

"Dr. and Mrs. Flynn, let me introduce to you the love of my life, Miss Tvoya Harrington, soon to be Mrs. Byron Munroe." I looked to my right and was embarrassed that I did not see them sooner. Dr. Flynn looked as if he read my surprise. He stood, took my right hand and kissed the back of it.

"Charmed and delighted to meet you, Miss Harrington," said the smooth doctor. His wife nodded as Byron pulled out a chair for me to sit down. My eyes met Byron to clue him in to the fact that I was not happy he neglected to mention to me that we would be double dating for dinner.

"So, you two will be tying the knot in about a month or so I hear," said Mrs. Flynn.

"Uh, yes," was all that I could get out when Byron continued and completed my response with, "The knot will be tied on August 13th to be exact."

Acknowledging that the question was asked of me, Mrs. Flynn continued never placing her eyes on Byron. "Are your plans finalized, dear?"

"Yes, we're about coming down to the home stretch," I answered somehow knowing that I was going to like Mrs.

Flynn in spite of how the evening came about. She was a depiction of unpretentious elegance and style. I perceived instantly that her attire, despite its simplicity, was very expensive. I may not have much to my wardrobe, but I do know good taste when I see it. Black also was her color of choice for the evening. I was wise to have chosen it as well. I certainly could get use to being a doctor's wife.

The four of us continued with charming small talk while eating an exquisite dinner. Pastoria was one of my favorites. The ambience, décor and service were outstanding. I had come here often for dinner with other suitors, before Byron. To hear him tell it, he was the one to introduce me to this fine establishment. I did have to admit that coming here prior to Byron didn't have the same poignancy as it did for me now. Yes, Byron made all the difference. The Flynn's were a delight. I enjoyed myself much more than I initially thought I would. It did in fact alleviate my stress after all.

Before long, dinner was over. Goodbyes were exchanged. Dr. and Mrs. Flynn had just pulled off in their car and we were now waiting for the valets to return with each of ours.

"That was a rather nice time, don't you think, Byron?" I said taunting my fiancé. Byron wasn't happy with the fact that Mrs. Flynn directed her whole conversation to me all during dinner. I believed Mrs. Flynn knew that I was totally taken off guard and had no idea we would be having dinner with them. She went out of her way to make me feel comfortable. Her sacrifice told me that she was accustomed to young, overzealous doctors such as Byron being impressed with her husband's position as Director of the Department of Surgery to the degree that their ostentatious behavior would get the better of them.

"Why didn't you tell me we were having dinner with the Director of the Department of Surgery and his wife, no less?" I said as I put my key in my front door. Byron followed me home in his car and had walked me up to my porch.

"I wanted to surprise you, baby."

"Yeah, you surprised me all right. I thought that we were going to have a nice quiet dinner, just you and me….," he interrupted my speech with a sensual kiss that was tinged with a taste of alcohol. I'd noticed at dinner Byron had downed a few but I chose not to make anything of it.

"No, Byron, don't!" was all that I could get out as I gently pushed him away and took a step backwards to get some distance between us.

"Tvoya, I can't stand this waiting."

"I know. It won't be much longer. You better go, before we get out of control."

"Man, I don't know about this, Tvoya. You're driving me crazy, baby." Byron took a step closer, grabbed both of my hands and placed them behind me. He then leaned in putting his face, nose to nose with mine. I turned my head away only to have his breath hot upon my neck. He gently leaned more into me and I almost fainted as the weight of his six foot two frame bent me backwards. I closed my eyes and almost forgot about my vow of celibacy right there on the front porch of my house.

"Byron!" Coming to my senses, I stood straight up and the forcefulness of my sudden movement took him off guard as he stumbled, letting go of both my arms. He started to fall backwards down the steps as I reached out to grab his shirt. We both laughed as he said, "You put a new meaning to the phrase, I'm falling for you." I almost couldn't resist his straight pearly whites that quickly disappeared making way for a pouty puppy dog droopy eyed grin.

"Goodnight, Byron," I said, fighting the temptation by sounding testy.

"Goodnight, baby," he said, resignedly.

I watched him from behind the screen door as he walked down the stairs back to his car. He was so good looking. He had to be the finest man I had ever met. Choco, chocolate dark with a hint of raisin hue was his skin. And smooth, too. I prided myself on having smooth skin. Well, after my makeup ritual, that is. But I was jealous of Byron's flawless complexion. There weren't any blemishes in sight. And his hair - jet black and wavy. He had the good stuff. There is sure to be an earthquake happening when we get together on our wedding night. As I closed the door, I wondered what our children would look like.

Once inside, I checked my answering machine for messages. There were none. "Thank you, Lord." I raised my arms to praise Him for giving me what I needed. Peace and quiet. As I drew my bath water, I thought of Valerie. I wondered how she was really doing. Lately, whenever I would ask her she would just say that she was fine and change the subject of our conversation. Maybe I should speak to Lamar. Yes, that's what I'll do. He'll tell me how she's really doing. I'll go by there tomorrow while Valerie's at work.

Immersing myself into the warmth and comfort of my bath water brought about thoughts of Byron and me. I was getting married. I could hardly believe it. Not that I thought myself unworthy of such an honor, but when I made my pledge to be celibate, I thought that it would be a long while before I would even entertain the thought of marital bliss. Again, though, I was reminded of the trade off. I had wanted to get married at my church, Mount Holiness Christian Life Center where Margo's father, Reverend Robert Underwood was the pastor. Anyone who wanted to get married at this church had to have three months of premarital counseling. This was absolutely foreign to Byron and he was adamant that it did not take all of that for him to know that he was madly in love with me and that he was ready to make me his wife. So I gave in and agreed to get married at his church, St. Paul's Episcopal Church, where the premarital counseling class was one hour. I informed my pastor, and although disappointed, he instead agreed that I should be obedient to my future husband. Reverend Underwood prayed with me, giving Byron even though absent, and me his blessing. When I broached the situation to my family, it was all together a different scene. My first mistake was to bring up the subject in the presence of my mother's eldest sister, my Aunt Marilyn. Because she is also a member of my church, I wrongfully assumed she would have the same convictions and would extend the same mercy as Pastor Underwood had. In addition, I sought to take refuge in the console of numbers. It was Mother's Day, and all of the Grant women had just arrived back at Aunt Lulu's from having brunch to celebrate. What was I thinking? The more the merrier? Not! How iniquitously mistaken was I? Aunt Marilyn, being the first to offer her opinion, was fit to be tied.

"Are you crazy?" she asked at the same time proclaiming that I actually *was* crazy. Not permitting me time to answer she continued, "How can you not get married in your own church? And get married in an Episcopal church at that!"

Chiming in Aunt Lulu added her comment to what was already becoming a volatile conversation.

"Ain't that the church where they just let a gay man become a Bishop?"

"Yes, it is!" answered Aunt Marilyn still leaving my say out of the equation.

"Wait, now!" interjected my mother, coming to my defense. "This is Tvoya's and Byron's choice."

"It seems to me, this is just Byron's choice and not Tvoya's," answered Aunt Marilyn looking directly at me.

Oh, and now the silence comes waiting for my reply.

"Well, uh, initially I wanted to get married at Mount Holiness, but Byron didn't want to wait for the three months of premarital counseling to set the date," I said with pleading conviction that was really no conviction at all. I was out numbered. I really did want to get married at my church but with holding Byron off intimately, I did not have a choice. I felt that I had to give in to him. And then the truth comes out with Aunt Marilyn's next breath.

"You're compromising because of your pledge to stay celibate, aren't you, T?"

"Well, yes," was all I managed to say as Aunt Lulu interrupted my statement of defense, which left me wondering…how did she know about my being celibate? My mother no doubt!

"What? You and Byron haven't even…."

"Lulu, don't go there," said my mother, jumping up from the sofa. "Furthermore, Marilyn, T has spoken to Rev. Underwood about this and he already gave them his blessing. So this conversation is over."

I was thankful for my mother's defense, and after that conversation it was never brought up again. Thinking of that, I drifted off to sleep being hopeful of my imminent life as a happily married woman.

4

"To Have..."

*M*orning reached its destination, and softly I was awakened to the undeniable voice of the diva herself, Ms. Patti LaBelle, belting out her story of unrequited love, "If Only You Knew," on my clock radio. I love that song. There was a time in my life when it was my personal anthem. I would cry myself to sleep by this song only to wake the next morning hearing it again, reminding me that I would have to go through another day reliving its words. But on this day, that experience was of a distant memory. How I got through it, God only knows...but through it I got. I laid in bed until the song ended, turned the radio alarm off so I could thank the Lord for another day before my feet hit the floor. Yes, it definitely was a new day in more ways than one. I prayed for someone like Byron to come into my life. And I believed God had delivered.

"Good Morning," I cheerfully greeted Byron, wondering why last night he had not called me one more time to say good night.

"Hey, baby, what's up?" he answered groggily.

"What's up? How come you didn't call me last night? You always call me after we've gone out." I was beginning to become embarrassed by my insecurity, noticing his response took a little too long for my liking.

"I couldn't call you because I was too out done."

"You were too out done? What is that?" Impatience and incomprehension was coloring my tone.

"I mean…I was too worked up from our kiss on your doorstep. I didn't want to call you before I went off to sleep just to be reminded I was again put off." Why was he pouring on the guilt?

"Oh, I'm sorry….but I thought you could handle this….Honey, we'll be getting married very soon. You can wait just a little longer, can't you?"

"This better be worth my wait," Byron tiredly announced.

Being shocked and hurt all at the same time, I decided not to go any further with this conversation.

"I'll talk to you later, Byron." He must've heard the annoyance in my voice.

"Baby, I'm sorry. Forget I said that."

"It's ok," I said, knowing good and well it was not.

"We straight?" he asked after a long uncomfortable pause.

"We straight, bye."

I hung up and did not answer the phone when it rang again, seeing that the Caller ID showed it was Byron. How many times were we going to go through this? How many times would I have to defend my decision to be celibate until we say our I do's? How many times?

The phone rang again. Not bothering to check the Caller ID, I just picked it up.

"Byron, please!"

"Hello, Tvoya?" I thought I recognized the voice, but it couldn't be…

"Yes, this is she. Who's calling?" I asked sounding pensive and suspicious.

"Tvoya, it's Royce. How are you?" said the deep baritone on the other end.

"Royce? Royce Strickland?" It can't be. I'd hoped he could not hear the banging beat that my heart was making as I spoke.

"Yes, it's Royce Strickland. How are you, Tvoya?" Royce said.

"I'm fine, Royce. I don't mean to be rude or anything, but why are you calling me, and how did you get my number?" I definitely did not need to be hearing from him, of all people. Wait until I tell Valerie, I thought.

"I got your number from your mother. I'm sorry if you hadn't wanted me to call you. I just wanted you to know that my father just passed away."

Can you say, open mouth insert foot, I thought.

"Oh, Royce, please forgive me….I'm sorry about your father. I heard he was sick, but I didn't realize…."

Cutting me off, Royce continued, "Don't worry about it. I can understand why you would be surprised to hear from me. Thanks for your condolences regarding my father. We were all expecting it. Oh, congratulations, your mother told me you're getting married very soon. I'm happy for you, Tvoya."

Man, why did he have to sound so contrite, forgiving and good.

He continued, "I always felt you were the one that got away," Royce said softly. I couldn't answer, I was in shock.

"I just wanted you to know about my father. Is it ok if I get back to you with the details of his funeral?" Royce asked.

"Oh yes, of course I would want to pay my respects. Your father was a good man, Royce." Yes, Mr. Strickland was a very good man, I thought.

"Thanks, I'll keep in touch. Talk to you soon, Tvoya." And with that, he hung up.

Mr. John Strickland had just passed away and his son was reaching out to give me the bad news? I could've heard it through practically anyone. My mother, or anyone of our neighbors. Why did Royce Strickland feel the need to deliver this message to me, personally? That is, via telephone. I had not heard from him in years. I wondered about this all day long but didn't speak about it with anyone I came into contact with and of course, certainly not with my future husband, Byron.

Later that same morning while visiting my mother at her hair salon, the buzz was all about the death of Mr. Strickland. And understandably so. Mr. Strickland was a very important man in our community. The Strickland family moved up the street from us only two months after we had been there. And it did not take Mr. Strickland long to make friends and influence people either. Right away, he began organizing block committees, holding association meetings and bridging the gap between us African American families and the White families that existed here before we arrived. He became the newly organized Federation of Block Association's first president, and then went on to become a councilman for our district. He was very instrumental in keeping the peace among the two races. Shortly after we started moving in, racial tension and trouble began to rear its ugly head. It started out with just a few pranks from the local white teenagers. Things like mooning us little black children from their cars as we walked to school. Riding past us and calling us "niggers". Us kids found the moonings hilarious, but once it was revealed to our parents what was happening, their response was not so funny. Things soon got much worse. Crosses were burned on our lawns. Car tires were slashed. Some of our teenage boys began to fight back. I remember one of Aunt Lulu's sons, Derrick, who is older than me had a vicious fight with one of the white boys that went to his high school. Derrick put the boy in the hospital and got himself arrested. Mr. Strickland helped Uncle Ray and Aunt Lulu put up the bail money to get him out. Mr. Strickland even had his lawyer represent Derrick free of charge, and the case was subsequently thrown out. All thanks to Mr. Strickland. After that, he organized athletic programs for all of the youth in the community, which were used mainly as a coming together, peace keeping tool to keep all of us occupied. Unfortunately, some of the whites were not going to mingle with us under any circumstances, and eventually these were the families that moved. Some even moved at night. But for the ones who remained and kept an opened mind about us blacks as a people came to realize we were just as hard working, goal orientated, proud and wanted and deserved to live a better life as they did. This became Mr. Strickland's mission, and now it was his legacy.

♥   ♥   ♥

"Yvonne!" yelled Dee Watson, from her station which sat two over from mommy's. She was my mother's most trusted and longest working employee in the shop. "Why didn't you ever give John some serious thought, gurl?!"

"Please Dee, let's not go there," my mother said as she motioned to her next customer to get in her chair. I listened quietly as I sat in the unoccupied station between the two.

"Come on, Yvonne, you know if you had given him some play, you could have been Mrs. Strickland."

"Yeah, I could have been the widowed Mrs. Strickland, how nice," said my mother, not bothering to even look Dee's or my way.

"I didn't mean it that way," said Dee defending her stance against my mother's sarcasm. "I just meant he was a good man and all you had to do was say the word and you would have been in."

"Whatever, Dee," she replied, tiredly. She turned toward me, and on her face I could see the impact this loss was beginning to have on her.

Dee was right. Mr. Strickland did have a thing for my mother. And she had a profound respect for him. But, in all the reminiscing, no one mentioned the thing Royce and I had for each other. Which suited me just fine. The Strickland's lost Mrs. Strickland to a heart attack the following year after they had moved in. Aunt Lulu organized a few people on the block to bring food over to Mr. Strickland and his two sons. This act of goodwill turned into a true labor of love as the single women, and some of the married ones too, would bring food, clean and do laundry...anything to bring poor John Strickland some relief. The times when my mother would jump on the band wagon, when she wasn't drinking of course, would afford me the opportunity to spend some time at the Strickland house checking out his oldest son, Royce. Aunt Lulu would tease my mother that Mr. Strickland would perk up only when it was her turn to serve. They didn't realize Royce would do the same when I would accompany her. While nothing ever became of my mother and Mr. Strickland, Royce's and my infatuation blossomed first from puppy-love and then into a full fledge loss of both our virginities and almost our minds kind of love. Royce and I would be boyfriend and girlfriend throughout our junior high school and high school years. Until college. Royce went away and attended Hampton Institute in Virginia, and I stayed in New York and attended NYU. It wasn't for the lack of monetary funds that I stayed in New York; my father did take care of that. It had more to do with my looking after my mother. She was drinking very heavily at about that time and I was the only one who she could count on. My father had stopped coming around, and if I wanted to see him I had to go visit him. And although Aunt Lulu and Uncle Ray lived upstairs, they tried as best they could to keep their distance. Alcoholics have a way of forcing the alienation of loved ones.

Passing the test of the first year without Royce and I being together, but making the effort to be as often as we could blindsided me the second year when I found out Royce had other plans concerning our commitment to one another.

It was homecoming weekend at Royce's school and Valerie, Lamar and myself made arrangements to be there to partake in all of the wild festivities. Somewhere along the way, between the homecoming game and party hopping, Royce and I managed to lose Valerie and Lamar. We would show up at a party only to find out we had just missed them. This went on for the whole of Saturday evening. Cell phones weren't out then, and even if they were we couldn't afford them so there wasn't any keeping in touch with one another. This was done only by word of mouth until we were back at Royce's dorm in the wee hours of the morning. When we finally connected by pay phone, Valerie and I agreed to travel back together the next day by train since she attended school out on Long Island. Lamar, who had taken the semester off and had to visit his grandmother who lived in the same city as Royce's school, was scheduled to take a later train. Valerie and I synchronized our watches before hanging up, but to no avail, for she missed the train fooling up with Lamar and had to take the next one, only to run into Royce with another girl who none of us had the pleasure of meeting the whole entire weekend we were there. Once home, Valerie informed me....Royce denied that anything was going on....Lamar tried to keep the peace between us all.....but the relationship suffered and as time went on, Royce and I grew further and further apart. The distance had taken its toll. My heart was broken, and I swore off all long distance relationships, and Royce Strickland, forever. And oh yeah...and there was my situation. The situation. Our situation. Gone situation.

Anyway, throughout the years, we would run into each other, make small talk bringing one another up to date on family stuff, nothing intense. It was clear to both of us that our chapter in our individual books of life were rendered complete. Royce and I had both moved on by writing new and distinctly contrasted episodes in which the characters, intentionally, were not each other. In some respects, in my mind it felt as if our story was a fictional tale I had read once...once upon a time. Now, Royce Strickland was back in the neighborhood to bury his father. My heart ached....for his loss and mine.

Trying to lighten the mood in the shop, as well as my own, I asked my mother if she had her final fitting for her dress for the wedding.

"No baby, not yet. Margo scheduled me for early next week," she replied as she ushered her customer to the shampoo sink in the rear of the shop. I followed to continue the conversation and to help her keep her mind off of Mr. Strickland's death.

"The girls are in the final phase of their dresses. Thank God!" I offered.

"Yeah, Margo told me last night that everything's moving along great... right on schedule." Something in her tone made me aware that she was still thinking about Mr. Strickland. I wanted to mention Valerie and how I was concerned about her, but with the news of Mr. Strickland, I didn't think that the timing would be appropriate. Plus, my mother didn't need a further downer. Instead, I offered to help with whatever needed to be done in the shop. I was bored to tears. Although I was a teacher, and most are accustomed to having their summers off, I surely wasn't. I usually worked the summer program at the high school, but because of the wedding, I did not put in for the time. It was fine in the beginning with the excitement of the planning, but now that things were getting wrapped up and the time was nearing, I was finding it harder to find things to keep myself busy with. Byron had taken on additional hours at the hospital due to our impending marriage. It wasn't as if he weren't working enough already. Come to think of it, I hardly saw him as it was. But I guess that was the price the wife of a doctor paid. I wondered if there was any support groups for us.

"No, baby, we're good here. All of my operators are working today, as you can see we're tight," my mother said but then stopped as a change in thought came to her mind.

"T, you know what you can do? Get in touch with Lulu, I'm sure she has already started organizing a group to go over to help Royce and his brother with the arrangements for Mr. Strickland's funeral. Maybe she could use the help." I wondered whether my mother's suggestion was equipped with an ulterior motive.

"I know when someone is trying to get rid of me," I chided in hopes of breaking the solemn mood.

"Oh, good, then. I'll see ya later, baby." My mother leaned over her shampooed headed customer to plant a kiss on my cheek, signaling that my time with her was up. She had not even heard what I had just said. I wondered as I said my goodbyes to the rest of the crew what was going on in my mother's head and heart.

5

"...And To Hold"

eath. Hearing of someone's passing always compelled me to count my blessings. And in doing so, I wanted so much to be with Byron. I wanted to tell him how sorry I was for the argument we had earlier that morning. But after trying him on his cell phone and reaching him was unattainable, my frame of mind further descended. Instead of speaking with Lamar about Valerie, I decided to stop by her office where she worked as a law administrator, and speak to her myself. I checked the time on my phone and was happy it was nearing lunch. I'll surprise Valerie and take her to lunch, I thought. I figured I could be there in about fifteen or twenty minutes, since she didn't work too far. I pulled into the parking lot of the building owned by the law firm she worked for at about 12:15 pm. Once inside the lobby, I jetted to the open elevator doors and pushed the button marked 3. I wasn't in the mood for taking the stairs today. Although, I needed to with the wedding fast approaching. My dress was finally completed and I couldn't afford any more alterations, especially with Faye wanting so much to be a witness to this earth shattering event. Thinking of that, when the elevator doors opened to the floor, I became sorry I didn't take the stairs after all. I made my way swiftly through the double doors that would put me right in front of her desk, hoping I had not missed her, only to find out I had. But then, I noticed her light was not on and the desk neatly organized as if unoccupied for half the day. I was met by Valerie's favorite senior partner, Mr. Merrill, who was well acquainted with who I was.

"Well, hello, Ms. Harrington. It's so nice to see you again," said the friendly Mr. Merrill.

"Hello, Mr. Merrill, how are you?" I said, not really interested in small talk. I wondered where Valerie was.

"I'm fine, and you?" he replied.

"I'm well, Mr. Merrill," I answered, hoping the pleasantries were coming to an end. But in spite of that, I continued, "Um, Mr. Merrill, is Valerie in today?"

"No, Ms. Harrington, she called in, taking a personal day. Said something about a family emergency. I hope it isn't too serious. I'm a little concerned, Ms. Harrington. Valerie hasn't been herself lately," he said with such sincerity, it melted my heart. I'm worried about her too, I thought.

"You know Valerie, she's probably just playing hooky somewhere." He did not share, judging by the look on poor Mr. Merrill's face, in my attempt to make light of Valerie's absence.

"Only kidding. Um, I was just in the neighborhood and thought I would stop by to take her to lunch. I'm sure it's nothing. Take care, Mr. Merrill. It was so nice to see you again," I said, quickly turning to get a safe distance away from him before the tears that were welling up in my eyes dropped down my cheeks. As I made my way back to my car, I wondered what they knew that I didn't, about my best friend. I had to find out.

I had just pulled up in front of Valerie's house when I realized I had not even called to announce I was on my way over. Get a grip, girl. I calmly turned off the engine to the car and pulled out my cell phone to dial Valerie's number. Oh great, my call went right into their voicemail system. Frustrated, I disconnected the call as Lamar's voice regaled the formalities of the "we're not available" speech. I waited a few minutes and tried the number again. The outcome was the same. As I sat contemplating my next move, I noticed Lamar's car was not even in the driveway but instead one I didn't recognize. My concern and curiosity was getting the better of me. When I couldn't stand it anymore, I decided to take my chances and ring the bell, unannounced. Mrs. Franklin, Valerie's mother opened the door. Her warm inviting face beamed as she welcomed me in.

"Tvoya! Chile, I'm so glad it's you." Mrs. Franklin's tight hug composed my anxious spirit. I didn't want to sound disrespectful but I wanted to ask her what was she doing at Valerie's.

"Hi, Mrs. Franklin." What are you doing here, is what I wanted to say next but decided against it. "How's Valerie, and what is going on with her?" I asked as I followed her into the kitchen.

"Can I offer you anything, Tvoya?" said Mrs. Franklin. "I just put Poetry down for her nap and I was getting ready to make myself a cup of tea. Please join me."

Mrs. Franklin took two cups and some chamomile tea from the cabinet. I only nodded my head as I warily watched her move about the kitchen. She seemed so calm, so reserved. There was nothing more I could do but to wait for her to answer my question in her own time.

She sat my tea down directly in front of me. It was steaming hot. She then carefully sat hers down as she took the seat across from me.

"Tvoya," she began slowly, "Valerie is at the hospital with Elizabeth."

"What? Who's in the hospital?" I said raising my voice.

"Poetry," Mrs. Franklin said lowly as she looked towards the hall that led to the upstairs bedrooms.

"Oh, I'm sorry," I said adjusting my decibels. "What happened? Why are Valerie and Elizabeth at the hospital?"

"Elizabeth had to have emergency surgery."

"Emergency surgery? Elizabeth? On what? I mean, why?"

My mind was racing. My mouth was traveling equally as fast.

"Calm down, Tvoya. You making me nervous, girl. That's why Valerie is at the hospital and not me. I just can't take it, and I sure's don't need you working the one good nerve I got left." Mrs. Franklin grabbed my hand as she spoke. "Before you rang the doorbell, I had just been speaking with Lamar. He took them over this morning. Me and Curtis got Elizabeth up by plane last night. Then, we rented a car. You know the doctors are the best up here north?! Lamar told me the doctor said everything went very well. They're just waiting on her results."

"What did she have surgery on?" I said, feeling a lot calmer than when we began this conversation.

"Um, just in her abdomen area. I'm sure it's nothing, but I didn't want those doctors down in South Carolina looking at her. They're all a waste of time. I mean they're just pure knuckleheads. I tell you, they're just all good for nothings."

"Valerie never even mentioned any of this to me. And I just saw her yesterday evening at her dress fitting," I reasoned.

"Well, you know Valerie. She's not one to let anyone know what's really going on."

But I wasn't just anyone, is what I wanted to tell Mrs. Franklin. I was Valerie's best friend. How come she had not told me about this?

"More tea, honey?"

"Oh, no, I'm fine. Thank you, Mrs. Franklin." I jumped to

my feet in time enough to take the tea kettle out of her hand.

"Let me get that for you. You sit down, I'm sure you're tired with all the traveling you just did." I poured her some more tea and walked her back to her seat at the table.

"Oh, thank you, Tvoya. I'm not so bad. Valerie and Lamar should be here soon, anyway. Lamar said Elizabeth was in recovery and doing well, and he and Valerie will be home soon. You know, Elizabeth will be released tomorrow. If you ask me, I think that's just too soon. They cut you open one day, and then they throw you out the door the next. I just don't understand it."

I observed her trance-like state. Mrs. Franklin was no longer talking to me. Beneath her calm exterior, she was very worried for Elizabeth. And so was I. For all concerned, really.

The two of us had been sitting in total silence for a considerable amount of time, when we both were jolted by the sound of a key turning in the door. It was Valerie and Lamar. Wearily, they entered the kitchen. Lamar plopped down in the chair between Mrs. Franklin and me, while Valerie stood with her back against the sink.

"Let me get you guys some tea," I offered as I moved back to the stove to retrieve the tea kettle. Valerie's and mine eyes averted each other's attention.

"I'm a need something stronger than that," Lamar said as he reached down to untie his sneakers. Valerie made no comment.

"Well, I can't help you with that," I answered as I sat back down.

Lamar was about to stand up, when Mrs. Franklin jumped to her feet and left the kitchen to get her son-in-law what she believed he needed. I watched Lamar intently as he tilted his head back and closed his eyes. Neither one of us said a word until Mrs. Franklin returned with a bottle of Johnny Walker

Red. She firmly placed it on the table directly in front of me, then walked over to the cabinet to retrieve four glasses. She began to pour but I waited just before she began to pour into the last glass, mine, to announce, I no longer drank.

"Oh, yeah, I forgot you don't indulge anymore, honey. I'm sorry." Mrs. Franklin's apology sounded more supercilious than contrite. Even Lamar concurred with my thought. I caught him smile as he leaned over to seize his glass.

Turning to Valerie, Mrs. Franklin asked, "You going back to the hospital tonight?"

"No, after Elizabeth was moved from recovery into a room and I was able to talk to her some, she told me not to come back until morning. I'm beat anyway. Tvoya, I'm sure moms brought you up to speed on everything. I can't hang anymore. I'm gonna check on Poetry, and I am down for the count. See ya later." Valerie pulled her weight away from the sink and slowly walked out of the kitchen.

"Mrs. Franklin, what hospital is Elizabeth in?" I don't know why I hadn't thought to ask this earlier.

"She's in Southeast General. Nothin' but the best for my baby," Mrs. Franklin proudly announced.

I only smiled at what Mrs. Franklin just said. I was deep in thought as I had just decided I would go up to the hospital myself to see about Elizabeth. I couldn't understand why Valerie was being so tightlipped about this whole thing. Should I mention to Mrs. Franklin I was going? I thought better against it. But decided to chitchat with Mrs. Franklin and Lamar just a little longer.

"How is Mr. Franklin, doing?"

"Oh, Chuck is well, thank God. He loves being retired. Driving me crazy though." Mrs. Franklin laughed.

Valerie's parents had both retired from the U.S. Postal Service just last year and moved down to Mr. Franklin's hometown in South Carolina. It was evident retirement suited her well. She looked so much younger than she had before she left. Mrs. Franklin is much older than my mom. Valerie would often joke about herself being an old folks' child. Valerie was the youngest of three children. Her brother Curtis was the oldest and then her sister, Elizabeth was next, seven years Valerie's senior. We use to have big fun hanging out with her. When Elizabeth partied, she partied. And we would try to hang right along with her. It was hard to believe she was now settled, living with her husband, Gary and their son, also in South Carolina. For many reasons, and on so many levels, did I have a profound respect for Elizabeth Franklin Scott. Once upon a time, she had been my angel.

Mr. and Mrs. Franklin, upon purchasing their new home in South Carolina, blessed Valerie and Lamar with selling them the old one for only a dollar; the home we now sat drinking tea, having small talk and worrying about the outcome of Elizabeth's surgery. I smiled at Mrs. Franklin's regarded reply concerning her husband as I took out my cell phone to check the time. It was going on 3 o'clock.

"I better go, Mrs. Franklin. I'm sure you want to get some rest before Poetry wakes up," I said as I walked over to the sink to place my teacup in.

"Ok, Tvoya. I guess I'll see you tomorrow when Elizabeth is released," Mrs. Franklin said. I detected a trace of disappointment in her expression. I guess she wanted to talk some more. But all I could think of was getting to the hospital to see Elizabeth for myself.

Lamar rose as I was leaving the kitchen. His hug was unusually tight, but I knew what he was communicating to me. He was aware Valerie was leaving me in the dark about all of this. But I intended to cut to the chase. Mrs. Franklin walked me to the door, we embraced and I was on my way.

Once I was back in my car, I again dialed Byron. Still I could not reach him. Aggravated, I threw the cell phone into the passenger's seat and drove to Southeast General Hospital. Too bad Elizabeth didn't have this emergency surgery at Byron's hospital. I could have gotten the low down straight from him. Not. Who was I kidding? I couldn't even reach him. Well for Elizabeth's sake, I was thankful she wasn't at Byron's hospital. Southeast General was far better than Queens Memorial. Byron would complain all the time about the short-handed staff there.

♥   ♥   ♥

"Can you tell me what room Elizabeth Scott is in, please," I politely asked the security officer that sat at the information desk. Without so much as an acknowledgment of my presence, he typed her name into the computer.

"She is in the women's pavilion on the north side of the hospital on the 2nd floor. Room 208." Never taking his eyes off of the computer screen, he rattled off this information as if I already knew how to get to the women's pavilion on the north side of anywhere.

Trying to keep my voice even, I asked, "So, how do I get there?"

Annoyance crept upon my being on the point of his giving me directions. Nevertheless, I thanked him and proceeded to find Elizabeth. I observed the droves of visitors who populated the corridors and elevators of this massive healing institution. I passing them, them passing me rendered me to consider what each person's story could be. Some were crying as concerned companions consoled. Some looked dazed consequent to learning of a loved one's inevitable fate. And others were celebratory witnesses to a newborn child coming into the world.

Once I reached the 2nd floor, I saw the nurse's station to my right. I sized up the population that manned the station and selected the nurse who looked to me to be the least stressed.

"Hello, I'm looking for a patient on this floor...Elizabeth Scott?" I asked the least stressed nurse. My assessment was precise. She welcomed me with one of the warmest smiles I had ever encountered from a stranger.

"Oh, yes, Mrs. Scott is in room 208 B, just to the right of you, down that corridor." My head followed her pointed finger as my cell phone rang.

"You'll have to turn that off," she said in a whisper, apologetically.

"Oh, I'm sorry." Before turning it off, I took a peek to see who was calling. It was Byron. That figures. I must have said this out loud triggering the nurse to ask me what I had just said.

"Uh, oh, nothing, thank you," I said as I turned to walk away.

She answered with a genuine, "You're welcome and God bless you."

That's what I'm talking about.... someone who knows God.

"God bless you, too."

6

"In Sickness..."

$\mathcal{R}$ oom 208. Here it is. I read the names on the tags before the doorway. A – Weinberg. B – Scott. I slowly leaned in to take a peek at the first patient. She was asleep. The television was on but I could not hear the volume of it. I entered the room slowly, passing practically on tiptoe, careful not to disturb patient Weinberg. As I neared Elizabeth's section of the room, my heart began to beat rapidly. I wasn't too keen on hospitals to begin with, and now to visit Elizabeth here, I was afraid as to what I might see. Her curtain was drawn, so I had to pass her bed to see her. She too was asleep. Her television, off. I looked behind me and in the corner was an empty chair. I quietly picked it up and placed it close to Elizabeth's bed. I sat down. I looked intently at Elizabeth's face; she was pale but peaceful. She had a tube going up her nose for oxygen and two IV's; one in each of her arms. I assumed for nourishment and for the administering of pain medication. As I sat, I noticed one would beep every so often. Note to self, ask Byron about that.

I continued to sit and sit. Not really sure as to what I was waiting for or waiting to do. Maybe Elizabeth would wake up and then we could talk. But she had just had surgery.

What was I thinking? She wouldn't have the strength to talk. As I continued to have this vacillating discussion with myself, a song came into my heart and into my mind. I began to sing softly the words to "His Eye Is On The Sparrow." When I stopped singing, the silence became deafening, except for the time to time beep that came from the IV monitor. I looked down at Elizabeth to see her eyes were now opened and she ever so lightly whispered my name. She then smiled and drifted back off to sleep. What I had been waiting for had come. Some kind of sign that said she would be all right. Although I knew she would not get the results from her tests until several days, I knew whatever the prognosis....It would be well. I arose from the chair and cautiously leaned over Elizabeth and kissed her forehead. She smiled. I carefully placed the chair back in the place of which I had found it, then tiptoed back past patient Weinberg, who was still asleep.

♥   ♥   ♥

"Tvoya? Tvoya!" Nearing the exit of the lobby, I turned around to see who possessed the deep baritone voice that was yelling out my name. Oh, no! It was Royce! Royce Strickland! This was so bizarre. What was he doing here? I stopped as he ran to catch up to me.

"Oh, my goodness, Royce?!" I said with a suspicious look of surprise.

"Hey, Tvoya. It's good to see you. What are you doing here?" he asked with the same suspicious look of surprise.

"I was about to ask you the same thing."

"I'm here to settle things regarding my father. They just released his body to the funeral home."

Feeling rather stupid for thinking foul play, I could not believe I had completely forgotten about Mr. Strickland's death. I'm sure by now my mother and Aunt Lulu had sent out the search squad looking for me. I was supposed to be helping Aunt Lulu organize the food and stuff to go over to Royce and his brother, Roger.

"Royce, I'm sorry. That must have been so difficult for you to go through. How are you doing?" I said, expressing regret.

"I'm doing ok, I guess. You gotta do what you gotta do. You know? But what about you? You didn't answer my question. What are you doing here? Did you just finish visiting someone?"

"Yeah, I um, just came from visiting Valerie's sister, Elizabeth," I answered, not really sure I did the right thing by giving him Elizabeth's name.

"What? Elizabeth's here? For what?"

"She had surgery earlier today." I was giving him way too much information.

"Surgery? What for? Is she ok?" Yep, Royce was still "Fifty Questions." The nickname Lamar of all people gave him, back in the day.

"I'm not at liberty to discuss Valerie's family business, Royce. You understand?"

"Oh, right. I'm sorry, I didn't mean to pry. I'm just concerned, is all. Give her and the family my regards when you see them."

"I'll do that. Look, Royce I've gotta run. I promised to run an errand for my aunt, and I am way late." I didn't want to tell him the errand concerned him.

"Tvoya, do you really have to run off? I was hoping we could have some coffee down at the café here. I know it would do me some good, to talk to an old friend at this time." Guilt, ran all through me. How could I say no? His

48

father had just died. How could I say no?

"Well, ok. Let me step outside first and make a few phone calls," I said retrieving my cell phone from my bag.

"Good! Good. I'll be waiting right here," said Royce sounding relieved I would have coffee and a conversation with him.

Man, I could not believe I was getting ready to sit and have a conversation over coffee with Royce Strickland. It had been years since we last seen each other. I couldn't think of what we could possibly have to say to one another. Considering, the situation seemed strange. What was stranger was that I was actually looking forward to talking with him. What harm could possibly come from it? Right?

The first call I had to make was to Byron. I had listened to his message and found out he was stuck with a rotating shift for the night. How convenient, I thought. I left him a message I would talk to him tomorrow. He mentioned tomorrow he was scheduled to be off. I didn't see the point in mentioning the situation with Valerie and her sister, Elizabeth, so I didn't. What could he do to help while working anyway? Nothing. However, I did need him. I wanted him to hold me. I wanted to cry in his arms. I wanted to tell him how much I felt for Elizabeth. I wanted him. Instead, I was getting ready to have coffee with the man who jilted me many years ago. And I wasn't even sure I had forgiven him. No, I told myself I would not go there. It wasn't right. Royce just lost his father. And my best friend's sister was in this hospital waiting to find out what was wrong with her. No, I was determined not to go there.

My next call was to my mother. She answered her cell phone on the first ring.

"Where have you been, Tvoya. Did you get any of my messages?" she inquired, annoyed I was just returning her call.

"Mommy, I'm sorry. I've been here at Southeast General...." I was cut off before I could explain what I was doing here.

"You're where? Are you all right? What happened?"

"Mommy! Calm down. Yes, I'm all right. I'm not here because of me. It's Valerie's sister, Elizabeth."

"Elizabeth?" she asked, cautiously.

"She had to have emergency surgery this morning. Mrs. Franklin and Curtis brought her up all the way from South Carolina."

"Oh, my goodness. How is she doing? Is she going to be all right?"

"Well, she's sleeping peacefully. They won't have the prognosis for a couple of days yet."

"My goodness. I hope everything will be ok."

"I'm sure it will be."

"So when will you be coming here to give me and Lulu a hand?" she said, switching gears rather quickly and sounding much like she needed a break. Aunt Lulu can be a tough taskmaster when it comes to organizing and cooking.

"Well, um....."

"Well, um what? You know Mr. Strickland passed and we have to make food for his boys and the family that will be arriving from out of town starting tomorrow."

"I know, Mommy, I know. But.....," she wouldn't let me finish.

"But, what T?" The exasperation in her voice proved she had had about enough of Aunt Lulu's bossing and she needed me there to run interference.

"Mommy can you just let me talk for two seconds? I met Royce as I was leaving the hospital and he asked me to have coffee with him." I spoke fast to insure she wouldn't interrupt again.

"Oh?" Her tone was definitely of a dubious nature.

Ignoring it, I continued.

"Mommy, I can't leave him like this. He just released his father's body to the funeral home. He needs someone to talk to," I said, not sure if it was her or me I was trying to convince.

"All right, baby. I understand. You take as long as you need. By the way, have you talked to Byron today?" Oh, she was good. But who did she think she was talking to? I chose to ignore the valid concern in her voice.

"I'll see you later, Mommy." And on that note I disconnected the call.

♥   ♥   ♥

"So what's your pleasure, Madam? This special café has only two choices of coffee, regular and black." I could not fathom that Royce was trying to make jokes at a time like this. Trying to play along, I answered, "Does that include decaf? I'll be up all night if I had anything other."

"I'll check."

"Make that regular," I smiled as I sat down at the table we had chosen.

"Regular decaf it is, for the lovely lady." Now why did he have to go and blow it by saying that?

I tried hard not to watch him as he served the coffee from the self service station just across from our table. But against my better judgment I watched him unwavering. Yep, he was still very good looking. He had a strong muscular build that would make any woman feel protected in his presence. I was amazed he still had his tiny waist. When we were in high school, Royce was a star athlete, a football jock. He was always one to keep himself in shape. It was very apparent he

51

still worked out vigorously since muscles were bulging all over. I was surprised his once blown out afro was totally gone. Royce now sported a Mr. Clean baldhead. I hated to admit it but it went well with his fine lined mustache and connecting goatee. My eyes and mind traveled down his whole physique and how he filled those jeans he was wearing. My mind screamed, now that's enough! Tvoya!

I couldn't let him catch me checking him out so I pretended I was looking for something in my bag as he approached the table.

"Here you go," he said as he passed me my coffee.

"Thank you," I answered as I closed my bag. "Royce, again, please know how sorry I am about your father."

"It's ok. But thanks, tho' I'm just glad it's over. He's in a better place, now."

I didn't know what to say. I just nodded in agreement.

"I know it's strange and awkward for us to be sitting here having coffee. But Tvoya, I appreciate your being here. I just needed to take a break. I thank God I ran into you." Ran into? It felt more like I had just been ambushed.

After a long silence, Royce again spoke. I felt so silly, not having anything to say.

"So when are you getting married?"

"Next month."

"Wow, that is soon. Your mother mentioned it was soon, but I didn't know how soon." Soon for who, I wondered.

"Yeah, well things are just getting wrapped up." It just dawned on me I hadn't thought about the wedding all day. Nor had I anything to eat all day for that matter.

"Who's the lucky guy?"

"His name is Byron Munroe. He's a doctor. A surgeon in fact." Why was I gloating, trying to impress Royce? Because it was true what he said earlier. I was the one that got away and I wanted him to feel it.

"I see you picked well for yourself." Ignoring his remark, I stood to my feet and confessed I was famished and was going to get something to eat.

"Can I get you anything?" Taking him by surprised he only answered, "Um, no."

"Suit yourself. I'll be right back."

This time it was Royce that had to do the scoping. I could feel his eyes follow me as I helped myself to the salad bar. I knew I had it going on and he was going to pay. It so happened I had on a slamming summer outfit that accentuated my well-toned aerobic, stair climbing, Pilate's, work it girl, body. Immediately following that thought, I began to feel a deep sense of remorse. How cold can you be, Tvoya? This man just lost his father and in a few days will be saying his final goodbyes and burying him. And all I could think about was making him jealous. Man, I needed to get a grip. For sure.

Back at the table, my tone and mood had changed towards Royce.

"How is Roger holding up? I hope as well as you," I said feeling more empathetic.

"Roger is handling his own. He and his family will be here late tonight. And Tvoya, I may look like I'm doing ok, but really, I'm not sure how I'm doing. I'm just going through the motions because there's so much to do, but it really hasn't sunk in yet," Royce said, never looking up from his container of coffee.

"I guess it'll take some time. Do yourself a favor and don't expect too much from yourself. Let God carry you," I said offering some comfort. Royce smiled at my comment.

"Thank you. That's good advice. Up until now, I was feeling sorry for myself and envying my brother that he had a family to share this with. But now I can finally get off that tip and thank God for having a friend in you, Tvoya."

A friend in me? What was he thinking? We hardly knew each other anymore. This was a huge responsibility for me to be considered Royce's friend.

"Surely you have a significant other you can lean on. A fiancée, a girlfriend, an ex-wife?" There. I said it. I had heard that over the years, Royce did get married. In fact, he married the girl Valerie saw him with all those years ago, he denied was even his girlfriend. Back then, he and Lamar kept in touch and Valerie solicited and circulated this information through the grapevine. But it was grapevine reported Royce's marriage soon became a living hell when his wife became controlling and territorial, ousting Lamar and even Royce's own family from his life. Oh, well…so sorry!

"No. There's no significant other. I've been divorced for a few years now," Royce said, "was doing some dating. But it was getting me nowhere. I decided to just throw myself into my work and business. It's paid off, but it can't comfort me during this time."

"I've heard your computer software business has been very profitable," I said, deciding now was not the time to pick him for information concerning his love life.

"Yeah, it's doing well. So well in fact I will be opening up a location here."

"That's nice." What I really wanted to say was…you should be just here to bury your father and then go on your merry way back over to the West Coast.

"After things are settled with Dad's estate, I mean," Royce said as if to imply that carrying on business as usual so soon after his father's death would be unthinkable.

"Oh, of course."

"Hey, answer this year's billion dollar question."

I looked up from my coffee wondering why Royce would make such an out of the blue statement.

He continued, "Where were you when the first African

54

American President was sworn in?"

I smiled. "Where were you?"

"No, I asked you first."

"Ok, I was in my school's auditorium watching the inauguration with the faculty and whole student body."

"You're a teacher?"

"Yes. Why do you sound so surprised?"

"Oh, I'm not surprised. Not surprised at all. Wow, that must have been something...to share that moment in history with children."

"Yeah, it was. This generation is so fortunate to see a Black man take the highest office in the free world."

"I'm sorry my dad wasn't able to attend the inauguration with me. He was too sick to travel."

"You were there?!"

"Yeah, me and a few of my boys took the trek all the way from the West Coast. It was awesome."

"I know it was. But, I'm sorry too your dad couldn't attend. He always believed this day would come."

"Yeah, all of his fighting for our rights over the years was for this very moment....to see a man of color, who was born with his natural African name, Barack Obama become President of these United States," Royce declared with a crack in his voice and a tear in his eye.

♥   ♥   ♥

By the time I arrived at my mother's and Aunt Lulu's they were finishing up their share of the cooking. Aunt Lulu was the first to acknowledge my arrival with a cynical and unwarranted wisecrack. "Oh, look what the cat dragged in."

"Now, Lulu, I had enough out of you for one day," my mother said, coming to my defense. "Mess with me. That's one thing. Mess with Tvoya and you're looking for a fight."

"Mommy, it's ok. I can speak for myself. Looks like you did everything," I said, looking around the kitchen.

"No. Not everything. You have cleanup detail, young lady," Aunt Lulu announced handing me the apron she just untied and took from around her waist. I could never understand how my aunt as small as she was could be the biggest tyrant in the family. My mother and I both towered over her, by a head. We could definitely take her, any time any place. That thought made me chuckle but I managed to conceal it well.

"No problem, I'll clean up. Why don't you guys take a load off?" I said, as I started filling the dishwasher. Aunt Lulu left to go upstairs to her place, leaving my mother and me to talk about the day's events.

"So, tell me again. What's going on with Elizabeth?" said my mother, as she sat down and placed her feet in the chair that sat across from her.

"Mrs. Franklin said that a few weeks ago when she came home she was complaining of bad stomach pains. Gary called the doctor, who told him to bring her in. But Mommy, Valerie hasn't mentioned anything about it to me."

"Didn't you guys meet for the bridal party's final fitting last night?"

"Yeah, we did. Valerie was there but she didn't say a word about this. But she's been gaining a whole lot of weight, like something's been bothering her."

"Well, what has she said about that?"

"Not much. She would just blow me off. Even Margo asked me if everything was all right with her."

"You know, ole' Margo, she don't miss a trick," she smiled shaking her head, continuing, "how did Elizabeth look when you went to see her?"

"She looked pale, but peaceful. She didn't look like she was experiencing any pain. She had an IV taking care of that."

"Baby, I'm sure Elizabeth will be fine," my mother said bending over to rub one of her feet.

"Yeah, I'm sure she will be. She'll be released tomorrow. I plan to go back over to Valerie's then. I hope I'll get a chance to speak with Elizabeth myself, since Valerie is being so tight lipped about this. I was there talking to Mrs. Franklin when Valerie and Lamar got back from the hospital. And do you know Valerie barely said a word to me?" I said as I loaded the last dish into the dishwasher.

"Tvoya, don't read into this anymore than you need to. I'm sure that when they know what's up, they'll tell you. And how is Royce?" she asked, hardly taking a breath to indicate her conversation would be switching gears. On the other hand, I knew this was coming.

"He's holding his own since Mr. Strickland's passing. If that's what you're getting at," I said with a measure of sarcasm.

"That's not what I'm getting at. I'll tell you just what I'm getting at. What on earth were you thinking, having coffee and…." I had to stop her right there.

"Mommy! Don't think I'm even interested in Royce Strickland. It was just two old friends talking and having coffee. Nothing more. Nothing less. Don't read any more into it. Understand?" I put my hand out to emphasize my point to her. I didn't mean to be rude. But I wanted my mother to be clear. I had no interest in Royce. Especially, since not one time in our conversation did Royce mention the letters I sent him after our breakup informing him I was pregnant. No, I had no interest in Royce Strickland. None whatsoever!

7

"...And In Health"

he next morning, as I was exiting the shower, I thought I heard a creaking sound coming from the living room. My condo wasn't that large, so no matter where you were in the place you could hear what was going on in any of the other rooms. I hurriedly turned the water off and stood quietly as the water dripped down my naked body. I was ashamed I was too afraid to even reach for a towel when I heard him call out my name.

"Tvoya, it's me, Byron." I exhaled deeply. I could have killed him. I cracked the door slightly just enough to peek my head through. "Byron, what on earth are you doing here?"

"What a way to welcome your man," he said trying to sound disappointed. "I was in the neighborhood and decided to drop by. I do have a key, you know. A key that you gave me, remember?"

"I remember. Give me a sec," I said as I dried. Thank God my bathrobe was hanging on the back of the door. I quickly put it on and came out to see Byron looking like he had been in a train wreck.

"Are you just coming from the hospital?" I remarked at his appearance as I toweled dried my hair. He had already made himself comfortable on my chaise lounge waiting for me to emerge from the bathroom.

"Come to Papa," Byron teased as he extended his arms lengthwise expecting me to run into them. Instead I gave him a quick peck on the lips then swiftly scooted past him and disappeared into my bedroom. Closing and locking the door behind me.

"Oh, that's cold, Tvoya. I just worked all night long and came straight over to see you, since we didn't get to speak to each other real time all day yesterday, and that's how you do me?"

"Yep!" I yelled through the closed door.

"All right, I'll remember that," Byron said sighing defeat.

I found a lightweight sweat outfit, I could quickly put on and after I dressed and was feeling much more in control I came out.

"Want some breakfast? If I knew you were coming I could have had something already prepared."

"Now, I have to make an appointment in advance to see you?" Byron complained.

Just then the doorbell rang. "You expecting company, or am I not the only one who drops by unannounced." Ignoring Byron's petty remark, I answered the door. It was Charlene.

"Hey, gurl! You missed big fun last night," Charlene said as she just brushed right past me entering the foyer of my condo. By this time, Byron had abandoned his lounge position and was now sitting on the love seat that sat adjacent to the foyer. This way he had a direct view of who was at my door. Charlene saw him and immediately stopped in her tracks.

"Oh my bad. I didn't know Fiancé would be here and this early too. What happened to that no touchy no feely arrangement you guys had? Couldn't wait for the wedding huh?"

"And a good morning to you too, Charlene," Byron retorted.

Paying Charlene no never mind. I invited her to stick around and have breakfast with Byron and me, much to Byron's displeasure. Having Charlene here in my opinion was best for the both of us.

"I can see that three's a crowd around here. And I know you two aren't into Manage a Trois'. So I'll just take one of these croissants, and I'm out," Charlene said as she walked into the kitchen to help herself to the breakfast goodies, I took from my mother's the night before.

Byron went back to the chaise lounge and closed his eyes. But like Papa D, my maternal grandfather used to say, 'all closed eyes aren't sleeping', so I knew Byron didn't want to partake in our conversation. Maybe I did the wrong thing by inviting Charlene to stay and have breakfast. Well, it was a good thing she wasn't staying after all. Although her presence kept Byron at bay, I did want and need to talk to him about yesterday's events.

"I'll get with you later, girlfriend, and you can tell me all about your crazy night," I said to Charlene while walking her to the door.

I resolved it would be better for her to tell me about what went on with her last night than for me to share what was going on with Valerie's sister, Elizabeth. Charlene and my relationship didn't go that deep. Which was why my mother questioned my reasoning for having her in my wedding in the first place; because Charlene would have a fit if she weren't. There are just some friendships one has to appease just to keep the peace.

"Bye, Fiancé!" Charlene yelled over her shoulder. No return reply from Byron was heard. I shrugged my shoulders and gave Charlene a weak smirk. She laughed out loud and then was gone.

I closed the door, took a deep breath and returned to the kitchen to cook my "Fiancé", his breakfast. I prepared in total silence. Byron made no sound either. Maybe he was mad at me for inviting Charlene to stay for breakfast. Or maybe he really was asleep. He did pull an all nighter, I reasoned.

When breakfast was done, I tiptoed lightly into the living room and stood quietly next to where he lay. He was in such a deep sleep, I hated to wake him. It was apparent he needed sleep over food. I went back into the kitchen, made myself a cup of coffee, ate a croissant and cleaned up. I wrote a note for Byron informing him I would be at Valerie's, my original plan for the morning. I left instructions as to where he could find his food, changed my clothes and was on my way. After I had driven off, it dawned on me that I hadn't given Byron a goodbye kiss. Didn't want to wake him, I suppose.

♥   ♥   ♥

As I neared Valerie's house I could see Lamar's car was parked in front. Great, they were all home. Earlier, I had spoken with Mrs. Franklin to find out how early Elizabeth would be released from the hospital. She told me Valerie and Lamar were already at the hospital, and Elizabeth would be released once her doctor had seen her. I promised I would be there as soon as I was able. When I arrived, Mrs. Franklin answered the door rather quickly and gave me a warm hug as I stepped into the house. Poetry was underfoot.

"How is Elizabeth doing today?" I asked Mrs. Franklin as I scooped Poetry up in my arms, prompting her delightful squeal.

"As well as can be expected, I guess. She's feeling a little discomfort. But you know Elizabeth, she's a trooper," Mrs. Franklin said as I followed her into the living room still carrying Poetry.

"Is Elizabeth sleeping? Can I see her? Where's Valerie?" I anxiously asked all at once as I gently lowered Poetry to her feet, who continued to cling to my pant leg, calling, "Auntie T, Auntie T," over and over.

"Valerie is getting her settled upstairs in the bed. Let me go up and let them know that you're here." I smiled weakly, watching as she left the room.

Poetry again got my attention, and I took to playing with her until I was summoned to come upstairs. I took her by her little hand, whispered to her to keep her voice low, and we proceeded to join the others in one of Valerie's spare bedrooms. I was surprised it was Elizabeth's voice I heard upon entering the room.

"What took you so long, Freshmeat?" she said as I cautiously walked towards her bed.

"Oh, Elizabeth!" Mrs. Franklin shook her head as she took Poetry's other hand and led her out.

Mrs. Franklin never did like the nickname Elizabeth chose for me, back in the day, when I use to hang out and hide out at their house to escape my mother's drinking escapades. Elizabeth would tease me with that name because she said I was so naïve and pitiful. Of course, she was just a teenager then, but after we grew up she apologized for calling me that. However, the name stuck. But I knew that her using it now was a term of endearment.

"You can come closer and hug my neck, you know, girl," Elizabeth said, motioning me by waving her hand. Just then Valerie came out of the bathroom that was hidden from view behind an armoire chest. "Hey, Tvoya, How ya doin'? I didn't know you were coming by."

I was surprised and a little peeved by her casual greeting.

Especially since she had been so secret agent about this whole thing. However, in spite of that, I was truly happy to hear my best friend was in better spirits. I understood she was very worried about her sister. Valerie had a way of being overprotective with the people in her life. And I suppose I was ok with that. I stopped to give her a hug as I made my way over to Elizabeth.

"How are you doing, Elizabeth?" My toned turned the atmosphere in the room to a more serious note.

"I'm all right, girl. I know you came to the hospital." I was shocked she knew I had come. Although she chose to stay quiet, witnessing by Valerie's expression, so was she.

"You really remember me being there?"

"Yeah, of course. Somehow I knew you would be."

"Well, you would do the same for me. I was really worried. Well?"

"Well, what?" Valerie interjected.

"Well, what?! What's the deal? What's going on?" I was getting frustrated with Valerie's evasiveness. Plus, I was speaking to Elizabeth.

"Hey, you two," Elizabeth called out, putting the kibosh on our implied feud.

"The doctors say they think it's ovarian cancer. But we are all waiting on the test results." I stared at Elizabeth in disbelief. I wasn't sure if it was because of what she had just said or the way in which she said it. So matter of fact.

I could hardly get the words out. "Ovarian cancer?"

"Yep, that's what they said." I still could not believe what I has hearing. And how could Valerie be so cavalier about the whole thing? Seeing my expression revealed to Valerie and Elizabeth all of what I was conceiving mentally.

"Tvoya, now don't you start worrying. I'm gonna be ok, besides the results haven't even come back yet. So please stop looking like someone just died." When Elizabeth mentioned that word, I instantaneously remembered why I was so anxious to see Valerie, yesterday.

"Well, since you mentioned someone dying…"

"What? Who died?" they both said in unison.

"Mr. Strickland. Royce's father passed away yesterday. And you'll never believe how I found out."

"Well, come on, girl. You gonna tell us or not. How?" Valerie asked.

"Royce, called me himself."

"You have gotsa be jokin'. Royce Strickland called you himself? You lying, girl! I mean really, I go in the hospital overnight and all of this goes down."

Cutting Elizabeth off, I interjected. "And that's only the half of it."

"Well tell us then," Valerie eagerly said. Elizabeth struggled to sit up straight so she could also get the 411. She cracked me up as she attentively listened all wide-eyed to my intense account of the events that took place within the last 24 hours. When I was done, she threw her head back on her pillow as if my whirlwind story left her exhausted.

"Hell!" she said, "if what I got is cancer, you know that I'm beating this thing just to find out how all this mess is gonna turn out." We all laughed. Like my Papa D would say, Elizabeth was a pip. A pip who needed to get her rest. I looked at Valerie, and she too needed to get some rest.

I promised them I'd stick around awhile and help their mother with the chores as long as they both promised they would get some rest. Elizabeth agreed. Valerie only suggested I go ahead downstairs to join her mother and Poetry, and that she will join us in a few. As I was coming down the stairs to find Mrs. Franklin, I could hear a familiar deep baritone voice coming from out in front of the house. No, it couldn't be. Or could it? I stood back from the entrance of the door so no one standing out front could see me, but I could get a good look at them. And it was so. Royce was standing out front talking with Lamar. I could not believe it! What was going on? Was Royce stalking me, or what? This was just too coincidental. But I knew better. A coincidence was God's way of remaining anonymous. Right? Ok, then, God, what are you up to? Wondering, I went into the kitchen expecting to find Mrs. Franklin. Instead, I encountered Valerie's older brother Curtis, eating.

"Hey, if it isn't T-bone," he said getting up to greet me with his mouth full of food.

"Hey, Curtis, how you doing?" I answered feeling genuinely happy to see him, despite his recollection of the nickname he had given me when I was a kid.

"You got some meat on that bone now, huh, T?" Curtis' version of my nickname was a spin off from Elizabeth's "Freshmeat." I only smiled and let him have his fun.

"Hey, congrats! Valerie tells me that you're getting married. You know, I always thought that you and I would one day be Mr. and Mrs." Was Curtis not only simple, but crazy too?

"Well, you know, Curt, you never did let me catch you," I said playing along. He waved me off as he sat back down to his meal. "Yeah, you know I was just too much for you, that's all, T-bone."

"Y'all, just need to stop," Mrs. Franklin said as she entered the kitchen, "is Elizabeth asleep and where's Valerie?"

"Yes, Ma'am, Elizabeth's resting. I told Valerie she should get some too, but she said she'll be down shortly. We were all talking so much, I think it was tiring Elizabeth out. So, I came down here looking for you. What can I do around here?" I said hoping I could make myself useful, especially with Royce being out front. I really didn't want to leave just yet.

"Sure, you can help me make some meals that Valerie can freeze so she doesn't have to cook while Elizabeth's here. You know she'll probably be spending a lot of time tending to Elizabeth. Curtis and I will be going back home in a few days, " offered Mrs. Franklin.

"Ok, then. Where do we start?" I said ready to jump right on in.

"We can start by going grocery shopping. Valerie doesn't have a thing in this here fridge," Mrs. Franklin replied as she surveyed the refrigerator.

My inner voice screamed within. Oh, no! I had to go outside and face Royce? Outwardly, I calmly smiled and nodded my head. Inwardly, my stomach was churning. I waited in total silence as Mrs. Franklin made the shopping list. I told her not to worry about the cost, I would take care of it. We went back and forth about it, but I finally wore her down and she rescinded leaving me to have my way. Now that that took all of about five minutes; the stall was no longer pragmatic. I had to go outside and face Royce. Why was my heart pounding so? I announced to Mrs. Franklin and Curtis I was on my way and bolted through the door like a racehorse out of the starting gate.

I rushed down the steps, whisked past Royce and Lamar nodding only a slight acknowledgement of them. Reaching my car seemed like a death-defying feat. But once inside, refuge was attained. Turning the ignition emanated the blaring sounds of music from the radio. My peripheral vision caught the sight of Royce approaching the car. His mouth was moving, but thanks to my arsenal of sound, I couldn't hear a thing from the outside world. I stepped on the gas and away I went. Looking through my rear view mirror prompted my prayer that the Lord would fix it so he wouldn't be there when I returned.

♥   ♥   ♥

What a difference a shopping trip made. Even though it was food I had been shopping for, it proved to be therapeutic, nonetheless. My mind and spirit was finding its peace as I conversed with the Lord while on the drive back to Valerie's house. I had to believe things with Elizabeth would be ok. I had to have faith that whatever the diagnosis would be when the test results came back it would be all right and the Lord would see Elizabeth through it. I had to believe Royce's appearances had no impact one way or the other on me and this situation. He was a part of my past. And all of those memories had to stay in their proper place... in the past. It was what is was, and nothing about it could be changed anyway so there was no need for stressing. I repeated this conclusion as if it was a mantra until I turned onto Valerie's street and up ahead I could see Lamar, Royce and now, oh my God... Byron standing in front of the house. Maybe I could just ride past and they wouldn't see me, I thought. But what about Mrs. Franklin's food? Tvoya! My mind screamed out, jarring me back to reality and the proof that I was reacting like a mad lunatic. Snap out of it! If I weren't driving, I would have smacked my own self. I was tap dancing on my own nerves and the dance was definitely getting old. Come on, girl, get a grip. I pulled up and parked my car right behind where Byron had parked. Being the first to see me, Byron walked over to open my car door.

"Hey, beautiful," he said as he gave me his hand as if he was a coachman helping Cinderella out of the horse drawn carriage. I knew, from this display of chivalry, Byron was full aware of whom he and Lamar were talking to; my ex-boyfriend, Royce Strickland. Byron was in bondage to the male ego and the spirit of competition. What he did next both surprised and infuriated me all the more. Byron planted such a sensual lingering kiss on me that anyone who did not know I was celibate would not believe that I was. Still, I played along. What was this control Royce had? First on me, and now on Byron. It was ridiculous that the both of us were performing for an audience of one, Royce, and for what? As Byron and I walked toward Lamar and Royce, I read the look on Lamar's face and it told it all. He was asking the same question.

"I see that you've met my fiancé, Byron," I said directing my attention deliberately towards Royce. I might as well get the confrontation over with.

"Yeah, you could say that Byron and I were kickin' it a bit," Royce offered. "Got any more bags that needs lifting?" he added acknowledging the bag Byron now held.

"No, man, I got it covered," Byron interjected as he walked past Lamar and Royce. Picking up his cue, I followed behind.

"You sure you got it, man? I mean after all, they are my groceries!" Lamar yelled from behind the hood of his car.

"No, you keep working on your machine, man. I got this!" Byron yelled over his shoulder.

I held the side door to Valerie's house open for him to enter. Once we were inside and seeing there was no sign of Mrs. Franklin, Curtis or Valerie, I asked Byron, "What are you doing here?"

"What, I can't come and see about my baby?"

"You pulled a double yesterday. You looked awful this morning. And when I left, you were out cold. From where did you get the sudden burst of refreshed energy?" Ignoring my inquisition, Byron, sounding like he was being left out of some major secret, quipped, "So, when were you going to tell me about your ex being back in town?"

"It's no big deal. I probably would've mentioned it to you

today, but discussing him now isn't a good idea," I reasoned, hoping Byron would understand. I did not want to make it an issue, especially not in Valerie's home. Not with what Elizabeth has been going through. I had too much respect for her than that.

"So, I assume you got the low down on Valerie's sister from Lamar," I continued.

"Well, that's what Lamar and what's-his-name was talking about when I rolled up."

"His name is Royce. Byron, please don't make this something that it's not," I pleaded.

"Something that's its not? That's an understatement, Tvoya. Here's this man, back in town for who knows what for, who knows you in ways I haven't been able to experience," Byron pointed out.

"So that's what this is about?" I said with teeth clinched to keep from raising my voice. "Byron, that is ridiculous." Cutting me off, Byron interrupted, by raising his voice, "Ridiculous? So, I'm ridiculous, now."

"Byron, please keep your voice down. Valerie's sister is upstairs resting and Lord only knows where the rest of the family is. Royce is back in town to bury his father. He just died yesterday." I paused for effect so Byron could let what I had just said sink in. "Byron, let's just continue this conversation later, ok?"

Turning my back, I began putting the groceries away. It was enough I had been trippin' all on my own, I sure didn't need this from Byron.

I moved about the kitchen, quietly, finding a place for each of the items Mrs. Franklin had sent me for. I could feel the nearness of Byron although his silence was irritably uncomfortable.

"Look, baby, let's just drop this. I only came by because when I awoke, I was missing you," said Byron, being the first to break the silence. I knew this was his way of saying he was sorry.

"Byron, I've been missing you, too, but I need to be here helping out Valerie and her family for now. Why don't you go back to my place and get some more rest? I'll meet up with you later," I said as I put my arms around his neck. He put his arms around my waist and pulled me closer towards him. To my surprise, he only gave me a light peck on my nose.

"Ok, you win. I think I'll go on home to my place, shower and crash. I'll call you on your cell when I wake up," said Byron as he walked toward the door. I only smiled as I watched him leave. I wondered if Royce was still out front with Lamar and what Byron would say to him now.

8

"Till Death Us Do Part"

"Mommy, are you ready?" I yelled as I entered my mother's house. As a rule, I wouldn't use my key if I knew she was home, but earlier she instructed me to do so when I came to pick her up for Mr. Strickland's funeral.

"I'm in here, T!" she yelled back from her bedroom. "Just finishing up my hair before I put on my hat."

Hat? I haven't seen my mother in a hat in years. I had to see what get up she had gotten into. I kicked off my shoes and placed them neatly besides her slippers that sat outside of her bedroom door. She never entered her bedroom with anything on her feet. She either carried her shoes with her into her bedroom or she would just leave them outside in the hall. I remembered that aside from her drinking this was another thing that drove my father crazy. Mom and her idiosyncrasies.

"Mommy, what hat are you…," I stopped mid sentence as I walked into my mother's bedroom and took in the sight. She was all dressed in black. Head to toe. And the hat. The hat was big and black and had a veil to boot. My mother looked like the Black Widow herself.

"Mommy, where are you going looking like that?" Just as I said it the doorbell rang. "I'll get it," I offered just so I could get out of that room before I fainted either from the shock or laughter. Opening the door, changed my disposition immediately.

"Margo!" I was so happy to see her. Maybe she could talk my mother into changing into something a little less dramatic.

"Hey, T. How you doing? You guys ready?" By Margo's joyous tone and look you would not believe she was going to a funeral.

"I don't know if Mommy is ready, just yet," I said gingerly. I wasn't exactly sure how I should prepare Margo for what my mother was wearing.

"What? Yvonne!" Margo called out to her. "You're not ready?"

"Who said I'm not ready?" my mother answered back as she entered the living room.

I looked at Margo and my eyes read, help! Margo gave out a holler and fell on the couch laughing. My mother put both hands on her ample hips and demanded to know what was so funny.

"You, girl. Where are you going dressed like that?" Margo managed to say as she fought to calm herself down.

"I'm going to John's funeral," my mother said without apology or regret for her outlandish ensemble.

"Yvonne, seriously, now don't you think that what you're wearing is just a little bit too much?" Margo was calm now and desperately trying to reason with her best friend.

"No, I don't. Now, I am ready, so let's go." My mother was resolved. For whatever reason, she was going to wear what she had on, and that was that.

For a moment, time froze. Margo and I only looked at one another until Margo said, "Ok, then, let's do this, but Yvonne let me warn you, you are going to raise more than a few eyebrows. Don't tell me later I didn't warn you."

My mother only sucked her teeth, rolled her eyes and opened the door. She held it open waiting for the two of us to go past. Once we did she locked up and followed. And that was that.

Once we were inside Margo's car, the tension that was brought on by my mother's outfit seemed to dissipate allowing us to chitchat a little about the wedding.

Margo began, "You and Byron have to get to the catering house and make your final selections for the menu. I've been in touch with them and they have availability this Friday evening. How does that work for you and Byron?"

"That's seems fine, so far, but I'll have to check with Byron. You know his schedule's been crazy. In order for us to be able to have a respectable honeymoon he has to juggle his time and help some of the other surgeons out so they will cover for him while he's away. I'll let you know..., let's see...no later than tomorrow afternoon. Is that ok?" I said trying to figure out when's the next time I could possibly even get a hold of Byron to confirm this with him.

Since our conversation the other day at Valerie's, he had been noticeably distant. After he had left, I stayed a few more hours helping Mrs. Franklin with the cooking and with looking after Poetry. Valerie and Elizabeth slept well into the evening, so I didn't get an opportunity to speak with either of them again until the next day over the phone. Before leaving Valerie's, I tried Byron several times on both his cell and house phones. There was no answer at either one. So I decided I would surprise him much the same way he did me and go over to his place. But when I arrived, Byron was no where to be found. I left him a note in his mailbox, hoping he would come home soon and read it. I went home and wondered all night about where he could have gone. It wasn't until well after midnight that he finally called me. Perplexed and at the same time perturbed, even so I tried not to chastise him. But when all he could offer me in a way of an explanation of his whereabouts was that he was just out driving around, I flipped. Was this how we were going to be after we got married? The question had to be asked, and if this was so, were we ready for such a step? Such a commitment? Of course, I was afraid of his response. I didn't want to lose Byron, but lately, I was beginning to see a side of him I didn't particularly care for. Was my being celibate really that much for him? Was I denying my man a part of me he so desperately needed? Why did it always have to come down to that? Why couldn't my future husband just understand this commitment and pact I had made with God and myself? Byron said he loved me. Then why couldn't he just wait another month? Our going back and forth on this issue was getting us nowhere. Finally, we agreed we would give each other some space and time, and hopefully with prayer things would get better between us. And that is how we left it. So, I guess it was safe to say we were still getting married.

♥   ♥   ♥

Before I knew it, we had pulled up to Mount Holiness Christian Life Center. The place was mobbed. Cars were double parked everywhere and people were spilling out from the doors of the church, waiting to get a final glimpse of the man of our community who had made such a difference in the lives of so many people. It was a good thing for us Margo was the daughter of Rev. Underwood, for as soon as we drove up one of the brothers from the security ministry was on point, opening our doors and seeing us out while another brother jumped in the driver's seat to find suitable parking for Sister Margo's car. Once we were on the sidewalk, Margo and I took each of my mother's arms and proceeded to ascend the massive steps that led to the threshold of this beautiful church that each of us called home. We both silently looked at her and realized that Mr. Strickland's death had really taken its toll on her. Her otherwise glowingly pecan tan skin now looked gray and ashen. My mother was grieving. I now felt so sorry for her loss. Mr. Strickland was a close friend.

As we walked through the doors that led to the sanctuary, people automatically moved out of our way. As we moved down the center aisle, all eyes were drawn to the three of us. To the right of me I could see my Aunts Marilyn and Lulu waving to us to fill the seats they had taken the trouble to save. But before I could even inform my mother of their intentions, she whispered, "No, I'm sitting in the front row." I could not believe what I had just heard my mother say. I looked to Margo for some sort of confirmation that my ears were not playing tricks on me. No such comfort came from her direction. She only whispered to my mother, "Ok, Yvonne, have it your way, but I sure hope you know what you're doing."

So to the front row we went. And sure enough to the astonishment of both Margo and myself, when we arrived at the front, Royce arose to receive us and three vacant seats with "reserved" posted on the back awaited us. As we took our seats, I dared not look back at my aunts. Along with others, I could feel their stares burn holes right through the back of our heads. My mother and Royce sure had a lot of explaining to do.

For two hours we sat and experienced the emotional gratitude of many who had come to pay their final respects to a man who had touched so many lives. They came from all over, from all walks of life. From prominent and significant to nondescript and nonessential. But all were important and worthy of Mr. John Strickland's time and influence. The testimonials that came from the hearts of these people were sincere, profound and deeply felt. It was a wonderful home going service.

When it came time for the final viewing and receiving of the family, it was apparent Margo and I were out of place. But not so for my mother, she graciously received the condolences of all whom acknowledged her presence. Then it was time for the front row to say their final goodbyes; Royce allowed my mother to be the last. I was flabbergasted. What private joke had I been left out of? She seemed to be overextending her last moments with Mr. Strickland's body, as she and I were the only ones left besides the funeral director and Rev. Underwood still left in the church. From where I was standing I could see her mouth moving but I could not make out the words. Then, without performance or travail, she calmly turned to face me and said, "I'm ready to go." She tucked her arm in mine and we walked slowly out of the church to meet the others as they waited for Mr. Strickland's coffin to be escorted out into the waiting Hearst.

Once we had regrouped with the family, Royce was the first to speak, "Miss Harrington, please, I want you, Tvoya and Miss Underwood to ride in one of the limousines to the burial."

Without hesitation, my mother answered, "No, thank you, Royce, I'm not going to the burial. I've already said my final goodbye to John. I'll meet you all back at the house, later."

Royce taking my mother's hand, smiled warmly, "I understand. I'll see you all back at the house."

Royce might have been disappointed she didn't take him up on his offer, but I sure wasn't. My mother and I needed to talk. And from the look on Margo's face, she needed an explanation as well. The ride back to my mother's house was comical to say the least. Margo and I bombarded her with a million questions all at once.

She only answered, "I'll tell you two everything after we're home."

When we pulled up into the driveway, there stood my Aunts Marilyn and Lulu waiting. The inquisitiveness of their expressions didn't look as inviting as Margo's and mine. Sure, we wanted answers, but they looked like they wanted blood.

My mother was the first to get out of the car. She walked right up to the doorstep occupied by her two imposing sisters.

Before either of them could part their lips to utter a solitary word, my mother put her hand up, eyeballing them each directly and said calmly and effortlessly, "Wait!"

By now, Margo and I had approached the steps but hearing my mother's command as if she was speaking to us prompted us to immediately stop dead in our tracks.

"I don't want to hear not one word from either of you," she continued. I was surprised she would even speak to her sisters this way. She didn't even blink an eye. I have never heard her stand up for herself against them before. Never in my life. My aunts, have always been opinionated and judgmental when it came to their younger sister. And she had always allowed them this power. I believed it had to do with her guilt over her having had a drinking problem. But where did she get this sudden strength and courage?

She proceeded to pass them, opened her door and went inside. On cue, we all obediently followed. She was taking off her shoes and walking towards her bedroom when I entered the house. No one said a word. As if by instruction, we all took a seat and waited for her return. The moment felt like a lifetime that it took for my mother to return to her eagerly awaiting inquisitors. All of our eyes were on her as she walked over to me and handed me a sheet of paper that had writing on it. I looked from her face, down to the page. It was a letter.

"You want me to read this?" I asked.

"Out loud," she answered. I opened the folds and began to read the words of the most unexpected, sensitive love letter, from any man, I had ever read.

"My Dearest Yvonne,

If you are now reading this letter it indicates that I have now passed over and have met my Maker. I wanted to express to you in the most efficient way that I could think of how much you have meant to me. Even though you have never taken me up on my offer to love you and honor you as my wife, doesn't mean I ever relinquished the feelings. Ever since the first day I laid my weak tired eyes upon your sweet angelic face I have loved you. I am grateful that although you could not return my love in the way I wanted you to, you never ceased in being a wonderful caring friend to me. As the days of my illness darkened, you were the breath and the light that kept me going. You were there for me probably better than a wife could be if I had had one. You shopped and prepared my meals for me, you cleaned for me, you read to me and you kept me company. Even though I had a full-time nurse to do all of that, you were the one that did it, and without complaint or fanfare. I know that not even your family knew of your commitment and care for me. But now that I am gone and this is over, I hope they come to know and appreciate how much you meant to me. I have left instructions for Royce to give you this upon my demise. And before I became too ill to make any sound decisions, I included you in my will. You will be contacted shortly by my lawyer, Maxwell McCoy, of Jackson, Nelson, and McCoy,

*who will inform you of all the details to my estate. I will be
waiting in eternity for you.*
   It is with much love, respect and peace that I write.

Love,
John"

I slowly folded the letter and stood to hand it back to my
mother. As she took it out of my hand I had a sudden urge to
embrace her, but because of the deafening silence,
regrettably I chose not to. Instead, Margo rising from her
seat on the couch did the honors. My mother fell limp in her
arms and released a heart-wrenching wail that sounded
foreign to any of our ears. Taking my signal for a second
chance, I embraced the back of my mother and rested my
head on the back of her neck, while Margo chanted, "Come
Lord Jesus, Come Lord Jesus."
   The three of us rocked back and forth in perfect unison.
Feeling the loosening of her hold, I raised my head to see
that my Aunt Marilyn was offering my mother a glass of
water, while Aunt Lulu was frantically fanning us all.
   Margo was the first to speak. "Sit, Yvonne," was all she
said as she ushered my mother to sit in the chair I had just
been in. She obeyed while clutching the glass of water as if
her life depended on it.
   In that instance, my mind flashed back to the way my
mother would grip her drinking glass when it held the
contents of her favorite alcoholic drink. Thank God that was
no longer her reality or mine, in fact. I forced my attention
back to the present to be a witness of the coming strength
that flooded my mother's soul as composure was regained.
She was coming back to herself, and again the room fell
silent, with the exception of a few sniffles that managed to

escape from her reacquired poise.

"Well, that was certainly something else," said Aunt Lulu as she sat back down, now turning the fan onto herself. Margo and I locked eyes. My eyes warned her, but to no avail since Margo was the first to burst out in contagious, combustible laughter. Soon all of us, even my mother, were on the floor laughing hysterically.

"I knew John had it bad for you, Yvonne, but I had no idea," said Aunt Lulu as she eased up on the belly wop.

"Gurl, I thought you had lost your mind....dressed all in black and whatnot," Margo joined in.

"Lord Jesus, Lord Jesus...only He knows what the two of you had. I told you, you should've married that man," Aunt Marilyn said. "Yes, John Strickland was a good man, yes, he was. He was a good man," she said over and over again. "But, no...you had to waste your life pining away for Thomas."

"Aunt Marilyn, don't you think Mommy has been through enough for one day?" I said hoping to shut her up. After all, Thomas was my daddy. I didn't have the nerve to defend him to my aunt but I didn't want to hear him being trashed either.

"Yeah, Marilyn, let's just let Yvonne get some rest," Margo offered as she stood. My mother was already making her way to her bedroom. She acted as if she hadn't heard a word of what Aunt Marilyn had just said.

"Come on, Marilyn, we promised to bring those cakes over to Royce and Roger and the rest of the Strickland family. They'll be back from the burial soon," Aunt Lulu surprisingly added.

"Yeah, I know what I said I'll do. T, you stay here and see about your mother. You know she got lots of regrets," Aunt Marilyn said as she walked towards the door that separated my mother's dwelling from Aunt Lulu's.

She stopped in front of me and whispered, "That's why she didn't go to the burial, you know. Yes, Lord, lots of regrets."

I was wondering about that myself. What was this, we all just witnessed? Was it grief or guilt?

After their departure, my mother emerged from her room wearing a brighter casual outfit than the funeral garb she sported earlier.

"Now, that's the Yvonne we all know and love," laughed Margo, looking my way for approval. I said nothing. My confused inquisitive state was getting the better of me, and I felt my mother owed me more of an explanation of her mysterious love affair with Mr. Strickland. Margo picked up on my mood and announced she was leaving to run a few errands. She said she had a wedding to do the next day and still had lots to do before tomorrow came. Finally, it was just my mother and me.

"Well?" I said, not giving my mother time to offer an explanation on her own.

"I know, T. I'm sorry, I kept my closeness to John from you. I just felt that with my drinking, I had already given the neighborhood enough to talk about. I didn't want to add to it with exposing my relationship with John."

"Mommy, I'm not the neighborhood, I'm your daughter. Anyway, what do you think they're doing right about now? You know once the Strickland family gets back from the burial and everyone gathers over there.... what do you think the conversation's going to be about?"

"I don't care, anymore, T. That's just it. I don't care anymore. Tvoya, I have spent my whole life trying to please everyone and doing what I thought they wanted me to do. That's why I drank...to escape that. When I was drinking, the alcohol...gave me...or what I thought it gave me at the time, was the courage to be, say and do whatever I wanted to. But that was a lie. Spending time with John showed me I had wasted a lot of time being afraid….just afraid. But T, I am sorry I didn't tell you. I don't know why but I couldn't at the time. Maybe I didn't want to be talked out of…" I heard what my mother was saying but I interrupted her anyway.

"Didn't want to be talked out of what, Mommy? I understand why you would have wanted to spend time with Mr. Strickland, but why couldn't you share it with me? I'm not getting that."

"I don't know, T. I just don't know," was all my mother could say. So I guess that was all there was left to say. So I picked up my handbag, my Bible and left.

9

"So...Help Me God!"

$\mathcal{I}$ could not believe my mother. How could she pull this stunt, and not even share it with me? How long had she been involved with Mr. Strickland? Was it before he became ill? How much time did she spend caring for him? No wonder she acted so strangely the other day at her shop when his death was discussed. No wonder Royce called her when Mr. Strickland died. How long did Royce know about my mother and his father? Why was I kept in the dark? I sat in the car right outside of my mother's house for what seemed like hours wondering. Wondering, if she even told Mr. Strickland about the...... My mind must have really been far away for I had not even seen Royce come from up the street when I was jostled back to the present reality when he crouched down and rested his arms on the ledge of my car's driver side window. I jumped! He nearly scared me half to death.

"Sorry, Tvoya. You didn't see me did you? You were worlds away," Royce curiously announced.

"Royce, you scared me," I said trying to reclaim clarity. "How are you? The service was really beautiful." I'd hoped I wasn't rambling, but I didn't quite know what to say. I had a lot of questions for him as well. But somehow, now didn't seem like the right time.

"I'm holding my own, I guess. Yeah, the service…it was done in style…just like my old man. Roger and I wouldn't have it any other way. What were you doing just sitting out here? Why haven't you and Yvonne come over?"

Yvonne? Since when did he get on a first name basis with my mother? Oh, yeah it must have been when she started taking care of his father. I can't take much more of this, I thought.

"I, um was just getting ready to go home. I'm not sure what Yvonne is doing," I said wondering if he picked up on my emphasis of sarcasm when I used my mother's name. I sure hoped he had.

"Tvoya, you weren't just leaving. I'd been watching you from my father's porch for quite some time. You were just sitting here. That's what made me come down the block, I needed to check on you."

Oh, great the gig was up! Well, so now he had been scoping me and he knew I had been sitting in my car for more than fifteen minutes, I guess it was fair game to ask him a question or two.

"How long have you known that my mother and your father had been keeping time?" There, I said it. I just blurted it out. Royce looked a little stunned.

"You didn't know?"

"No, I didn't know," I repeated in mocking fashion.

"Well, what did your mother tell you?"

"She didn't tell me anything really. I read the letter your father left for her."

Smiling, Royce retorted, "Pretty incredible, huh?"

"Incredible? What's that's suppose to mean?!" I snapped.

"I mean, nice, sweet. Tvoya, your mom made my dad very happy in his last days."

"Oh yeah? Well how come I'm the last one to find out about it?" Royce tried to say something but I didn't allow him. "And how long have you known?"

He tried to answer, but again I continued, "I can only imagine what the conversation is about at your house, right now."

"Well, to my knowledge, no one has said anything. And now that your aunts are over there, I'm sure nothing will be said. I think you're making more of this than it really is."

"I'm making more of this than it really is? First, my mother shows up dressed as the Black Widow herself. Then she, along with Margo and myself is ushered to the front row of the church as if she was your father's wife. And then, instead of just telling me, she has me read a love letter from your father out loud to Margo and my aunts. And to top it all off, your father's lawyer is due to contact her regarding his estate. I don't know about you, but Royce, really this is all just too much."

"Phew, chill, girl! I thought you weren't gonna take a breath. Tvoya, Dad had been in love with Yvonne ever since my mother died. Maybe even before. It was no secret before she died, they were planning to divorce. Even though Yvonne really never took his advances seriously, she really did care for him too. She was there for him when he became sick. And I am personally grateful to her for that. She made a difference in my dad's life, especially in his last days. He told me himself and he gave me explicit instructions regarding her... if and when he would pass away."

An awkward lull loomed over our debate after Royce made his declaration to the allegiance of my mother to his father. My quest to win this argument became futile and embarrassing. I glanced at Royce only to find his expression mirrored my selfish reaction. I was being a fool. All at once, I realized although Mr. Strickland was dead, I was actually jealous of him and my mother and at the same time, scared for myself. In a month, I would become Mrs. Byron Munroe. Could I be the wife he needed me to be? Could I be there in sickness and in health?…for richer, for poorer?…..till death us do part? My revelation also forced me to mourn the idealism of my parent's relationship. It would never be. I'd always fantasized they would get back together…even in spite of the fact my father was remarried. In my mind, Faye could be replaced by my mother at anytime. But I knew this changed everything for my mother. I now understood why she couldn't tell me about it. I wondered in all of the time my mother spent caring for Mr. Strickland, did it ever come up that I was once pregnant with his grandchild. It began to dawn on me that part of my frustration with this whole scenario centered on my own private pain and secret. Looking now into Royce's face led me to believe maybe there was a chance after all these years, I would receive some sort of retribution for all I had suffered. But I pondered, when would it be realized?

"Royce, I'm sorry, but you'll have to excuse me. I just realized how wrong I've been about this whole thing. I need to go back in and apologize to my mother," I said as I hurriedly rolled up my windows and got out of my car.

"Whoa, can I see you this evening…just to talk, old friend to old friend?" He said as he followed me back up the driveway to my mother's house.

"Um, I don't think so, Royce," I pleaded. Not this again, I thought.

"Oh, come on, Tvoya. I'm sure Byron won't mind you just having dinner with an old friend who, by the way, is grieving." Oh no, he did not go there. Did he?

"Let me get back to you after I talk to my mother. Ok?" I reasoned.

Maybe this excuse could buy me some more time.

"Here, call me, later." He handed me his business card. "Call me on my cell phone."

"Ok, I will," I said as I opened the door to walk into my mother's kitchen.

Just then Royce grabbed my arm turning me to look directly into his face, and said, "Please do, Tvoya. Please do."

♥   ♥   ♥

"Mommy?!" I called out as I entered the kitchen finding it was empty. She was not in there. I walked cautiously inside the living room and still she was not there. I stood listening and then unexpectedly, I heard music. It was coming from her bedroom.

"Mommy?" I said evenly and as quietly as I possibly could while approaching the doorway to her bedroom. I did not want to wake her, if she were asleep. I obediently took off my shoes and laid them softly next to hers before I entered. My eyes had a hard time adjusting to the darkness that permeated the room. All the drapes were drawn. I had her hotel-ish window coverings to thank for that. My eyes filtered what little light came in from the hall, and now I could make out my mother's figure lying on her bed. Her radio was programmed to and played jazz from her favorite station. But something else up surged along with the music. My mother was crying. I knew she was aware of my presence, but she offered no recognition of it. I got on my knees and knelt down beside her and whispered I was sorry. She turned over. While wiping her already streaked stained mascara eyes, she sniffed and said, "I know you are, baby. I know."

She moved over giving me room to join her. I was reminded of those times when after watching a scary movie and having nightmares about it, I would come into my mother's room begging her to let me sleep in her bed. Just like now, she would just move over and let me take the warm spot that I would swear was prepared just for me. Only now, she needed the comforting. I was indebted to be there for her as I cradled my mother in my arms, allowing her to grieve the loss of a love that could have been. For she carried the guilt of knowing that a crucial but obligatory secret was withheld from his knowledge.

10

"Not To Be Entered, Unadvisedly"

I was aroused by the delicious smells that floated from my mother's kitchen up through itchy nostrils that longed to follow its leading. Struggling to sit up, I caught a glimpse of the time from my mother's alarm clock. It was 7:30pm. I could not believe I had slept for six hours, and during the day too. I could not remember the last time that happened. I could hear muffled voices as I neared the door. Not meaning to eavesdrop, I stopped to listen to whom the voices might belong to. Well, one for sure belonged to my mother, but the other I could not quite make out. Then I began to recognize it. It was Royce! My God, what was he doing here now? Just then I remembered his earlier invitation to take me to dinner. Will he never give up? I knew I was safe here in my mother's bedroom. She would never give me up to Royce anyway. Besides, she probably thought I was still sleeping. I waited patiently until I heard the side door to her home close. Good, he was gone. I cracked her bedroom door ajar and peeked out. At first I couldn't see anyone, then my mother moved into view as she sauntered around the kitchen cooking my favorite dish, Lasagna. I emerged from the room, allowing the aroma to fully engulf me. Ah, it was a wonderful smell. And equally as wonderful was to see my mother up and doing what she did best beside hair…cooking. My mother could sure burn some pots.

"Well, hello sleepy head. Did you get a good rest?" Her greeting made me smile.

"Well, hello yourself. Speaking of self, you sure seem like you're back to your old…"

"Bite your tongue, young lady, ain't nothin' old about me." Yep, what wonders a good cry and some rest did. My mother was back.

"Are you making what I think you're making?"

"Sure am. Your favorite."

"Mommy, you didn't have to do that."

"And you didn't have to come back and console me either. But guess what…," her and I were on the same wavelength for we both finished her sentence, "I'm glad you did." We embraced, signally that all was well in Harringtonville.

"Can I help you with anything?" I asked hoping I could make myself useful.

"No, you just being here is enough," she said as she opened the refrigerator to take out the fixings for a salad.

"I can prepare that," I offered. She consented and went to check the oven.

"T, gurl, you're so popular. Folks were looking for you left and right. First, Valerie called. Then, Byron. And Royce just left. He said something about you and him having dinner together tonight. Does Byron know about that?"

"Nothing was confirmed with Royce. What did Byron say? Did you tell him I was sleeping?"

"Yep. He said he would catch up with you later tonight. He was at the hospital still. What's wrong, baby?" my mother asked responding to my sigh.

"Nothing really." I didn't want to worry my mother with my insecurities about Byron and me.

"What do you mean, nothing really? Tell me T, what's going on? It doesn't have anything to do with Royce does it?"

"Mommy, can you lay off of the Royce tip? Everything is fine with Byron and me."

"Just checking. I know that Royce still has it bad for you. I just don't want you getting caught up in the memories." Did my mother just say what I think she said, that Royce still had it bad for me? So it just wasn't my imagination, Royce did have an ulterior motive for asking me out to dinner tonight.

"Speaking of memories….the ones I have of Royce aren't too favorable, Mommy. Now you of all people know that."

"I'm just checking. T, you're getting ready to marry a wonderful man, and I don't want you blowing it by letting someone from your past…and may I remind you, someone who did you very wrong, intrude on your present happiness."

"Mommy, please."

"No, T. John would tell me from time to time that Royce would ask about you. And Royce even confessed to him that he made a very big mistake by letting you go."

"Did he ever mention the…"

"No! That's what I'm talking about. He always asked about you, but never anything else. It seems to me, Royce Strickland is not worth your time. He certainly is not the man his father was. That's for sure."

"Ok, Mommy can we drop this subject?" My reasoning pleaded that enough was enough. But my mother wasn't convinced, for she continued.

"T, I learned something very precious and important during this season in my life when I was there for John in his final days. Love is not to be taken for granted. Sometimes we spend a lifetime chasing what coulda woulda only to find coulda woulda doesn't and never will. I did that with your father, and look where it got me. When I coulda been with a man who truly loved me unconditionally. And in the end, I realized and am thankful for knowing that I did love him too."

My mother's words intensely pierced my heart sending shock waves directly to my soul. Only trouble was, with only a few weeks to go to my wedding my mind was not on Byron, it was instead now on Royce.

♥   ♥   ♥

"Hey, gurl. I was hoping I would hear from you soon," Valerie cheerfully declared upon hearing my voice on the other end of the phone.

"Yeah, Mommy told me you had tried to reach me earlier," I said as I sat down on my chaise lounge after making myself a cup of hot tea. It was late and I wasn't sure if Valerie would still be up, but I certainly was glad she was. I needed to talk to her. I began to feel guilty for even making the call, once she did pick up. I know Valerie had a lot on her mind, waiting for the results of Elizabeth's surgery. She sure didn't need me hounding her about my itty bitty problems. She picked up on it anyway.

"Tvoya, what's up with you?"

"Valerie, how are you doing? Has Elizabeth been having any pain?"

"Here and there. But, she's fine. Would you please tell me what is going on with you, and what was the deal with your moms today at Mr. Strickland's funeral?"

Following Valerie's lead on her changing the subject, I said, "Valerie, you would not even believe this, when I tell you. Before Mr. Strickland died, my mom and him were spending some time together. In fact, he left her a love letter and something in his will. Valerie, they really did love each other. I was shocked and pretty mad at my mom for holding out on me. But now I'm ok with it all." I proceeded to give Valerie all of the details in great length and when I was done, there was nothing but silence.

"Hello, Valerie? Are you still there?"

"Wow!" was all that she uttered. Valerie was stunned to say the least.

"Um, Tvoya, I know all of what's been happening has been a pretty heavy thing to have dropped on you. And I know my being quiet about Elizabeth's health issue hasn't help either. You're getting married very soon and I didn't want this to have a major impact on you and Byron. You deserve to just concentrate on your wedding and nothing else."

I appreciated what Valerie was now saying, but there was so much that my mind was processing, dissecting and making assessments on. Should I tell her about the insecurities between Byron and me? Should I tell her about Royce hounding me? Of course I should. This was Valerie I was speaking to. But I didn't want to burden her and I certainly did not want to drudge up the past.

As if reading my mind, Valerie broke my train of thought. "Freshmeat, give it up. What's on your mind?" I knew just what Valerie was referring to, but instead I figured this was not the time. Anyway, it was with Elizabeth that I should have been discussing what I was really thinking about.

"All right! All right! I should know by now I can't hide anything from you."

"Well, you're the same with me."

"True. True. Well, Val, I'm not quite sure how to say this. But I'm having second thoughts about Byron and me." There was no need to involve Valerie in what I was planning on discussing with Elizabeth. This was a much safer subject to discuss with her.

"Gurl, that's normal, right before a wedding."

"I don't know Valerie. Shouldn't I be ecstatic and all?"

"Yes and no." What did she mean, yes and no?

"What kind of answer is that?"

"I mean marriage is a big step. It's probably the biggest step you'll ever make in your life, so it's to be expected to have jitters."

"Valerie, this is more than just jitters. This is more like….do I really love him? And can I love him for the rest of my life?" And what about Royce? I dared not mention his name, but I had to admit to myself, he did factor in to the equation.

"Of course you love Byron. He's the man of your dreams. Gurl, you better just stop worrying yourself about all of this, and just go ahead and get married."

I was dismayed by Valerie's reasoning. She didn't get it, and she was the one that always got it. I was beginning to think that I couldn't talk to anyone about this. It was no use in taking this conversation any further with Valerie. She believed I had found happiness in Byron Munroe, my knight in shining armor, and for that there would be no getting through and maybe it was just as well. Valerie didn't want to admit it, but I knew she was more concerned about Elizabeth's health, and rightfully so. Right now, my problems and concerns played second. To Valerie, I had always been the friend in need, and she was always my protector. She was there for me when my mother's drinking became too much and I needed a place of refuge. She was there for me when I needed consoling after my father left my mother and me. She was there for me after the breakup with Royce. Somehow, I think that Valerie thought she still

94

needed to be there for me but not in the way I needed her now. What I needed was for her to see what I was saying objectively and not subjectively. However, I understood and in so doing, I agreed to play along.

"You know, you're right Valerie. I am getting ready to marry a really wonderful man. I must be crazy to be having these thoughts," I said trying my best to sound that I myself was thoroughly convinced. However lame I thought I sounded to myself, Valerie was convinced and for the moment that was fine.

"Oh, Freshmeat, just enjoy the ride," Valerie chimed.

Yeah, I guess however bumpy, I lamented.

11

"To Live Happily…"

I wasn't hearing what I thought I was hearing, was I? I had just awakened to the blaring ring of the telephone only minutes after I had just fought to get into my R.E.M. sleep. And as glorious and satisfying as it was, I had to shake myself hard so that I could get all of the sordid details of this drama Charlene was trying to convey.

"Wait, Charlene, slow down. Did you just say you need a place to stay? What happened?" I asked as I wiped the drool from my left cheek. I hope Byron still loves me after he finds out about this little tidbit about myself.

"I got evicted today, Tvoya! I have to be out of here within twenty-four hours or they're going to lock me out with all my stuff inside. I need your help."

This was not a first…Charlene needing my help. But now, she sounded so desperate. Charlene only sounded this passionate when detailing the happenings associated with a wild night of partying.

"Ok, ok, calm down. Of course, I'll help you. You can stay here until you get things together."

Oh, no, now how was I going to explain this to Byron as if we really needed Charlene's problems complicating our life right now? But I certainly could not leave her in such a jam.

"Oh, thank you, thank you, Tvoya. I promise this will be just a temporary arrangement. I'll be out of your hair within a matter of weeks." Did Charlene forget I was getting married in just a matter of weeks?

"Pack up some of your clothes and your necessities and come over tomorrow. What are your plans for your furniture?" I asked the question, but earnestly I was hoping that I wasn't factored into the answer.

"I plan on making some calls to a few storage places in the morning. I think I can manage to get something arranged," she said now sounding a lot less frantic.

"Good. Listen, Charlene I'm gonna be all over tomorrow so call me on my cell and let me know what time you plan on coming over with your things. I'm sorry, but I won't be able to help you pack."

"No problem. I just appreciate you letting me crash there for awhile. Thanks so much, Tvoya. I feel so much better, now. I'll see you tomorrow."

"You're welcome, Charlene," I said. As I disconnected the conversation, I wondered what really happened with Charlene. I realized then that what she did tell me didn't actually make much sense.

♥   ♥   ♥

"You did, what?" yelled Byron while answering all in the same breath. "You consented to Charlene staying here with you?" Byron continued his yelling as he paced back in forth in my kitchen.

"Calm down, sweetheart. It won't be for long. She'll be out of here in just a few weeks," I reasoned.

"Do you realize we are supposed to be getting married in just a few weeks? Or has that just slipped your mind?" Byron sarcastically retorted.

"Byron, don't be like that," I pleaded, trying with every fiber of my being not to allow his last comment to have an affect on me. "I can't just let her be put out with nowhere to go. That just wouldn't be right."

"So when will we have any privacy or...." Byron didn't finish his sentence, but I knew in what direction he was going with it. He was getting ready to go there again, on the intimacy tip. I chose to overlook it.

"Never mind," he continued, "do what you want. Don't mind me. I don't seem to matter much these days anyway."

What was Byron talking about? He did matter. He mattered very much to me. We were getting ready to become husband and wife for life. Why was he making everything so difficult? With the way we had left our last conversation, I was surprised he would just show up, unannounced this morning. I had expected to hear from him last night, but he didn't call. After speaking with Charlene, I fought hard the temptation of calling Byron last night. Instead, I called Margo. I was due to give her a return call anyway. I thought by calling Margo, my do good Samaritan act would be confirmed and I would leave the conversation feeling better than when I had hung up with Charlene. Her response to Charlene coming to stay for a few weeks wasn't unlike that of Byron's. She was totally against it. I explained to her also that Byron and I were disagreeing about nearly everything, these days. To keep the peace, her advice was to ask my mother to house Charlene, instead. This I thought was definitely a bad idea. Worst than Charlene staying with me and Byron being against it. Charlene and my mother sharing living space? Oh, the horror! But worst was now getting Byron's reaction. We were getting no where on this topic. I thought if we could talk about the wedding, his mood would soften.

"How about some breakfast, snookums? You must be hungry, after your all nighter," I said trying to sound loving, but then remembering he didn't even give me an explanation as to why he didn't call me last night.

Pushing that thought into the back of my mind. I added, "Margo needs us to go by the catering house to pick out our menu for the reception dinner. How's this Friday for you?"

"It's fine," he said with an air of disinterest. But, we both knew all was not fine.

♥ ♥ ♥

I inadvertently disconnected the call while reaching in my bag for my cell phone. After retrieving it I checked the Caller ID to find that it had been Charlene, trying to reach me. She must be ready to start bringing her things over, I surmised. I sure hoped Byron would not still be there. Earlier, we both ate our breakfast in total silence. And it was unbearable. Finally, I retreated and decided it would be a good thing to just leave the house. I had a lot of errands to run anyway, and I wanted to get back before Charlene got there. Byron didn't seem to object; at least he didn't verbalize it. But he didn't offer to get out of the way before Charlene showed up either. It was as if he was waiting to see if it was really Charlene who would be moving in. No! I must be trippin'. He couldn't possibly have thought that. Nah!

Charlene picked up on the first ring. "Hey, gurl, where you at?"

"I'm on my way back to the house now. Are you there already?" I asked, silently praying that Byron was gone.

"Yeah, just me and Fiancé." Oh shoot! He was still there.

"All right. I'll be there soon. Um, Charlene, can I speak with Byron?"

"Sure can. Heeerre's Fiancé."

"Yeah?" Did he have to sound so put out?

"Hey, I didn't think you would still be there," I said trying to sound still unaffected.

"Why not? Do I have to go?"

"Byron, you know better than that. I just didn't think you would want to be around when Charlene got there. Since you're so against her moving in." Now I was the one exuding sarcasm.

"Whatever, Tvoya."

"Hey, gurl, see you when you get here." Byron had passed the phone back to Charlene and didn't even say goodbye. Lord, what was I going to do?

12

"... Ever After?"

As I pulled my car up to the curb right in back of Charlene's car, I could see Byron sitting on the top step that led to the entrance way of my condo unit. And he looked none too happy to boot. I'm sure this heat didn't help either. The northeast was suffering from a fourth day straight run of an unbearable heat wave. The temperature was hitting a record high of 98 degrees on this particular day, with the humidity reaching to 100. So why wasn't Byron in the house where the air-conditioner was pumping? Charlene sure wasn't out there baking, and I couldn't blame her. On days like this, I tried very hard to stay out of the heat. The only exposure I could take was from the air-conditioned car to the air-conditioned house.

"Hey, you!" I said trying my best to greet Byron on a lighter note than I had previously left him.

"Hey, yourself," he answered, not divulging either way, the sway of his mood pendulum. At least he stood up as I approached him.

"She's inside," he offered.

"And how come you're out here...in all this heat?"

"I like the heat." Liar my mind screamed. Ok, Byron have it your way. His eyes met my smirk, but that was as far as he would allow them to travel. He knew better than for our eyes to meet. If they had they would have confirmed that he was already busted. Instead of exposing Byron, I said nothing more as I crossed the threshold to my humbled abode that now a friend in need would also inhabit.

Charlene and I had a rather shallow three dimensional relationship. She needed. I had. She took. I understood this and I was ok with it. Some thought she took advantage of me. This probably was so, but my reasoning was if someone was in need and I had the resources to help them, then who was I to deny them the help. I learned from the Lord that everything belonged to Him so it really wasn't mine to give or not to give anyway. Hence, us becoming roommates.

Charlene and I went back to our college days. We met while attending NYU, and we even worked together for a short while at a travel agency in Manhattan. In the beginning of mine and Charlene's relationship, she grated on my nerves in the worst way. But as time went on, I came to understand her and she me. We were total opposites. I came from a broken home, she always had her two parents that lived together. The problem, however, in Charlene's world was they were both too busy for her. Her aunt was the only person she could rely on. She was old fashioned and stuck in her ways, as Charlene put it, and this cramped Charlene's lifestyle. We had contrasting tastes in just about everything. Food, clothing, and men. Everything Charlene ate was accented with hot sauce. Everything Charlene wore revealed more of her than needed to be. And the roughnecks were her choice companions. Which reminded me, I would have to make it clear to her that she would have to entertain elsewhere.

When I walked into my living room, I found Charlene sitting on the chaise lounge, remote in hand watching a fight scene on the Jerry Springer show with the volume way too high.

"Hey, girl, I see you have made yourself comfortable."

"Hi, Tvoya, I didn't hear you come in," Charlene offered while frantically depressing the volume button on the remote.

"Yeah, that was way too high."

"Sorry, roomie. Is Fiancé still outside? I told him he didn't have to wait for you out there. I wasn't going to bite him," laughed Charlene.

"Gurl, you better leave my man alone," I half-heartedly joked.

"Gurl, ain't nobody want your stuffy, stuck up, surgeon no way. Where can I unpack?" Charlene was a mess. I knew she wasn't a threat to me. While we were college mates, Charlene and I sure shared a lot of things, but men weren't among those on the list. So, why was Byron so afraid of her, I wondered.

I showed Charlene to the spare bedroom and where she could unload the surprisingly few belongings she brought along with her.

"Where's the rest of your clothes?" I asked as Charlene began to waste no time in putting her things away.

"Some I put in storage, and some I took to my aunt in Brooklyn on the way over here."

"So now, how did you get yourself evicted?" I finally had to ask, since she sure was taking her sweet 'ole time in telling me.

"Well, as you know I've been out of work for a while, and my unemployment recently ran out. Which got me behind in my rent. Uh, say about six months," Charlene answered sheepishly.

"Six months! Why did you let it go for so long? And what happened to that Sugar Daddy you had?" I snapped, instantly regretting being so abrupt with her.

"Sugar Daddy ain't as sweet as he used to be. You know men, if you ain't putting out, you don't get no funds. Oh, yeah but you don't know nothin' bout that, with your celibate self," Charlene said responding to my dubiousness. Touché.

"Sure you right, I don't know nothin' about what Sugar Daddies do or don't do. And being celibate has nothing to do with it. Charlene, what you really need is Jesus. Gurl, you has gots to get your life right!" I retorted.

"My, my, aren't we testy. If you would just give Fiancé some, you wouldn't be so uptight," Charlene threw back.

"Uptight? I would say you're the one who's uptight, with your evicted self." I just couldn't resist.

"Oh it's like that, uh?" laughed Charlene. "But seriously, Tvoya, you need to consider giving the poor man some. After all, he'll be your husband soon enough anyway. I'm sure God wouldn't mind. It's not like you're a virgin anyway."

I could not believe Charlene. I swallowed hard, took a deep breath and decided her comment did not deserve a reply. No, but she was right. I wasn't a virgin. I had my share of intimate relationships that ended up no where but with my self esteem quickly snowballing, descending emphatically into a collusion, of course.

"Charlene, how long will you be needing to stay? Like you just mentioned, I will be getting married very soon. If you can get your finances together by then, maybe you can rent it from me," I said offering her a solution to a problem her and I both knew would not be solved in that short amount of time.

"I got some things brewing in the pot. I'll be out of your hair in about two weeks tops. I promise, roomie."

"Good!" I answered skeptically.

♥   ♥   ♥

Now where did Byron go? I wondered as I opened my front door to call him inside only to find he was not there. This was getting real old, and I didn't know how much more of this I could possibly take. He must of taken off quite some time ago, since there was no sign of his car going down the street. Come to think of it, when I pulled up earlier, I didn't even see his car parked anywhere near my place. Did he get a ride from someone else? He couldn't possibly have walked. What kind of game was Byron playing? Should I call him on his cell? Or should I just let him cool down? I decided I couldn't let him just leave like that. I called him on his cell. It rang and rang, then went to his voicemail. So he had it turned on, but he wasn't answering. All right, so he wanted to play. Byron didn't know I was the master at playing games like this.

"Where's Fiancé?" Charlene inquired as she stepped out into the heat. "Boy, it's hot out here. Gurl, let's go to the pool." My first reaction to Charlene's suggestion seemed irresponsible and something that I didn't care to do. But then as sweat beads began to develop across my brow and not necessarily because of the heat, her proposition became all the more appealing. There wasn't anything pressing I had to do today and a swim would definitely take my mind off of Byron's antics.

"Charlene, let's do that!" We raced inside like teenage girls, giggling as we threw on our swimwear. I chose my black and white bikini with the black sheer drape scarf for the bottom. There was about a two-block walk from my condo unit to the pool area, and one had to wear something over their bathing suit when walking the street. I yelled this tidbit of information to Charlene knowing she would have no shame in just walking the street in her bikini. I decided on my white sundress to conceal my suit, slipped my feet into a pair of cheap flip flops I hadn't yet worn all summer and then threw a few incidentals into my beach bag. I was ready. Charlene and I met in my living room. I was surprised she was dressed rather modestly for Charlene, but then again she knew I lived in a family community. Good.

"Ready, roomie?" Charlene asked enthusiastically.

"Yeah, let's go!" I quipped, just as eagerly.

The walk to the pool was rather pleasant. It had been a long time since Charlene and I just kicked it. She filled me in on her eviction dilemma, and I was even more convinced she was truly grateful for my help. I told her I would be praying for her. She wasn't too impressed with knowing that, since she prided herself on not embracing any one form of religious expression. Really, Charlene was her own god. This never sat too well with me, but nevertheless, I always hoped and prayed the light would come on in her heart; had to keep trying though…to enlighten her all the more.

We were overjoyed that as hot as it was, there weren't many people at the pool. Immediately following our arrival, we commenced to jumping right in and swimming a few laps.

"Phew, I hadn't realized how tensed I was until just now," I said to Charlene as I reached the other side of the pool to join her.

"Gurl, I know what you mean. Ain't nothin' like a good swim. Well maybe one thing can match it," Charlene said teasingly.

"Please not that again," I said as I rolled my eyes.

"Ok, ok. I'm sorry, roomie. I won't go there anymore. It's your thing. Do what you wanna do," Charlene surrendered. I hoisted myself onto the side of the pool and sat for a while with my feet still dangling in the water. Charlene stayed in the water and floated away on her back. I sat there watching her and wondered what it must of felt like to not have a care in the world. Charlene sure had the patent on that. Must be nice. I, on the other hand, had lots to think about. Here I was getting married in a matter of weeks, and my fiancé and I weren't getting along. But whenever I thought about Byron, something incomprehensible would occur. Royce's face would be the image that would come to mind. Weird. And then there was Elizabeth and her health issue. Trying hard to push that thought from my mind, I decided to try Byron again. I dried myself off and made the call. Still no answer. This time, I decided to try his house. Again, no answer.

Charlene startled me as she plopped down in the pool chair next to mine. "He's avoiding you, isn't he?"

"Yeah, he's mad I'm letting you crash with me for a while."

"Tvoya, I'm sorry that I'm intruding like this....," Charlene's voice drifted off.

"Don't worry about it, girl. You need a place to stay and I have the room. That's that! Byron is just going to have to get over it."

"I know!" Charlene exclaimed with a burst of newfound excitement. "Let's go dancing tonight."

"No, I don't feel much like dancing," I said, thinking this activity was the last thing I wanted or needed to do.

"Gurl, you are about to become an old married woman, so this could be your last chance to cut that rug," Charlene expressed as she swerved her hips to the music that played in her head. I had to admit, it had been a long time since I had gone out dancing.

"I see that I got your attention. Yeah, gurl, let's go out and get our groove on," Charlene said as she continued to pop her fingers and dance. Now she had the attention of all the patrons at the community pool. Oh Lord, I know I shouldn't go, but I sure can use the diversion.

"Hey, how about a compromise? Let's go check out that new jazz spot on Springfield and Linden." I prodded, hoping Charlene would see the wisdom in us just chillin'.

"Ok, that'll work," she agreed. And I was happy she took the bait. What I needed was to just relax and take in some cool soothing melodic sounds that only jazz could deliver. It wouldn't be the best thing for me right now to go clubbing. For me, that would mean working myself into a frenzy in an attempt to release some pent up tension brought upon by Byron's infantile behavior. No thank you. I might wind up doing something I would regret. Yes, indeed, 'cause at this notable juncture in my life, regrets is what I was trying hard to avoid.

13

"The Union Of This Man and Woman"

$\mathscr{F}$or me, being at Razz was quite a distinctive diversion. However, not so for Charlene who on the way over, enlightened me to the fact that in all of its three months since opening, she had been a regular. I should've known, a new club in the area would not have escaped Charlene's patronage. There wasn't a club in the Tri-State area she had not been to. Charlene was indubitably a club connoisseur. If she had not been there at least once, then it did not exist. True that!

Immediately upon entry, one could observe that this jazz spot was not your ordinary, run of the mill nightclub. Instead, it was the embodiment of supreme class and distinction.

"Charlene! How come you never mentioned this place to me before?" I asked as I allowed my eyes to wander and take in the gratifying motif.

"I didn't think you were still interested in hanging out anymore. I mean you being all engaged and all," Charlene teased, as she also allowed her eyes to wander but for different reasons than I.

"Being engaged doesn't mean being dead. I still would like to know what's going on." I lamented not knowing why I needed to defend myself.

"Oh, gurl, the guys in this place are fione, tonight," quipped Charlene as she scanned the floor. I could have further inquired on her assessment of tonight as opposed to other nights, but decided against it. Let's just have a good time, my mind kept telling me.

Since it was the middle of happy hour and the dinner hour was approaching, the host asked, "Would you ladies like to be seated in the dining room or would you prefer a small table here in our cabaret? If you're not interested in a full course meal, our happy hour offers a nice buffet I'm sure would be pleasing to your palate."

So just beyond this reception room was the cabaret section. How quaint. On the stage in the center of the room a quartet was currently playing. And they were very good. And young too. Judging from the level of professionalism displayed by them and their sound, one would assume they were much older. But these cats, (as my father would put it) didn't look a day over twenty. It was refreshing to see and hear old standards played by young bloods. We mustn't forget the sounds of those who came before.

After we were seated in the cabaret section, I couldn't help but look around for my father. He would love a place like this. Knowing him, however, he had probably already been here a few times, with Faye in tow, no doubt. Faye was the type of woman that didn't let her man go too far without her being there with him. But no, they weren't anywhere that I could see. And thank God for that. Tonight, I surely didn't need them hawking me. Tonight, I just wanted to kick back and enjoy a quiet night out. Then I was reminded I was out with Charlene, and maybe quiet would not be the appropriate adjective to describe what this night could possibly have in store.

Charlene and I agreed the buffet would be suitable and were escorted to a table that sat just outside of the entrance to the dining room. I was pleased that from our table we could scan the whole view of the cabaret section. I also noticed that anyone in the dining room could not only enjoy the sounds of the quartet but they could also see the jazz set being played from their dining table. Very strategically well done. I wondered who owned the place. I was very impressed.

Since vowing celibacy and being engaged, Charlene was right, I had not been into the club scene. But it wasn't only that. I was in a different place in my life's journey and clubbing seemed immature and obsolete. Besides, the adventure no longer served me as it had before. I had found my Mr. Right, and I wasn't looking anymore. So all the men, even here who were standing around profiling with a drink in one hand and gangsta leanin' scoping their prey, no longer had the same appeal they once had. I'd played this game, many times before. Sometimes I would win and most times I would lose. Now that this time had passed, the memory of it was more romanticized than it actuality had ever been to begin with. Was that true with all memories? I often wondered.

Charlene broke my reflective insight upon her announcing that she was ready to get her grub on. I wasn't quite ready to eat, so I told her to start without me. She was gone before I could really get it out. But I knew better, Charlene had her sights on someone and she was ready to make her move. I just sure hoped that by the end of the evening, she wouldn't be asking me if she could bring them home. In my opinion, Charlene's judgment wasn't always very sound.

"Hey, Tvoya," the voice said, as a I turned my head in its

direction.

"Royce?" I said in utter amazement. He was bordering on serious stalking.

"How are you doing?" he said as he sat down. I didn't remember inviting him to do so, nor did he even ask.

"Royce, what are you doing here?" I tried, my best to be polite, but our run ins were getting on my nerves.

Being teasingly sarcastic, he retorted, "Hello, Royce, it's so good to see you again. How have you been?"

"Ok, I'm sorry. But really, what are you doing here? Royce, you are starting to spook me. Everywhere I seem to go, you show up. What's up with that?" I pleaded, hoping he understood where I was coming from.

"Maybe it's karma, coincidence. I don't know, Tvoya. Maybe, it's just meant to be. I know you don't think that I'm stalking you." My silence told him my true thoughts.

"Well, I'm sorry, then. I didn't mean to intrude. I'll check you later, Tvoya." Royce stood up and then slowly and calmly walked away. I felt terrible, but not bad enough to call him back. He really needed to leave me alone.

I watched him methodically as he walked past the stage to take a seat at a table that sat void of anyone other than himself. Tvoya, I thought, that was mean. He just lost his father. He's back in town and after being away so many years, he hardly knows anyone. He probably just needed to get out to clear his head and take his mind off of losing his father. And then he saw you, a friendly, recognizable face. And you just literally told him to get lost. Way to go, girl.

"Hey, sweetness." Transfixed in my thought, I didn't see the new person who had just parked themselves at my table. I looked to my left to see, an old familiar face, Kenny Mendola.

"Oh, hi, Kenny. I didn't see you sit down. How have you been?" Kenny was always ok with me, and I was suddenly happy this deterrent was sent to take my mind off of the condemning conversation I was just having with myself about the way I just treated Royce.

"Welcome to Razz, Tvoya! I was wondering when I would see you down here." Kenny was wondering when he would see me down here? Did he visit this establishment that often?

"No, I'm not a club rat. I know that's what you were thinking." Right away, I was embarrassed for what I was thinking and I cringed at the fact that I was cold busted.

"Um, I didn't mean to give you that look," I said, trying to mend my fences.

"Not a problem. I was referring to the fact that since I've been in business, I haven't seen you come through the door."

I smiled as I realized he was telling me he was the proprietor of this tasteful establishment.

"Kenny, this is you?"

"Yeah. That's what I was trying to tell you. How do you like it?" Kenny said as he leaned back into his chair crossing his legs while squaring his shoulder to exert his ownership all the more.

"Congratulations, Kenny! I didn't know that this was you! It's real nice. Real nice."

"Thanks, Tvoya. I'm glad you like the place. And I'm glad you finally got down here. Don't see much of the old gang anymore, so when I do, it's all good."

Yeah, that's what Kenny and I were part of. The old gang. I wondered if he knew Royce was here as well. Since he was part of the old gang, too.

"Kenny, did you see that Royce Strickland is here too, tonight?" I offered.

"Yeah, I checked Royce out earlier. I invited him down myself. We kinda kicked it after his father's funeral, and I invited him down to check the place out. And I did check out how you just dis'd my man." Wow, I was beginning to feel like a specimen under a microscope.

"Oh, you saw that?"

"Yeah. Whatz up with dat?"

"It's a long story, but I didn't mean to dis him. It's just that....," I was beginning to rattle on, when I thought my eyes caught the sight of Byron walking around the bar area. But when I focused more intently, he seemed to have disappeared.

"You were saying, Tvoya?" Kenny said trying to keep our conversation flowing.

"Oh, I'm sorry, I thought I saw someone I knew." I didn't want to say fiancé. Why? I wasn't quite sure. "So, Kenny...I'm really glad for you, the club and all."

"Yeah, I felt the neighborhood needed a jazz spot like this. You know, your father's been down here a few times."

"I figured he would have been. My dad does love his jazz."

"Yeah, Mr. Harrington is one cool dude." Kenny looked away into the direction that Royce was sitting, before offering his next probe.

"Is it true? I heard you're getting married."

"Uh, yes, I am. Next month to be exact." I was happy to have the conversation directed away from Royce and my father.

"Wow, that's soon. It'll be here before you know it. I hope you'll be happy and that he's good to you, Tvoya. You know... you're good people." He glanced back towards Royce's direction.

"Hey, Kenny. The place is hot tonight!" Charlene said as she placed her plate down and gave him a kiss on his cheek.

I should have known Charlene would already be bosom buddies with the owner. Kenny returned the greeting.

"Charlene, we were just talking about you," Kenny

offered. We were? I thought. Kenny continued, "Tvoya, Charlene was the one that told me you were getting married. We found out the first night she came to check the place out that we had something in common. You."

Getting married and moving out to Long Island would definitely be a much-needed change for me. Still living here in the neighborhood kept my business too front and center for my comfort. All I could do was smile at Kenny's assessment of his relational tie to Charlene. Not that Charlene needed to know me to be relationally attached to anyone. She was quite the social butterfly all by herself. By now, I was figuring I must be becoming the talk soup of my community. What did I expect, anyway? My mother owned the hottest beauty salon in the neighborhood. Followed by her newly exposed love affair with Mr. Strickland, the late councilman. Whose son, my ex, was now in town, stalking me. Did I need to go on? Was it me or was I just a legend in this community in my own mind?

Probably so. Probably so.

14

"For Richer..."

*K*enny politely excused himself after observing that by frantically waving a white towel, one of his bartenders was trying to get his attention.

"Ooh, he is so fione, Tvoya. You know I'm gonna get with that," Charlene said claiming her stakes on Kenny, as she sat down to begin attacking her food.

That girl can eat and never gain an ounce. But she was right about Kenny. He was a very good-looking man. He always had been. But I was never attracted to him. One reason, I was stuck on Royce Strickland, and the other, back in the day Kenny was conceited. He knew he was cute. Kenny was the product of a bi-racial marriage, which resulted in his looks reflecting the best of both nationalities. His mother, African American and his father, Italian. When by now most of the brothers were sporting shaved heads because of hereditary dictates, Kenny's silky locks were still long and thriving. Especially now that hair was making a comeback. Kenny was taking full advantage of it. Mom's shop was his spot. See, you can't get nothing past no one in this neighborhood. It was too tight knit.

"Girl, you think every man on God's green earth is fione," I replied to Charlene.

"I can't help it if I appreciate the male specimen," Charlene said rolling her eyes, as she chewed on a fried chicken wing, "and who was that man that came over to the table before Kenny?" Charlene inquired. Why did she have to see Royce and me talking? I had made the choice of not even mentioning Royce to Charlene. Charlene had loose lips and I was afraid she would mention Royce's name in the presence of Byron.

"Oh, him?" I tried to sound as nonchalant as I possibly could. "Just an old friend that noticed I was here."

"The exchange between the two of you seemed so short. Who is he?" Charlene wasn't going to let up was she?

"Charlene, I thought you were scoping for men prey. Don't tell me you were checking on me the whole time." I tried my best to keep the tone of my voice as steady and my attitude as light as possible, but Charlene was on to me.

"Oh, my God, that was Royce wasn't it, Tvoya?" Charlene announced her newfound revelation as if she had hit some sort of jackpot. The live music had just ended and now a soft melodic piano was being piped in. I was sure the couple at the next table had heard Charlene's proclamation. Charlene had never actually met Royce, but she has seen photos of him. Since it was around the same time Charlene and I had become classmates in college that Royce and I ended our relationship, she had heard about his whole life story.

"Yeah, Charlene, that was…I mean that is Royce Strickland." We both looked in his direction. Our movement was perfectly synchronized.

"Gurl, I'm going over and introducing myself. I practically know the brother already anyway," Charlene said as she wiped her mouth and stood up to straighten her dress. She was already part of the way to his table before I could even open my mouth to say anything to stop her. And what could I have said anyway. Charlene was right. She did practically know him. I was so hurt behind our break up that I would mouth off about it to whomever would listen. And since Charlene was always available, she was the perfect candidate for a sounding board. It was in that moment it occurred to me why I had asked Charlene to be in my wedding. She had been there for me back in a time that was terribly dark and my sanity was in serious question. Yes, Charlene had a right to meet the infamous Royce and I had no right stopping her.

I watched surreptitiously as Charlene made her way to Royce's table and sat down. Without an invitation to do so, no doubt. They had so much in common, I thought. Charlene looked so animated, as I'm sure she was explaining to him how she knew him and why she was introducing herself to him. I could no longer bear to look, so instead I decided to check my cell phone for messages, hoping Byron had tried to reach me. Nope. He hadn't called. I was really beginning to worry about him. Maybe he was right. Was I not paying my man enough attention? Putting everyone else's needs before him? We really needed to talk. But when? He was putting in more and more hours at the hospital and now with Charlene moving in…did I make a mistake in that as well?

I was glad to see that the young gentlemen of the jazz quartet were beginning another set. At least this would give me something other than my cell phone, or Charlene and Royce to look at. Just as I was beginning to settle into the groove of the music, I felt a strong grip at my arm and a powerful tug that abruptly lifted me up out of my chair. "What the hell?…" My neck quickly snapped thrusting my head upward for my eyes to find the assailant that so swiftly and literally swept me off of my feet. It was Byron and he was moving….and moving me right along with him…in tow that is!

"Byron!" I screamed, desperately trying to pry his fingers

from the vice grip hold that he held to my arm. My circulation was beginning to get cut off and he was really hurting me. My feet were moving so fast struggling to keep the pace he was setting for me that my heel broke in the wake.

"Byron! Let me go! What is going on with you? You're hurting me!" I screamed out.

He was mumbling something I could not make out and when he turned to look at me, I could see his eyes were red and fiery and his breath smelled of alcohol. I had seen this look before. But where? I couldn't place it but it's familiarity frightened me. What had gotten into Byron? Why was he so forcefully dragging me out of here? He had managed to bring me just beyond the bar area when I heard Royce call out, "Byron! Man, let her go!"

Byron's abrupt stop forced his release of my arm, which resulted in me aggressively crashing down to the floor... Hitting my head. Then all I could see from my upward bound view was all hell breaking loose.

"Tvoya, are you all right?!" Charlene was on her hands and knees, screaming loudly in my ears. I looked at her but she looked funny. Fuzzy really. I could hear voices yelling, feet scuffling and glass breaking. Then nothing.

"Tvoya! Tvoya! Can you hear me? Are you all right? Are you all right? Can you hear me?" The voice kept saying over and over again.

"Of course, I can hear you. Will you stop yelling at me and repeating yourself? Let me up. I'm fine," I said groggily, annoyed and terribly embarrassed. I began to hear the voices yelling again, but this time from a distance.

Charlene and Kenny helped me up and walked me over to a black leather sofa that sat in the reception area of the club. I could hear someone telling the crowd that I was ok and it was over and for them to go back to their tables and enjoy themselves. The music started playing again. Kenny then told someone to close the door to the reception area. Once the door was closed all I could hear was a soft hum that fell into the rhythmic time of a thumping that vibrated through my now hurting head. I felt something cold pressed lightly to my forehead. It felt good. I closed my eyes and then remembered what brought me to this place.

"Where's Byron? What happened?" I said as I struggled to sit upright. The sharp throbbing felt in my head told me that I should think better of this. I gave in, and laid back down.

"Royce and my bouncers took him outside to get some air.... and straighten him out, if you know what I mean." Kenny reported. His tone sounding disgusted.

"Tvoya, I think Byron was drunk," Charlene said, slowly almost apologetically.

"You think?" Kenny interjected. "Yeah, my man was dead drunk all right. Who was he anyway? I guess somebody doesn't like the idea of you getting married soon. Huh, Tvoya?"

"Kenny, that was Tvoya's fiancé," Charlene informed lowering her voice wanting me not to hear.

"True Dat?" Kenny asked now slowly sitting down next to me. All I could manage to do was nod my head, yes, as stinging hot tears ran down my cheeks. How could Byron do such a thing? Was he that mad at me? Had I driven him to this? I closed my eyes, wanting to shut the whole world out. Then I heard the noise from the club become clearer as the door opened and someone entered the room.

"How is she doing?" said the voice that entered. I recognized it right off. It was Royce. Again, I struggled to sit up. But the searing pain in my head jetted from one ear to the other. I could see Royce but only barely as his image kept swirling past my eyes hindering me from keeping him in focus. He was now sitting next to me. But why was his mouth moving, but no sound coming from it? Who was dimming the lights? Turn them back on, I was trying to say, but I couldn't hear myself either. Then again, nothing.

15

"...or Poorer"

"*Oh, my God! I'm late. I'm late for my wedding! Why didn't the limousine come and pick me up?" I pick up my Bible and begin flipping through the pages. But what am I looking for? There is it! The phone number for the Holy Matrimony Car Service Company. I begin dialing. I put down what now appears to be a telephone book. Then instantly I am at the front doors of my church, Mount Holiness Christian Life Center. There are no cars parked out front. The church is deserted. And on top of that, the doors are locked. I frantically pull on the oversized handles, but I can't get the door to budge. Then without warning, the doors fly open and a man I don't recognize is standing on the threshold offering his hand to me. I smile and place my hands in his and I begin to feel an overwhelming peace wash over me. We walk, hand in hand, through the next set of doors. Just before us is a long winding aisle that looks normal at its first appearance. But as we walk down this aisle, this man and I find the runner that is being rolled out just as we take each step has flaws. It buckles. It has bumps, rocks and tiny holes that the heels of my shoes keep getting caught in, forcing me to trip. I notice the pews of the church are filled with my family and friends and as we walk pass them, they cheer. Finally, the man and I get to the altar where Pastor Underwood has been waiting. He tells us he has been waiting a long time for us to get here. The man and I look at each other and smile. "I now pronounce you husband and wife," Pastor says. And then he hands us a baby bundled up in a receiving blanket. I take the baby. We look down at it and then we kiss. And then I notice that the cheering has stopped. We turn to walk back up the aisle, but now everyone is gone and it's dark. We try to take a step, but we can't get our legs to move. We look at each other and then turn to look out into the vastness of the church, but we see that there is nothing but darkness. I begin to see there is a huge pair of blood red eyes that has flames of fire coming from the sides of them coming towards us. The eyes keep moving closer and closer and closer to us. "Help! Help!" I scream over and over again. I turn to my new husband who begins to pat my hands gently saying, "Tvoya, it's all right, I'm here."*

"Tvoya, it's ok." I began to hear Royce's voice get clearer and clearer as I struggled to open my eyes.

"Royce, where am I? What are you doing here? Where's Charlene?" I begin to barrage him with a dozen questions.

I must've bolted straight up from a lying position because Royce was telling me I needed to lay back down. The sudden wave of nausea, suggested that I should listen to him. I did.

"But…"

"Tvoya, just lie still, I'll explain everything to you. Just be patient," Royce said while patting me on my hand.

It was at that moment I realized I had just awakened from a dream. Was Byron dragging me through Razz a dream as well? Royce continued, but I could tell he was gingerly picking and choosing his words. I prayed he would just spit it out.

"Tvoya, you're in the hospital. The doctor said you have a minor concussion, but they want you to stay and relax a little while longer so they can observe you."

As Royce recounted the events that brought me to the hospital, my eyes began to burn with hot tears that I rigidly tried to keep from coming. The question that kept repeating in my head was why did Byron act like this? I didn't want to utter his name to Royce so I thought to ask for Charlene.

"Where's Charlene?"

"She's speaking with the doctor now."

"Royce, can you bring her and the doctor in? I have a lot of questions."

"Sure, Tvoya. You just relax," Royce said before disappearing behind the curtain that was drawn all around me.

I felt so embarrassed and stupid and I had a lot of questions to ask, but asking them of Royce was out of the question. He was the last person I wanted to speak to about this, but at the same time, I was truly grateful he was there.

Royce kept to his promise and before I knew it Charlene and one of the emergency room doctors were pulling back the curtain.

"Gurl, how you doing?" Charlene asked as she gently gave me a kiss on my cheek. "You were knocked out for a while there."

"Hello, Miss Harrington, I'm Dr. Goldman. I understand you're ready to hear what's going on with you."

"Yes, my friend just told me you think that I have a minor concussion."

"Yes, that is correct. When you fell, you hit your head pretty hard. Got quite a bump in the process."

I wanted to ask about Byron, but I'm sure the doctor had no idea about the sordid details. In fact, I wondered what

Royce and Charlene told him. Then it hit me. What hospital was I in? Was I at Byron's hospital, Queens Memorial?

"What hospital am I in?" I asked, hoping no one would pick up on my reason for asking. My coming to Byron's hospital would not be good for him. I couldn't stop wondering where he might be at this time.

"You're in Southeast General, Miss Harrington," said Dr. Goldman. Oh good. "And we are going to take good care of you. We just want to keep you just a little while longer. Just for observation. Do you understand, Miss Harrington? A concussion is nothing to play with. You experienced a temporary loss of consciousness, when your friends brought you in."

He was right, I didn't remember being brought to the hospital.

Dr. Goldman continued, "But after examining you, I don't see where there has been any trauma to your brain." Dr. Goldman must have read the expression of concern and confusion on my face for it warranted him giving me more of an education on head injuries.

"All of your vital signs are intact. Both your pupils are the same size and you are not showing any unusual eye movement. And just now when you were speaking your speech wasn't slurred. These are all very good signs. How do you feel, Miss Harrington? Are you feeling dizzy or experiencing any nausea?"

"Um…, yes, a little of both."

"Well, that is to be expected. Do you remember anything about the fall you had?"

"Vaguely," was all I could manage to say. Besides my mouth felt like it was stuffed with cotton. I badly needed something cold to drink but Dr. Goldman only continued, "Do you remember what happened before you fell or after?"

"Um, can I have some water, please?" I asked weakly

while gently rubbing the back of my head.

"Sure, you can."

Charlene, who was quietly standing guard at the entrance of my private curtain space, offered to go and get me some.

As soon as she was back, I sat up to retrieve the glass from her hands. Aah, that was so good.

"I'm sorry, doctor, what did you ask me before I asked for the water?"

"Not a problem, do you remember what happened before you fell or after?"

Oh yeah, that question. Was this a trick question? Was Dr. Goldman trying to see if my story matched the one given to him by Charlene and Royce. And did he know that my fiancé who was responsible for this, was a doctor as well?

"Um, I remember walking very quickly and then I must have tripped and fell," I answered slowly and then closed my eyes. I didn't want the doctor to read that I remembered more than that. Forgive me Lord.

"Ok, you just lie back, keep the ice pack on the bump and get some more rest. I'll probably release you in a couple of hours. So, I'll be back every now and then to check on you until then."

Without opening my eyes, I only nodded my head to let him know I had heard what he had just said. Then I could hear him pulling back the curtain and walking away. I then slowly opened them to see Charlene peering down at me.

"Tvoya? Can I get you anything else?" Charlene said as she placed the palm of her hand to my forehand as if checking to see if I had a fever.

"No, I just want to go back to sleep," I said as I could feel a wave of drowsiness sweep over me. Just as I began to close my eyes, I could see Royce come back from behind the curtain. I smiled a lazy smile at him. He smiled back. It was comforting. *Nighty, night. Lights out again.*

16

"Dearly Beloved"

he time between my dozing back to sleep and Dr. Goldman returning to my room seemed no more than a wink. He released me giving instructions to Charlene and Royce as if they were my mother and father. He again checked my vitals, signed my chart and had a wheelchair waiting to cart me up and out of that place. Even if I needed to stay overnight, I wondered if my HMO would have covered it. Probably not. A teacher's insurance left a lot to be desired these days. Anyway, I was beginning to feel more and more like my old self, and it wasn't until we were in Royce's car did I even question the whereabouts of my own. In addition, I was like crazy hungry and "feining" for some french fries.

"The doctor said all you can have is something light like soup, salads, fruits," Charlene announced sounding more like my mother than my mother would. She was riding shotgun and I was sprawled out in the backseat.

"Don't worry about your car. After Charlene and I get you settled at your house, I'm going back over to Kenny's spot to get it." Royce caught my eye in his rear view mirror, winked and smiled. I smiled back weakly more due to my embarrassment than the throbbin' in my head.

Once we arrived at my place. Royce was the perfect gentleman. He ran around from his door to my door and hurriedly ushered me out instructing me to place all of my weight onto him. Being this close to Royce with my arm around his neck made me feel secure and at the same time woozy. Charlene was already up the stairs holding the door open as we made it to the last step. As we entered my living room, I noticed the clock on my wall unit and was disturbed that the time was 4:10 am. And still there had been no mentioned of Byron. I wanted so badly to ask Charlene about him, but with Royce around, I hadn't the nerve. Then I remembered that he was going to pick up my car. That would be a good time for me to drill Charlene. I advised Royce it would be ok to let me down on my chaise lounge. He did as told. Charlene went to work in the kitchen finding me something suitable to eat that would be in line with the command given to her by Dr. Goldman. Royce plopped himself in the chair adjacent to me watching me intently. He didn't say a word but his expression spoke volumes. I again smiled that same dumb smile not knowing what else to do. Then I decided to get the Spanish inquisition over with.

"All right, go ahead… tell me that I made a complete fool of myself tonight."

"Tvoya, I don't think it was you who made the fool of themselves." Right away, I knew he was referring to Byron.

"I don't know what to say…Byron has never done anything like this before." I was trying hard to plead his case. But as I did, anger started to rise up within me and before I could hold them back, the tears began to flow.

"Tvoya, if you ask me…you could do a lot better than Byron," Royce said with disdain as he moved to sit down next to me on the chaise lounge, at the same time offering me his handkerchief.

"A lot better? Like you, Royce? Huh!? A lot better like

you…who left me years ago, pregnant with your child and never looking back?" I screamed while slapping the handkerchief out of his hand.

"What's goin' on out here?" Charlene bolted into the living room, stopping short to take in the scene.

"What was that? Tvoya? What did you say?" Now it was Royce who was doing the yelling.

Why did I have to go there? This was all water under the bridge. I was over this episode in my life. Over Royce. Over the rejection. Over the disappointment. Over the life changing choice I had to make without him. I was really mad at Byron and was now taking it out on Royce. But maybe I was mad at Royce, too.

"Royce, I think you better go now," Charlene said as she ushered him towards the door. Royce stopped just before opening it and said, "Tvoya, we have gotsa talk."

"Yeah, yeah, you can talk to her when she's feeling better. She has a concussion, remember?" Charlene opened the door for Royce, pulling his shirt sleeve.

"Ok, ok! I'm out. I'm gonna pick up Tvoya's car, but when she's feeling better, we are gonna talk." I could hear Royce going down the steps making this threatened proclamation.

"Now, what was that all about?" inquired Charlene.

"Charlene, please can I have something to eat? I'm starving and please no more questions. My head is killing me."

I quickly scoffed down the chicken noodle soup and bowl of assorted fruits Charlene had prepared for me. Boy did it hit the spot. Her coming to stay with me in spite of her extenuating circumstances couldn't have come at a better time. It was funny, but this was the sort of thing my best friend, Valerie would be doing for me, but she was home with more pressing matters weighing on her. Which reminded me that today would be the day the family was to find out the results from Elizabeth's surgery. Oh God, I hope it would be good news.

With being newly nourished, I felt I had the strength to take the dishes into the kitchen and join Charlene in cleaning up. Besides, I needed to keep busy and my mind off the fact that Byron had not yet given me a call. I knew this because the light on my answering machine was not blinking, indicating no new calls.

"Tvoya? What are you doing in here?" Charlene scolded, not impressed that I had made it to the kitchen.

"I'm feeling much stronger since the food. Thanks, Charlene." I sat the dishes in the sink and felt I had better take a seat soon or my words would become contradictory.

"Glad that I could help," Charlene said as she watched me steadily.

"Charlene, why hasn't Byron called?" I now was ready to hear Charlene's take on this. I know she had been waiting to give me an earful.

"Gurl, Byron's probably somewhere passed out. Tvoya, he was really wasted," Charlene declared with pity. Pity wasn't something I wanted at the moment. What I needed was an explanation. Just then the doorbell rang, and I knew it was Royce bringing me the keys to my car.

"Charlene, can you...."

"I'm on it, Tvoya. I'll get rid of him. You've had enough for one day." Charlene was through the door before I could say anything else. I sat still to listen to the exchange between Charlene and Royce. But I couldn't hear much. Then I heard the door close and shortly thereafter Charlene was back in the kitchen asking me where I wanted her to put my keys.

"You can leave them right here on the table. How was Royce's demeanor?" I asked Charlene, like I really cared.

"It was hard to tell. He asked if you had eaten. I told him, you had. He said he felt better knowing I was here with you and he will check on you tomorrow. Then he was down the steps getting into Kenny's car." Charlene's recount had a trace of 'what's going on with you two' to it, which I chose to ignore.

"Charlene, thanks again for everything. I'm gonna take two aspirins and go to bed. Please get some rest yourself. Good night."

All I wanted to do at that moment was reach my bed and crash. Charlene was probably right. Byron was drunk, so I probably wouldn't be hearing from him until later this morning anyway and I needed a good sleep in order to deal with him. It would be soon enough for all the explaining that needed to go around. Byron to me. Me to Royce. And everything to Charlene. I knew she couldn't wait. Me neither, really.

♥   ♥   ♥

I awakened to the ring of the telephone, only it wasn't coming from the phone resting on my night table stand. It was coming from the kitchen. I could hear Charlene's voice, now coming closer. She opened my bedroom door slowly, just enough to fit her head in.

"I'm awake, Charlene. Who's on the phone?" I had almost forgotten Charlene was staying with me.

"A Mrs. Munroe?" Charlene's question sounded suspicious. Now I was really wide awake.

"That's Byron's mother," I whispered back to Charlene, holding out my hand to take the phone. Charlene then made herself quite comfortable on the end of my bed. I shooed her out, but she wasn't budging. I guessed I couldn't blame her. This was becoming a saga of epic proportions.

"Uh, hello? Mrs. Munroe? Is everything all right with Byron?" My heart was racing a mile a minute. I was so afraid that maybe he had gotten himself into an accident and his mother was now calling me to give me an account of the bad news.

"Hello Tvoya." Her tone was slow and steady. One could easily recognize her West Indian accent with her elevation of the last syllable of my name. I loved to hear her speak.

"Yes, Byron's all righta. He is just nursing a bad head. Ya know. Darling, he is quite embarrassed for his behavior on last nighta. Ya see. He told me whata happened and he is sooo very sorry. Can you forgive him, Tvoya?"

"Forgive him? Um, I don't mean to be disrespectful, Mrs. Munroe, but why isn't Byron calling me himself?" I was confused. I looked over at Charlene. Her expression was mirroring my thoughts and feelings, and that was because she hadn't heard a word of what Mrs. Munroe had just said. I did, however, and I certainly didn't understand this logic....having his mother call me? Was Byron nuts?

"Tvoya, darling. He just asked me to call you...to a soften the blow. Ya know."

"Is Byron there with you? Please put him on the phone." I was trying hard to remain composed but this was just too much. Charlene raised an eyebrow, indicating to me my tone had not sounded pleasant.

"No... a Byron is not here. He's at his home."

"You mean he called you to ask you to call me? Why didn't he just call me?"

"Now, Tvoya, please calm yourself, darling. Seeing by the waya you're reacting, maybe it was just as well I called ya first."

"I'm sorry, Mrs. Munroe. I don't mean to be taking this

out on you. But this is between Byron and me. Please tell him to call me. Goodbye." I pressed the off button on the phone and threw it on the bed.

"I don't believe this. He had his mother call me. She said to soften the blow. What's up with that, Charlene? Is Byron crazy or what? He drags me through Kenny's club, throws me to the floor, resulting in me having a concussion and now…he doesn't call me, but his mother does?"

"Tvoya, gurl, you had better calm down before you give yourself a stroke." Charlene was trying her best to settle me and get me back to lying down. "What did she say? But wait, tell me without raising your voice. Ok?"

I agreed and told Charlene what Byron's mother had said. Which was really nothing. Nothing that could explain to me why Byron had acted so foolishly last night and why he didn't have the nerve to fess up and come to me correct.

Now the phone and the doorbell were ringing, simultaneously. I reached for the phone. Charlene went for the door.

"Mrs. Munroe, please have Byron call me. I don't think this situation is going to get solved with you as our go between." I made the mistake of not checking the Caller ID before answering, again.

"Tvoya?" This isn't Mrs. Munroe," the voice said on the other end. Immediately, I knew who it did belong to. It was Royce. Had I'd known it was him I would have let this call go through to my voice mailbox.

"Oh, hi Royce. I thought you were someone else." I surely didn't want to have a conversation with Royce either, but seeing all he had done for me earlier, I guessed I owed it to him to be nice. And then, of course, there was the other matter I blurted out in my frustration. I silently prayed he wouldn't bring it up. The Lord knew I couldn't deal with it at this time.

"How are you feeling? Better, I hope," Royce sounded pensive but quite genuine in his concern.

"I'm coming along. Listen, Royce, I want to thank you for all you did last night. I really appreciate it, but I'm gonna be ok. No worries. All right?" I said trying to make light of the whole fiasco.

"Have you heard from Byron?" Royce wasn't going for making light of it.

"Um, no not yet." My attention became divided as my mother walked into the room, followed by Charlene, who stood behind her mouthing that she tried to detain her.

"Um Royce, I've got to go. I'll talk to you soon. Bye." I hung up from Royce to face the music from my mother. Rehashing this whole account was getting boring. And I knew she'd probably heard an earful at the salon already. Question was whose version did she hear, and whose would she be relaying to me?

"Tvoya, is what I heard true?" my mother began before I could put down the phone.

"I don't know, Mommy, that depends on what you heard." I rolled my eyes as I threw back the covers to swing my legs off the side of the bed.

My day had definitely started. There was no rest for the weary where she was concerned. She came all the way over here demanding the truth and that was what she was going to get. Even if it involved us all realizing that Byron could possibly have a drinking problem. I wondered what my mother would think of that.

17

"Speak Now"

I couldn't bring myself to look at my mother as I told her the sordid details of what occurred the night before between Byron and me. And gathering by the way her eyes were transfixed to staring at the floor as I snuck a glance in her direction, she couldn't look at me either. I knew she was feeling the guilt of hearing what the repercussions of someone who was drunk could do to those they claim to love. She had been through this many times before. But solely on the back end for she never grasped what she was doing while she was doing it; only when she was told about it later would she scramble to recollect her memory, recognizing the consequences of her intoxicated actions.

"Is it true that Royce was there?" my mother asked breaking me out of my rambling.

"Yeah, Royce was there, too." Boy, the salon got all of their details straight. She didn't seem to be surprised by anything that I told her. She had already heard it at the shop. Guilt was the only thing that I could attest to what was displayed on her face. She and I then sat in silence. Charlene took this as her warning sign. She announced she had prepared breakfast and that she had to go tie up some loose ends with her getting her things into storage. I thanked her and then she was gone, leaving my mother and me privately to our thoughts. The phone rang again, breaking the conflicted hush my plight had placed on us both. I was dismayed that my mother reached for it and answered before I could get the chance. She could care less that it was my phone.

"Hello?" said my mother with a moderately light and airy expression that would be hard to trace her previous mood. I observed her purposely to figure out who was on the other end. Immediately her demeanor changed and I knew then, it had to have been Byron. My eyes locked with hers as she searched to find a clue that would reveal to her I was ready for this upcoming conversation. I nodded that I was. However reluctant, she gave me the phone, left the room closing the door behind her. Thank you, Mommy. I needed the privacy.

"Hello, Byron." No hint of airy and light in my expression. My tone was filled with bewilderment and agitation.

"Um, hi Tvoya. Can I see you?" I could hear him swallow hard while taking deep breaths.

"Can I see you? Is that what you just asked me, Byron?" Now I was the one taking the deep breaths. "How about how is the concussion I caused you to have last night?"

"Oh, baby, I'm so sorry about that." His voice was trembling and I could hear that he was crying. "Please....Tvoya. Please forgive me. Let me come over. I need to see you."

"Byron, what was that all about...last night. Why did you just show up at Razz and act like such a damn fool? Why Byron?" My voice was slightly raised but I was careful not to let my mother hear me.

There was a long pause. I was waiting for an explanation.

But was I being too hard on him? This was the man I was getting ready to marry. Should I be cutting him some slack? Maybe this was just an isolated incident. I didn't really believe that Byron would intentionally harm me. I didn't really think that he had a problem with alcohol. Did I? The wedding was still on, wasn't it? We could work through this. Right?! Together!

"Byron, yes, please come over." My tone had found a way to be soft again. He responded to the change.

"I'll be right there, baby. I'll be right over." And then the connection was broken.

I sat on the side of my bed for an considerable length of time, rationalizing it all. I came to the conclusion I wasn't going to be able to figure any of this out until I at least had a bite to eat. Sounds of robust gastric nuances were escaping from my tummy, and I was hungry as I didn't know what. When I emerged from my bedroom I found that my mother was waiting for me in the kitchen. She had made a pot of coffee and held a cup up to me as a peace offering from her seat at the table. I accepted, feebly smiling. She jumped to her feet as I took the chair next to the one she had just abandoned.

"Let me fix your plate. It looks like Charlene cooked up a delicious meal here," my mother said as she made herself busy fussing over me.

"Thanks, Mommy." I was too engrossed in the conversation that was going on in my head between Byron and me to say anything else to her. Instead, I just stared at the far wall of my kitchen, sipping my coffee.

"What did Byron have to say? Is he coming over?"

"He didn't say much, and yes he said that he was on his way."

"Oh, good! Then, I better get out of your way."

"No!" I surprised myself with my response. It must have

surprised her as well for she dropped the fork she was getting ready to place to my left. "Mommy please stay awhile." My mother searched my face. "Tvoya, are you afraid of Byron?" Afraid? Of Byron? I didn't really think this was the case. But maybe she was right. Maybe deep down inside, I was afraid. But of what? Didn't I want the truth? Didn't I want to find out if my fiancé had a drinking problem? I needed to know what was happening between Byron and me.

But as I sat there contemplating the circumstances, I began to realize this wasn't only between Byron and me. Elizabeth's imminent health crisis and Royce's return had become formidable factors in this inopportune yarn.

"Mommy, please…no questions. Just stick around, ok?"

"All right, baby, all right."

♥　　♥　　♥

After finishing breakfast, I made my way to the bathroom to take a nice hot invigorating shower. As the pulsating water permeated my shoulders and back, the tension of the night before seeped its way out of every one of my pores. I knew I didn't have much time to spend drenching away the residue of this not so distant memory; shortly I could possibly be relieving it all again, with my forthcoming conversation with Byron. However, I did emerge more relaxed than when I went in. The lingering dull headache that had made itself comfortable in my head had even departed. I dried, lotioned and dressed, and was now feeling ready to face Byron. From behind the bathroom door, I heard the doorbell ring. I was glad my mother had agreed to stick around. She could run interference if things got too uncomfortable for me. I waited for them to finish their formalities, however I'm sure it was unsettling for them both. Soon silence came and my entrance was anticipated.

I walked slowly into the living room. Byron's back was facing me. He had not yet heard me come in. I stood still watching him. My eyes scanned for my mother. She probably made herself scarce by retreating to the kitchen. Good. Byron then felt my presence and quickly turned around.

"Tvoya! I didn't hear you come in." Byron stood perfectly still as if his legs willed him to. I was disappointed he didn't come towards me.

"Byron?" If he thought that I was going to walk over to him, he didn't know me very well. I sat down on the sofa facing where he stood. I observed his fingers twitching. He then became aware of his exposed nervousness forcing his hands into his back pockets.

"Sit down, Byron," I said trying very hard to hide my annoyance with his self-inflicted distance. He did as I asked, sitting all the way on the chaise lounge provoking further my aggravation. Why didn't he sit next to me on the couch? I gave a silent sigh and moved to sit next to him on the chaise.

"I'm so sorry, Tvoya...about last night. I don't know what else to say. I had a little too much to drink and wasn't myself. Please forgive me. I promise this will never happen again," Byron said amidst his tears. I began to feel very sorry for him. Maybe I drove him to this. Maybe my celebrating abstinence and Charlene's moving in and the tension of our upcoming wedding nuptials all contributed to Byron's error in judgment.

"I forgive you, Byron. I forgive you," I whispered as I positioned his head unto my shoulder. Next thing I knew, we were embroiled in a passionate, I can't live without you kiss. He did after all apologize. What more could I ask of the man?

18

"To Love And Cherish"

"Mommy! The coast is clear. You can come out now. Byron's gone."

My mother was through the double doors of my kitchen before I could get the entire phrase out. She and I both knew she was eavesdropping the whole time anyway.

"Boy, that was quick. Did you chase him away?" she asked as she wiped her hands on a dish towel.

"I told him he looked a mess and that he should go home and get some rest. He's expected at the hospital this evening."

"Oh? Is that all you told him?"

"Well, he did apologize. I felt sorry for him. Byron has been under a lot of pressure lately. And I'm partly to blame for that."

"Tvoya, baby, never take the blame for someone's drinking. If I've learned nothin' else since my sobriety is that the alcoholic can blame no one but themselves."

"Who said Byron's an alcoholic? That never even entered the picture. He just had a little too much to drink and his jealousy got the best of him."

"His jealousy? Maybe because Royce was there? Tvoya, if you don't put a handle on this Royce situation, he is going to ruin your wedding and relationship with Byron."

"Oh, about Royce….Mommy, I kinda went there with him.., I mean…I mentioned he left me pregnant…not looking back."

"What!?" I heard the dish towel snap as it whipped around my mother's backside as she drew her hands to rest on her hips.

"I know. I know. Don't even say it. It was stupid. But last night after he brought me back from the hospital, he said something that made me fly into a rage, and I just blurted it out. I guess the trauma from the concussion and my being mad at Byron just hit all at once. I know… I shouldn't have said anything."

"Well, maybe it's just as well this comes out now," my mother sighed as she sat down beside me on the chaise lounge. "I guess you and Royce never did have closure. This is probably what you need to put a rest to the past so you can step into your future with Byron. But remember Tvoya, it wasn't like he wasn't aware of it in the first place. He did leave you to make all of the decisions by yourself."

"Mommy, don't you have something better to do today, than to baby sit me?" I didn't mean to sound like I didn't appreciate my mother's concern or her advice. But I did need a break from all of this. Besides I needed to call Valerie to see if Elizabeth had been to her doctor for her results.

"Yeah, baby. I do need to get back. But you shouldn't be left alone."

"Mommy, I'm fine. Charlene will be back soon."

"Oh, yeah! And what's with Charlene staying here? She started to tell me something or the other when I got here. But I was more concerned with what was going on with you to much listen to what she was saying."

"It's a long story, Mommy. Anyway, when Priscilla gets here, she's gonna need to stay with you."

"Well, thanks for asking me," my mother rolled her eyes as she stood to pick up her purse. "Are you sure you're feeling all right?"

"Never better, Mommy."

"Now, I know that's a lie."

♥   ♥   ♥

My mother's leaving left me to my own contemplative rationalization. And then I decided I wasn't going to dwell on any of this any longer. It was... what it was. Byron made a mistake. He apologized. I accepted his apology. What I needed to be thinking about but chose not to was what my next conversation with Royce would be like. My mother was right. I did need closure with Royce. Although this was a long time ago, he never got to hear my what for. And the time had finally come. God was in control of everything, and I was trusting that my blurting it out last night was for a worthwhile purpose. But first I needed to check over at Valerie's about Elizabeth. She could be possibly getting some bad news and I needed to be there for her. But I was sure it was good news, she would be destined to get.

"What?! Elizabeth, did I hear you right?" I almost dropped the phone.

"Yeah, Freshmeat. The docs confirmed it. I have ovarian cancer." Cancer? How could this be? No! It couldn't be!

"How are you...I mean, what....," I couldn't get my mouth to move with my thoughts.

"It's ok. Tvoya." I couldn't believe how calm Elizabeth sounded.

"I'm coming over."

"No, now is not a good time. Just before you called, Valerie and I just got finished telling Ma and Curtis. It hasn't really sunk in with them yet and I still have to call Gary."

"Sure. I understand." I wasn't so sure it had even sunk in with Elizabeth. "I'll let you get back to the family. I'll talk to you later. And Elizabeth, please if you need anything or you just need to talk, please call me. I'm here for you. And please tell Valerie, I'll get with her later."

"Thanks. I'll be sure to do that. We'll talk later," Elizabeth said before hanging up.

Cancer? I was dumbfounded. Could this day get any worse? I could only imagine how this whole thing would affect Elizabeth's family. At that thought of reasoning, the doorbell rang. I looked through the peephole of the door and was startled at the volatility in which I had opened it. Then before either of us could say, hello, I was blubbering and boo-hooing in Royce's arms. Royce was the first to speak, breaking my hypnotic crying jag.

"Tvoya, baby. What happened? What's wrong. Did that mother…"

"No! It's nothing to do with Byron," I said trying to regain my composure. What was I doing anyway in Royce's arms? Was I crazy? I backed away from Royce to obtain a reasonable measure of safe distance between us. He grabbed the screen door before it had a chance to slam in his face.

"Can I come in?" He stood waiting for my consent. Confusion painted his expression. Uncertainty colored mine.

"Sure, come in." Royce followed me into the living room. I wasn't sure as to what I should say next. Could I trust Royce to this painful revelation of Elizabeth's health? It seemed that since Royce's return to the neighborhood, Lamar and him were growing quite tight again. But still…would it be all right to share their personal business with him? But, I needed to talk with someone. My emotions had run the gamut within the last twenty-four hours and I couldn't take it anymore. But what will my spilling my heart out to Royce accomplish? It could possibly make matters worst between the two of us. I sure didn't want to lead Royce on. And this could open up Pandora's Box and lead us to discussing the past. Was I ready for all of this? Could I expect Royce to be understanding and supportive of all that I was going through? Anyway, what was he doing here?

"Royce, I'm sorry for what just happened. I'm kinda out of sorts. But…um, what are you doing here anyway?"

"I came to check on you. I knew if I called you again, you would just put me off. So I decided to make a surprise visit."

"You came to just check up on me, huh?" I stared at Royce with an eye of apprehension. "Royce, please, I'm just fine."

"Tvoya, just now when you opened the door, you were not fine. What's going on?"

"Nothing, Royce."

"Come on, Tvoya. I think you need to get out and get some air. Let me take you for a ride."

Maybe that wouldn't be such a bad idea after all.

♥　　　♥　　　♥

The weather had unquestionably improved from the day before. The temperature and humidity had lowered considerably and the crispness of the air quality made it a lot easier to breathe. While sitting in the front seat of Royce's BMW, listening to the soft jazz that played from a CD player, I began to take deep solid calculated breaths. Inhaling through my nostrils, exhaling through my mouth. Slowly, I began to mellow out. I had no idea as to where Royce was taking me, and for a few minutes I didn't care. I was finally beginning to relax. My head was quite at home on the seat's headrest and slowly my eyes became heavy. I allowed myself to be lulled into a dreamy state of unconsciousness as my body relaxed into a weightlessness sleep.

"Tvoya, we're here." The whisper of Royce's voice tickled my ears. I slowly opened my eyes to find his lips brushing ever so slightly across my cheek. I moved away discreetly being careful to not offend him out rightly.

"We're here?" I asked as I turned my head and groggily looked out of the window, "and where may I ask is here?"

"Oceanfront Park, that's where." Royce turned the key in the ignition to turn the motor off. The boardwalk stretched out right in front of us. And beyond the horizon of it's railing one could see the rushing in and out of the ocean waves.

"Are you ready to take a walk?" Royce asked noticing I was still in a dreamlike state.

"Yeah, I'm ready. Some exercise will do me good."

Royce smiled and nodded as he got out of the car and came around to my door to help me out. He opened the door and held his hand out for me to place mine in his. His hands were so soft yet firm and commanding. You could sense the strength of his spirit through them. It comforted me at the same time as it worried me. Bringing back feelings of long ago. Feelings that had long been thought to have been forgotten now realized more suppressed. Upon recognizing the possible danger, I quickly removed my hand from his and subsequently stuffed them both into my pockets. Thank God for summer sweats with pockets. I smiled secretly at my private joke.

"Wow, I haven't been down here in years," I said, "I've completely forgotten about this place."

"Good! So you haven't brought Byron down here," Royce

said beaming a broad smile. I had to admit, he was still so very fine. I shot him a quick look of dissatisfaction toward his comment but decided not to respond verbally. It would have only been tempered with sarcasm of which I declared I was free from. He got the message and for a while we walked in total silence. Both of us deciding it would be safer to just observe and take in the extraordinary panoramic view of the beach and its ocean. The population was rather sparse. A man and his dog played fetch with a Frisbee. A couple played tag with the ocean as they jumped over the waves each time the tide came in, and a little boy and his mother made sand castles as dad slept.

We reached a park bench in the middle of the boardwalk and I decided it was time to sit down. Royce decided it was time to talk. Eager for this, I was not. There was too much to say, and I knew there would be too much emotion ushering it in. Oh, why did I agree to come for this ride with Royce anyway?

As I came to expect and none disappointed, Royce was the first to disrupt the serenity this muted time granted.

"Tvoya? Can we talk? I mean…you're so uptight. What's going on with you? I want to help." Royce seemed so sincere. Could I really trust him with all I was encountering?

"Look Royce. I'm a… just feeling a little, uh…. overwhelmed and vulnerable right now. I don't know, um…. if I can really explain to you, uh…. what's going on with me." I was so embarrassed by my stammering. I thought I was going to break down at that very moment. I wasn't sure if Royce picked up on this. If he had, it didn't stop him from pressing me further.

"You said something after I brought you home earlier that I think we oughta talk about." Royce's tone was without a doubt calmer than it had been when I blurted out what I was sure he was referring to.

"Royce, please. Let's not go there. You're talking ancient history. It's over and done with. There's nothing to talk about."

"There's nothing to talk about? Tvoya, you yelled at me that I left you pregnant. And with my baby?!"

"Like you didn't know," I interrupted, finding myself up on my feet.

"No, Tvoya. I didn't know." Royce now too was standing. We stood looking at each other intently for what approximated an eternity. Who was Royce trying to fool? Did I not hear him right? Did I not hear him say, he didn't know?

"Oh, please Royce! You mean to tell me that after all these years, you're now gonna stand there and lie to me and tell me you didn't know I was pregnant?" My eyes were burning and at the same time blinded by the stinging tears that had began welling up inside. They were now on overflow traveling liberally down my flushed cheeks. I was hot. How could he stand there and tell me that he didn't know? Who did he think he was talking to? The ditzy schoolgirl I used to be? Yeah, maybe that was it. Yeah, maybe he had lost his mind. And thought I had as well.

"Tvoya, I'm not lying to you. I didn't know." His voice was barely audible. He then sat back down slowly staring straight ahead at the sea. I began to feel a little woozy and I sat down as well. Again silence permeated our existence. Royce placed his hand on mine.

"Tvoya, I'm sorry. Let's start again."

Start again? What the hell was Royce talking about? I moved my hand from his and shifted my entire body, whereas now my back was facing him. At that point, I didn't know if I was angrier at him for drudging up the past or myself for showing such emotion….such vulnerability. My God! I was over this. This happened so long ago and I had dealt with it. I had already   long since moved through the process of bereavement. It was like experiencing a death. I had been through all the range of emotions….Anger, denial, depression, mourning, acceptance, and I had survived. I survived! So why was I traveling through this time warped tunnel? Why was I now crying uncontrollably? Wait now, why was I now enveloped by the muscular strength of Royce's arms? He was holding me and I was holding on to him as if I couldn't live another minute without him. By now, he was stroking my hair and whispering softly into my ear that everything was going to be all right. Why was all of this happening, now? Now, that I was promised to marry Byron Munroe. Why this now, Lord? I dared not ask out loud, but only within my heart.

I slowly managed to pull myself away from Royce's soothing embrace. Truth was I didn't want to leave it. I wanted to stay and melt and sink and wield into his all encompassing frame. I wanted to hear him say he was sorry for not answering any of the four letters I wrote to him about the baby. I wanted to hear him say he was sorry for letting me go through the ordeal all alone. I wanted to hear him say he still loved me and that he had married the wrong girl. I wanted him…..

"Tvoya, I didn't know about the baby, please tell me…if you can, what happened." I looked into Royce's face and found that he was crying as well. I looked into his eyes and I didn't recognize him. He was so foreign and unknown to me. His mouth was moving. He was saying something, but I couldn't hear what that was. I could hear the waves pounding the waiting sand. I could hear the squawking exchange of the seagulls conversing in flight. I could even hear the ring of my cell phone and at the same time, I heard nothing, except, the silence of nothing spoke volumes of something. Something of sincerity. I heard that Royce was telling me the truth. He didn't know. He hadn't known. He never knew about our child.

The culminated events of the preceding days had me living more in the past than in the present. My past was with Royce. My present and future was to be and should be with Byron. And due to this moment, both worlds were about to collide.

Royce did deserve answers. But, did I have to be the one to tell him? It amazed me that it took this long for him to find out something that everyone else involved thought he had already knew. First off, my mind could not tell my mouth fast enough the words that needed to be expressed. The years and the pain that rode them took their ole sweet time resurrecting. Tucked away in a nice place were the memories. I had worked so hard at keeping them there….in tact. They did not want to come out. Skeletons and some memories had a way like that. You push them in, away and out of sight but they keep rearing their ugly heads. Until you need them is when you come to find out they have decided all on their own they want to stay hidden. Disappointing you, they turn on you and they leave you to fend for yourself. Bringing them out is tougher than you expected. You tug until it hurts so that you soon realize you didn't need them after all. Then the dam just breaks and all on its own the force of the pent up past with all its rage of emotions crashes through the barricades you worked so hard at putting up. And nothing and no one can stop it.

I told Royce how soon after that last weekend I spent at his school, I became aware I was pregnant. With time, it had become clear our relationship was over. I had to be sure as to what my motives were. So it took me three months to even write the first letter. Did I want Royce to know about the baby because it was his or because I wanted him back? It took me all of the three months, just to figure that out! I wanted both. I wrote the first letter, and received no response. This blow of rejection sent me into a tailspin. The only person I had to lean on was Valerie. Even though she was away at school, we were on the phone every night. At that point I had not even told my mother. My father wasn't clued in until the very end.

My cell phone rang again. This time, I remembered Byron and thought I should pay it some attention. It wasn't Byron, but instead Valerie. I chose to answer it. Royce looked at me as if I were from Mars. I smiled weakly, hunched my shoulders while wiping away my tears.

"Hi Valerie." I tried my best to make my voice sound light. Royce got up from the bench and started walking down the boardwalk.

"Hi, T, can we meet somewhere so we can talk?" Her voice was laced with urgency.

"Sure, Val. Is everything all right with Elizabeth?"

"Yeah, Um she's resting right now. T, meet me at the restaurant around the corner from my house. Ok?"

"Ok, I'll be right there." I disconnected the call and watched Royce as he leaned against the railing with his back still facing me. Our talk would have to wait. Sorry Royce.

19

"I Do...Don't I?"

*R*oyce was thoroughly disappointed I abruptly ended our trip down memory lane. And even though I was quite resigned to traveling through our time capsule…, let down, I was not. There were more pressing issues that needed attention, and I needed to hear what Valerie had to say. Royce agreed to take me to meet Valerie and after a while, finally relented in offering to pick me up, when I insisted I would find a way back home from there. Upon his dropping me off, I promised I would get back to him as soon as I possibly could, but not before I got him to promise he wouldn't stalk me for this information either. He swore, scouts honor and then he was on his way.

When I entered the vestibule of the restaurant, Valerie was waiting there with a apprehensive look of concern. She had witnessed my getting out of Royce's car, but said nothing about it when we greeted one another with a hug.

"Hey, gurl. I hope I didn't keep you waiting." I decided then I wouldn't mention Royce either.

"No, you're right on time. Let's go in," Valerie said as she held the door open so that I could walk in front of her.

The hostess met us beyond the foyer beckoning us to follow her. She led us through the entire restaurant and what seemed to be strange for a Saturday afternoon, it was almost empty. So why were we being taken past all of these available tables, I thought to myself. Finally, we were led to two heavy looking doors with brass columns for handles. Our hostess stopped and looked for what seemed like Valerie's permission to proceed. I also looked at Valerie to see that she nodded... affirmative.

"What's going on here?" I asked, but was not given an answer before I was gently shoved through the heavy doors into a beautiful banquet room full of women shouting, "SURPRISE!" in total unison. Yeah, they got me. They got me good!

I looked around the room as everyone seemed to rush at me all at once. At first glance, it appeared that every woman I had ever met or known was present. My mother, Margo and of course, my aunts, Lulu and Marilyn, as well as Charlene, and some of my teacher girlfriends were there. Even Faye was in attendance. And to blow me totally away, my cousin, Priscilla was there. Who was missing was, Valerie's mother and sister, Elizabeth, and understandably so.

Although I was there physically, I indubitably wasn't there mentally and spiritually. This transition, I was not expecting. It totally caught me off guard. I was expecting to get some information from Valerie on Elizabeth's health, but instead, I was ambushed by my own bridal shower. Why didn't they just cancel it? I was just coming from having a concussion. I'm sure everyone there knew about that fiasco. And if that weren't enough, I had just come from playing true confessions with Royce. No wonder, Valerie didn't mention Royce's dropping me off. I should have known better. I was greeted first by my mother hauling a garment bag instructing me to change. I had forgotten that I was way too casual for this sort of affair. I grabbed the bag from her and followed the hostess to the restroom, but not before I stopped to greet my cousin, Priscilla, who I had thought would not be in town until at least next week.

"Pris! What are you doing here? No wonder I couldn't get you to tell me your definite arrival date and time."

"Hey Cuz! Surprise!"

"Tvoya! Will you go and get changed so we can get this here party started?" My mother intercepted our little exchange. I proceeded on to the restroom, like a good little bride to be would. No doubt, Valerie, Charlene and Priscilla were in tow.

Once we made it to the restroom a barrage of questions came at me from every angle. "Where were you?" "Why couldn't we reach you?" "Even, Byron didn't know where you had gone." Oh no! Byron knew I was missing in action. Great!

While I struggled to get changed quickly, Valerie and Priscilla insisted I give them an explanation of my whereabouts. They also wanted a blow by blow account of the incident that occurred between Byron and me at Razz. I looked to Charlene, figuring that she had already given them the 411. She only shook her head, saying, "No, gurl, this is all you." She seemed to be gloating that she knew something more about me than my best friend Valerie knew. And poor Priscilla was totally in the dark.

"I just came from the airport and the word over there is… Byron kicked your butt," Priscilla announced, "let's go and hunt that negro down." Priscilla was always looking for a fight. Just like her father, my Uncle Joe. And come to think of it, was exactly how he got killed….looking for a fight.

"Pris, it wasn't like that at all. Byron got a little jealous. He was a little drunk and one thing led to another. It was all very innocent." I didn't want my cousin getting the wrong impression of my fiancé. She hadn't even met him yet and already there was a stained impression on her brain regarding him.

"T, I heard you got a concussion from his manhandling." Priscilla looked at Charlene when she said this.

"Let's just drop this for now, all right?" I said as I touched up my makeup. Looking back at each of them through the mirror made me realize how blessed I was to have these women in my life.

"Yeah, we'll drop it for now, but later we've gotsa talk. We better hurry up before your moms comes in here to get us all. We've got a bridal shower to get through." Valerie spoke and that was all that was said for now on that subject.

As we all walked down the hall from the restroom leading to the banquet hall that held my bridal shower, I dropped back to allow Charlene and Priscilla to proceed Valerie and me.

"How is Elizabeth doing? You know you shouldn't even be here," I whispered to Valerie. I was taken aback that Valerie was here involved in giving me this shower with her sister just having received the bad news that she has cancer.

"She's doing ok. Freshmeat, we'll talk about all of that later. I want you to enjoy your bridal shower. All right? Now you have a lot of guests to greet." Valerie's words were in support of me but she looked troubled and I felt so guilty for going through with my wedding.

At that moment, for the first time, I seriously considered postponing the wedding. But with all that had been going on of late, who could I possibly share this new revelation with? Everyone loved the idea of Byron and me and although we had just went through a moment of distress, for many this would be excused and overlooked.

"What took you so long?" my mother asked handing me a plate of food.

"Oh, thanks, Mommy. I'm starving," I said as I grabbed the plate and went to woofing down the grub as fast as I could.

"So, T, where were you?"

"You'll get mad if I told you. So I'm not gonna."

"You weren't with Royce, were you?" my mother's asking held obvious contempt. I reached over and gave her a peck on her cheek.

"Mommy, thank you for this wonderful shower. Everything looks absolutely amazing." Maybe flattery would take her mind off of Royce and me.

"Tvoya, I'm warning you. You're playing a dangerous game." A game! Was my mother tripping or what? Who knew better than I that this was no game? This was....this was....this was my life. Past. Present. And future.

I traveled through the mass of women receiving my congratulatory well wishes and words of wisdom on what it would take to sustain a marriage. I was genuinely appreciative of all that was said to me. I treasured each and every bit of advice. But I felt so far removed from it all. Was I really getting married? Was I really ready for such a big step? Was Byron the one? He didn't nearly know all there was to know about me, and I was sure I didn't know all there was to know about him.

"You're troubled, T. Am I right about it?" Aunt Marilyn sat down next to me.

"Oh, Aunt Marilyn. I just have so much on my mind."

"You gotta take it to the Lord, chile. Tell him all about it."

"I have. And I'm not getting any answers," I whined.

"Maybe you have gotten your answer. You just don't like the answer you got. T, you don't have to go through with this wedding, especially if the Lord is telling you not to. 'Cause, if you go through with it, you will live to regret it."

Could it be expectant that Aunt Marilyn would be the only one I could talk to about my doubts of marrying Byron? She was the only one I knew that had a true connection with

God himself. She was so spiritual and at the same time so grounded.

"Aunt Marilyn, can I get with you tomorrow to talk to you about something?"

"Sure baby, come on with me to service tomorrow. I guess you heard that our guest speaker will be Reverend Sapphire Pierce-Vertrell."

"Yeah, ok. It's a date."

"All right now." Aunt Marilyn squeezed my shoulder as she walked away. And I began to feel a little bit better.

♥   ♥   ♥

The shower was well underway and everyone was having a good ole' time. Opening my gifts was a hoot. My level of embarrassment increased with each gift of lingerie I opened. Each outfit was more outrageous than the one before. The ladies got a kick out of my blushing. It had really been a long time since I'd worn any of that stuff. Since being celibate, these unmentionables no longer were a part of my wardrobe. I was ashamed to admit even if just to myself, I once owned this type of wear. And the men that had the privilege of viewing my wearing them certainly didn't deserve the honor. I wished I could go back and retrieve my virginity and dignity. But since I can't.... celibacy is the next best thing. In my opinion and my understanding of what the will of God is in this area, this honor, privilege and right belonged only to my husband.

The whole affair was beginning to wind down and I was making the customary thank-you's and glad you could make it regards when Charlene announced her disappointment in the fact that we had not had a male stripper to entertain us.

"I told you she was scank," Priscilla bickered as she approached me and Charlene.

"I beg your pardon?" Charlene snapped back.

"I wasn't talking to you. I was talking about you. So you can just take your begging pardon self and go somewhere." Priscilla was ready for a fight, again.

"Priscilla, why are you trying to start some mess? How was your flight?" I interjected trying to change the subject. Charlene rolled her eyes and walked away.

"Good," Priscilla remarked, "T, I don't know why you even asked that witch to be in your wedding."

"Yeah, Pris, the operative word being *my* wedding. Did Mommy tell you, you will be camping out at her place?"

"Yeah she did. That's what I'm talking about T. Charlene only uses you and you continue to let her. I don't understand it."

"Pris, Charlene is my good friend. I'm sorry if you don't understand it. But here's the deal. Don't go there with your nonsense again. You got me?" I had to set my cousin straight. This feud, Priscilla had going with Charlene was as old as dirt. Priscilla never did get over the fact that someone she was diggin' on back in the day when she would come and visit me had a thing for Charlene, and not her. And believe me, when Charlene was made aware of it she used it to the max. But this was old school water under the bridge, and was not priority in my book of things that concerned me. I had more pressing things weighing on me. I had to figure out if I was really going to go through with this wedding or not.

20

"To Honor..."

My bridal shower was now over and those left in attendance were my mother, Valerie, Priscilla, and Margo. Charlene left shortly after I had finished opening all of my gifts. She said she had a date. Valerie teased that I should take inventory of my lingerie for Charlene could've swiped a few items. Priscilla doubted Charlene even had a date and suspected that was just an excuse to keep from helping me home with my gifts. My mother complained Faye didn't lift a finger to help with anything, all the while Faye griping she wasn't allowed to be a part of my wedding dress fitting. My mother was thoroughly pleased to inform her that my dress was already finished, and for sometime now. And Margo hung out and laughed at all of us. When the time was appropriate, I grabbed Valerie and we went out to her car to talk.

"Valerie, I can see you're very worried about Elizabeth. Why were you even here today?"

"Freshmeat, this was your bridal shower. I wouldn't have missed it for the world."

"Val, I really appreciate it. I really do. But I...." Valerie put her hand up to stop my rambling.

"Tvoya, it is what it is with my sister. Trust, I was grateful I had your bridal shower to come to today. I couldn't stay in the house with them, anyway. It was just too depressing."

"But she's gonna beat this. Isn't she?" I asked somewhat perplexed by Valerie's admission of being intolerant of Elizabeth's situation. I was not prepared for what she said next.

"T, the doctors have given Elizabeth only three months to live."

Did I just hear Valerie say that Elizabeth had only three months to live? No I didn't hear that! So why did it feel like the oxygen around me was quickly diminishing and my chest was about to cave in from the deep breaths I found myself having to take.

Valerie's head then fell onto my shoulders as she began to sob. I placed my arms around her and rocked her gently as I too began to cry.

Why had Elizabeth been dealt this cruel hand that soon would be played out, literally? It wasn't fair. Elizabeth couldn't be dying! She just couldn't be!

Valerie was the first to regain her composure. She lifted her head from my shoulder, fished in her pocketbook for her tissues, passed one to me and blew her nose.

"Tvoya, there is something else, you should know." I wiped my eyes quickly and thoroughly.

"What's that, Val?" I asked cautiously.

"The family has agreed that because of the situation, you should meet Jonathan." Now I knew for sure that I was going to just drop dead right then and there.

"Meet...Jonathan?" I was stammering and my head was beginning to hurt, bad.

"I'm sorry to have put this all on you at once." Valerie was still crying and I couldn't answer her. I didn't have anymore words. I was fresh out. Besides, for someone who was supposed to be getting over a concussion, I did entirely too much talking for one day. But I did manage to say this.

"Valerie, I have to go home. I have to go home now!" I was on the verge of becoming hysterical. Valerie picked up on it. She stopped crying and was shouting for me to wait as I was high tailing it out of her car. I didn't even bother to close the door.

As I reached the entrance way into the restaurant, I was met by my mother and Margo who were carrying the last of my gifts to my mother's car. When they saw that my eyes were red and that Valerie was in close pursuit behind me, they of course stopped me to calm me down. I told them just as I had told Valerie…. 'I needed to get home.' My mother inquiringly looked to Valerie, who by now was becoming just as unglued as I was. Margo grabbed her as she began to sob again.

"What in the world is going on here?" Margo asked as she struggled to keep Valerie's sanity in tact at the same time that my mother tried to do the same for me.

They took the both of us to her car. Margo took Valerie's keys from her and announced she was going to lock up her car. My mother suggested we all go back to her house. Priscilla was the last to come out of the restaurant. She was flagged over to the car and given instructions to follow in her rental. Poor Priscilla didn't have a clue as to what was going on, but by the way my mother gave her the orders she dared not ask.

The car ride to my mother's house was tempered with sniffles and a lot of nose blowing, all contributed by Valerie and myself. My mother and Margo were startling quiet until we were all settled in her living room. Margo had made everyone some tea and all that was heard was the clanking of the teacups to their saucers.

"Would someone like to explain to me what is going on, here?" My mother asked, only after she was assured that Valerie and I had totally calmed down.

Valerie was the first to speak. "Mrs. Harrington, I'm so sorry that I totally lost it back there. But I was telling Tvoya that Elizabeth has only three months to live."

There were gasps from my mother, Margo and Priscilla. I began to softly cry again. Valerie looked my way and her eyes welled up with tears once again as well. My mother who had been sitting across from Valerie moved next to her on the sofa, placing her arm around her to console her.

"I'm so sorry, Valerie. Is there anything we can do?"

"That's not all, Mrs. Harrington," Valerie went on, "we…that is my family…thought that given the circumstances…Um, Tvoya ought to meet Jonathan." Valerie's admission was met with a hush that alluded that everyone was dazed and overwhelmed. However, my mother was quick to reclaim poise.

"Your family, thinks Tvoya should meet Jonathan? Well what about our family and what we think?" My mother's tone was sharp but not at all insensitive. I hoped Valerie could sense that.

"What Yvonne means, Valerie, is that this needs to be discussed between both of your families."

Margo interrupted and continued on, "We are all so sorry to hear about what is happening with Elizabeth. This is so heartbreaking. It's a terrible thing."

"I'll do it. I'll meet Jonathan." I interrupted Margo's attempt to keep the peace.

"Tvoya, what are you saying?" My mother stood as if her towering over me would make any difference. My mind was made up.

"If that is what Elizabeth wants, then that what's I'll do. I'll meet Jonathan."

"Tvoya, think about what you are consenting to do. Does Byron even know about Jonathan?"

"Mommy, this is not about Byron. This is about truth and doing what is right."

The truth was I wasn't thinking about Byron and how this will affect our relationship. I was thinking more of Royce.

"Tvoya, this is big. Don't you think you need to take some time to think about this?" Margo was reasoning.

"I know this is big. But Elizabeth is dying and the clock is ticking. It's not my call to sit around and wait on this." I jumped to my feet and went into the kitchen. I could hear Valerie say that she thought that she should leave. I came out to beckon her into the kitchen with me.

"Valerie, I'm sorry I tripped earlier and that it sounds like my mom's against it. We all have to get use to all of this."

"I understand. I didn't mean to lay this all out on you. The one you should be speaking with is Elizabeth. She'll call you when she's ready."

"Right. I'll wait for her to call. I do want to see her. But I'll respect her boundaries. She's dealing with a lot."

"Thanks, T."

Margo entered the kitchen to tell Valerie she'll take her back to her car. After they left, I unequivocally told my mother to butt out.

"Tvoya, now listen to reason," my mother pleaded as I came back into the living room.

"Mommy, my mind is made up. Case closed!"

"Aunt Yvonne, let it rest for now." This was the first thing Priscilla had to say since we got to my mother's house.

"Thank you, Pris. Can you take me home?" I was painstakingly exhausted.

Priscilla had a million and one questions that I did not have the energy to answer. She soon relented when she realized that I wasn't budging. I was grateful she herself was tired and decided to go back to my mother's house to knock off early. Besides, I assured her that my mother would be more than happy to fill her in as to all the drama that was currently surfacing in my life. She had a knack for this type of story telling. Hence, being the owner of a beauty salon. It was the perfect profession for her.

♥   ♥   ♥

I tossed and turned all night, attempting unsuccessfully to getting some sleep. I checked my phone messages. Byron went in for a double. Good. Royce was leaving town for a few days to take care of some unexpected business that cropped up. Great. He vowed to be in touch. Whatever. I needed the break. And then there was my father's message I was kind of expecting. Since while at my bridal shower, Faye heard some about my unfortunate experience at Razz, I knew it would only be a matter of time before he would call demanding I rethink my commitment to marrying Byron. He needn't worry. I was certainly entertaining the reservations I myself had. Not only because of that incident but because of Elizabeth's situation and her now wanting me to meet Jonathan...and my literally being in the middle of telling Royce. And there was that last minor detail that was major; I had never told my fiancé I had a child that I had given up for adoption thirteen years ago.

"...and Obey"

*B*right eyed and bushy tailed, I was on Aunt Marilyn's doorstep punctually at 10:30 am. Throughout the night, my mind vacillated between whether or not I should marry Byron and how should I tell him about Jonathan, to how was I going to complete telling Royce that he had a son. All the while the dark cloud of Elizabeth's terminal illness loomed, breaking my heart. She had been a true angel to me and the only mother Jonathan had ever known. Albeit sleep was endlessly illusive and utterly scarce, I felt fresh and ready for the world. Going to the house of the Lord always put me in a disposition that everything will be all right.

As I drove over to Aunt Marilyn's house, I thought of Elizabeth more and more. I wanted so much to talk with her privately and in person, but I did not want to push or pry. I was committed to waiting until she summoned me and determined to fight the temptation to do otherwise.

"How are you feeling, chile?" Aunt Marilyn opened the door immediately after I had rung the bell. In fact, her promptness startled me.

"Oh, hi Auntie, am I too early?"

"No chile, I was waiting for you. You eat breakfast yet?"

"I grabbed a muffin and some coffee. I'm good."

"I had something light too. Ok, let's go, then. I want to get a good seat. With Reverend Pierce-Vertrell coming, we're expecting a full house." I only nodded my head in agreement. I had heard a lot about this Reverend Pierce-Vertrell, but I never witnessed her ministry. I had been a Christian for a while now, but I was still skeptical when it came to visiting ministers, especially if they claimed to be prophetic. I believed God gave us a brain to use to be critical, objective and smart over such matters. However, I did trust my Aunt Marilyn. She had the gift of discernment. If this Reverend Pierce-Vertrell was a phony, Aunt Marilyn would have already exposed her to Pastor Underwood. She had been a deaconess for many years with this church. Even before Pastor Underwood became the pastor. So her spiritual acumen was proven and well respected at Mount Holiness Christian Life Center.

When we arrived, the church was all ablaze with the Spirit of the Lord. The head prayer warrior, Mother Annabelle Motley, was at the pulpit leading the congregation in corporate prayer. Aunt Marilyn and I were ushered to the front row of the church by a member of the usher board. I smiled to myself as I remembered that not long ago I had been seated in this same section along with my mother at Mr. Strickland's funeral. Despite the fact that this was my church home also, I had only sat in the front row these two times. I always sought comfort somewhere towards the back. The congregation went from corporate prayer to corporate worship. The atmosphere was charged with an undeniable electricity I had never became aware of before. There was something different about this morning. At the time, I could not put my finger on it. Still, it was distinctive. I was in expectation of the incredible and I had no idea I was going to encounter a visitation from the extraordinary.

General announcements were made. The offering was taken and then it was time for the message. I didn't remember her taking her seat next to Pastor Underwood, but when I did notice her occupancy our eyes met and an air of familiarity was felt. Did I know this Reverend Pierce-Vertrell? Where did I know her from? Our eyes met again. She smiled and then closed her eyes. Aunt Marilyn noticed the exchanged and leaned over to whisper, "She has a special word for you, chile."

"Right," I answered in disbelief.

"Just you wait. You'll see I'm talking right."

I decided not to challenge my Auntie any further as I began to become enthralled by hearing the biographical testimony of this Reverend Sapphire Pierce-Vertrell. She had led some life. Broken home. Abused. Abuser. Drug addict. Ex-con. Redeemed. Set free. All the while, hosting an amazing gift from God. She looked no more than 40 years of age. But 55 was her admission. After her introduction she stood...regal. Her stride to the pulpit was confident and at the same time humble. We were a well taught congregation, standing to our feet applauding what God was about to do in His vessel. She motioned with her hands for us to take our seats, and we did in unison as would a choir be...obedient to its director.   The room fell silent, waiting for what was next. Reverend Pierce-Vertrell took two steps back from the pulpit, threw her head back, opened her mouth and belted out one of the strongest vocal notes I had ever heard. She held it on the single letter word "I". And finished with "surrender all." She did it again. And again, until we were all once again on our feet. Some were singing. Some were softly crying. Some were wailing. Some were walking down to the altar to kneel. Reverend Pierce-Vertrell came down the five steps from the pulpit to meet those who had come to the altar. The music minister was on point as he orchestrated the choir to sing this song all the way through, as Reverend Pierce-Vertrell prayed over each one. When she was through and everyone was back at their seats, she slowly walked in the direction of where Aunt Marilyn and I were sitting. She stopped just in front of us and announced that God had something to say. She reached for my left hand with her right. I stood frozen. Numb. Aunt Marilyn whispered that I should place my hand in hers. I complied with this command and was led by the Reverend up the same five steps leading back to the pulpit. Once we were there she motioned for Pastor Underwood and his assistant pastor to stand behind me. My mind was racing. What was she getting ready to do? I felt like I was being prepped for surgery. Then I noticed that the music had stopped and the choir was now silent.

In the distance, I could hear a few "amens" and "glory" being shouted. Reverend Pierce-Vertrell again announced that God had something to say. Everyone and everything fell silent. I could hear my heart beating wildly and I thought everyone else could hear it, too. She took both of my hands now, and told me to look into her eyes and for me not to turn away. I wondered why? Was she going to change into something so terrible that I would be compelled to do what she just told me not to? I wasn't sure. I did as I was told and when our eyes met this time, peace flooded my soul. It was like looking into the eyes of an angel. Her eyes were deep, comforting, and mesmerizing. I know, so cliché. But true. I knew then why I had been instructed not to turn away. If I had, doubt would have been exchanged for this assurance of faith. I knew in my spirit that God needed me to hear His word not only with my ears but with my heart as well and locking my eyes with hers kept the hold and His promise.

Reverend Pierce-Vertrell then said, "This is what thus saith the Lord. 'You my child are preparing to get married, but the something old is the something new. You will get married my child, but not now and not to this one. I have the something old for you. Also, something that has been borrowed is coming back into your life. There will be a time of being blue…sadness, but this will break forth into great joy. I say this as a confirmation of truth. Stay close to me, my child. Seek me and I will be found.' " She then dropped my hands and laid her right hand on my forehead. I barely felt her touch when I began to feel a current of warmth that permeated my body. I felt woozy almost like I felt with the concussion. Then the positioning of everyone and everything including me, shifted. I was now looking from the floor up. So this is how it felt to be slain in the spirit. Amen!

22

"With the Guidance of God"

"*B*oy, that was some service," Priscilla remarked as she stuffed yet another forkful of pancakes into her mouth. I wondered if I was the only one that noticed Priscilla hadn't stopped eating since our food was brought to us. No wonder Margo had a time with her alterations. Priscilla should have been in the final stage of her fitting, but Margo was still dealing with the West Coast shop's equivalent to our shop here, regarding Priscilla's increasing growth to her frame. Valerie had the same issue with her weight gain, but it didn't pose the same problem for Valerie's gown was here in New York. Priscilla was sure putting a hurting on those pancakes and on Margo's patience.

Aunt Marilyn, Priscilla, my mother and I had decided to go out to eat after church. During the service, I didn't think my mother and Priscilla were even there. It wasn't until we were on the outside, greeting friends and acquaintances, did I see Priscilla come rushing up to me to exclaim how excited she was about witnessing the ministry of Reverend Sapphire Pierce-Vertrell. I was excited too, but at the same time apprehensive about what I should do next.

"Yeah, God was definitely in the place today! Huh, chile?" Aunt Marilyn said addressing me.

"I don't believe anything that came out of that woman's mouth. And T, don't you either. You just go ahead and proceed with your wedding plans." My mother was quick to refute what we all just witnessed to be from God.

"There'll be nothin' but trouble if you ignore what was just said to you. What you have to do now is pray that God give you the strength and the will to be obedient to him," Aunt Marilyn replied, even though she never laid an eye on my mother.

"How should Tvoya just change up everything? She's already just weeks away from getting married to Byron." My mother put the emphasis on Byron's name as she continued, "You would think that God would give you more notice," my mother laughed.

"You talking blasphemy, Yvonne. When our plans are not His plans, God has a right to stop it whenever He pleases. Just be grateful, He didn't stop it on the day of the wedding," Aunt Marilyn said this time glaring at my mother. Did anyone even care what I thought about the matter?

"Is that why you never got a marriage proposal, dear sister Marilyn?" Oh why did my mother have to go there?

"Mommy!" I said jumping to Aunt Marilyn's defense.

Aunt Marilyn held up her hand to halt my interjection.

"That's ok, T. It's ok. You all see what's happening here, right? First, the enemy is trying to distract you, Tvoya. And second, this is just Yvonne's guilt talking."

"My guilt? What on earth are you talking about, Marilyn?" my mother asked sounding very annoyed by this whole conversation.

"Yes, your guilt. And you know exactly what I'm talking about. You had this secret thing going on with John Strickland and you let that man die without ever telling him

170

he had a grandchild. A grandchild you both share at that," Aunt Marilyn calmly announced while sipping her coffee.

"Aunt Yvonne! You and Mr. Strickland? When did this all happen?" Priscilla put her fork down for this one. I shot her a look that said, 'we'll talk later'. Priscilla read me right and continued to devour the rest of the food that lay as prey on her plate.

"Besides, chile, have you even told Byron about Jonathan?" Aunt Marilyn continued, now directing her question to me.

"Telling Byron is not what I'm worried about. It's telling Royce that troubles me," I answered.

"And what is it you have to tell Royce?" my mother interrupted, "he didn't want to have anything to do with you when you were pregnant. Remember?"

"Mommy, I just found out he didn't even know about my being pregnant," I said, "we were kind of in the middle of having a true confessions moment when I was summoned by Valerie for my bridal shower. So I never finished telling him."

"You mean to tell me he told you he didn't know that you were pregnant with his child? That's a bold face lie, if I ever heard one, T," my mother angrily spat.

"I believe he's telling me the truth. All he knows at this point is that I was once pregnant," I answered softly, trying to diffuse the time bomb that was ticking away in my mother's mind.

"Yeah, right," my mother answered back, this time a little more subdued.

"And you haven't yet told Byron?" Priscilla asked, piecing all of what she had been missing together.

"See, that's what I'm talking about," Aunt Marilyn jumped back in. "If Tvoya was so in love with this Byron and getting ready to get married, she would have told him about Jonathan by now. Don't you think?"

"I see your point," Priscilla responded.

"That's why you had better heed the Word of the Lord, chile. He's trying to show you your own heart. Byron is not the one, because if he was, you would have told him everything from the start." Aunt Marilyn's face beamed to have shared this revelation.

"How do we know that this just wasn't a set up?" My mother trying again to refute what God had just told me.

"A set up? What do you mean?" I asked wondering what my mother had cooked up in her sometimes limited faith mind.

"Yeah, isn't Pastor not in agreement with your getting married in a different church? He could've just told this Reverend whatever her name is to tell you all of that," my mother reasoned.

"Oh, my God. We didn't just hear you speak against our pastor. This conversation is just getting too blasphemous for me," Aunt Marilyn retorted as she fished in her pocketbook and came up with some money to throw on the table. "Here! This should cover my meal. I'm leaving! Yvonne, you just went too far with that one!" Aunt Marilyn spat and left.

"Mommy! That wasn't right. How can you say something like that? You of all people. You seem to forget how God used Pastor Underwood in your deliverance from alcohol. Besides, he's your best friend's father. Margo would have a fit if she heard you say that about her father." I paused to let what I had just said sink in with my mother.

"Why is it so important to you that I marry Byron and ignore what I just heard at the house of the Lord?"

It became clear this wasn't only about me. This was about my mother as well. All of this was like opening up Pandora's Box. She would have to face the fact that she was in a fog during much of this ordeal. The truth was she wasn't much support to me. Back then, my mother chose to nurse her alcoholic demons rather than to help me make the decision of my life. If it had not been for Elizabeth, Valerie and Mrs. Franklin, I probably would have had my child aborted. I remember this was the very thing my mother suggested I do. Her guilt was huge. It included her not telling Mr. Strickland and her not supporting me, and she would rather see me get married to Byron, the wonderful doctor who she believed was sent so we could all live happily ever after. Not. In that moment, I had made my decision. Even though I'd thought God answered my prayers for a husband with Byron, I had to grasp reality and admit…I was wrong. I would not be marrying Byron Munroe after all. Pandora's Box was now opened. Wide!

23

"Who Gives This Woman?"

I spent the next few days in serious prayer. There had not yet been any word from Valerie or Elizabeth concerning her health or my meeting Jonathan, and it was fortunate and timely that Byron was working so many hours at the hospital. Even though we spoke on the phone daily, the conversations were brief and light. He did, several times, inquire about the plans for the wedding but I managed to put him off. I felt bad that I hadn't come clean yet to tell him it was over between us. I guess I was trying to let him down easy. However, knowing Byron, this would not be received by him with ease, not to speak of the drama that would categorically ensue. I just wasn't ready for that. I needed to find peace with my decision and be able to stand my ground however the outcome of this would be.

"Byron, I didn't know you were coming by," I said as I opened the door to find Byron standing there holding a beautiful bouquet of flowers.

"Can't I surprise my bride to be?" Byron said before planting a firm kiss upon my lips. I was trying my hardest to remain cool as my mind shouted, 'tell him that it's over, tell him that it's over, now!' I thanked him for the flowers and proceeded into the kitchen to place them in a vase with water. They looked so beautiful and I felt so guilty. I returned quickly. Byron had made himself comfortable on the chaise lounge.

"So, where's Charlene? Is she still mooching off of you?" Byron asked sarcastically.

"Charlene is still staying here, if that's what you're asking," I responded tiredly.

"Tvoya, I really don't understand you."

"What don't you understand, Byron?"

"We'll be husband and wife in only two weeks, and Charlene is still here taking up space and cramping our style."

"Cramping our style? What do you mean by that?"

"You know what I mean, baby."

"No I don't Byron. Please tell me just exactly what you mean."

"Baby, we can't even get our groove on, with her staying here."

Oh, how did I let this conversation get there. We were beginning to argue over something so ridiculous. It really didn't matter now anyway whether Charlene was here or not. Beside the fact he wasn't getting any, I had to tell him and make it very clear that we would not be getting married.

"Byron, please let's not argue. Um…there's something I need to tell you. Well, there's a few things that I need to tell you...about my past….and something else about the present and our future."

"Baby, I don't want to argue either," Byron said as he got up from the chaise lounge. He walked toward me with that gleam of lust in his eyes.

"Please, Byron, I need you to hear me on this."

"Ok?" Byron stopped and gazed at me in bewilderment. I walked past him and sat down on the couch.

"Byron, sit down."

"Tvoya, what's this all about?" His eyes told that he knew what was coming. Well, part of what was coming, anyway.

"Byron," I began, gingerly, almost sympathetically, "there's something about myself, I never told you." I waited for him to say something. He didn't. I continued, "Byron, I have a child."

"What?" Byron replied in astonishment. I watched his demeanor grow dark.

"Um…thirteen years ago, I gave birth to a boy. His name is Jonathan. But, I gave him up for adoption."

"Ok?" Byron said slowly, taking this all in. He said nothing more, willing me to continue.

"I have always known the family that I gave him up to. But now his adopted mother has cancer and I have been told by a family member, she wants him and I to be reunited." I thought it best that Byron not know what family my son was with. I didn't want him going to Valerie and Lamar asking all kinds of questions.

"Ok? So, who's the father?" Byron casually asked. How did I know he would soon ask this question? "Royce is his father. But he doesn't even know about all of this, yet."

"He doesn't know that he fathered a child that was given up for adoption?" Byron's asking sounded suspicious.

"No, he doesn't. Please Byron, it's a long story."

"And you don't care to go into it right now. Am I right?" Byron now sounded betrayed.

"Right. I don't care to go into it right now or ever. Which leads me to what I am about to say next. And please Byron, this doesn't mean that I don't or have never loved you. I…um…just feel... uh, I just…um…know that we should not get married." There I said it, stammering and all. I said it! It was out!

"You mean, we shouldn't get married right now, right?" I could not believe what I was hearing. I had thought what I had just said was clear enough.

"Byron, I'm sorry. No, what I mean is we should not be getting married at all. I'm calling the wedding and our relationship off." Now, that should do it.

"Tvoya, what are you saying? Is this because of what happened at the club?" I could only shake my head, no.

"If this is about your adopted son and Royce, we can get through this together. We belong together, baby." Byron had now moved closer to me. I felt my body get tense. Maybe I should have had someone with me while I broke it off with him.

"No, this isn't only about that. It's about God. He told me this wasn't right. It's not His will. I never even asked Him if you were the one," I reasoned.

"Ok? So this is about getting married at your church. I told you I didn't want to wait as long as it would take to have the premarital counseling there. Maybe we could speak with your pastor and he could wave it. And we can make the change to your church." Byron was now pleading.

"Byron, it's over. We are not getting married anywhere!" My tone was stern which surprised me as well as him. Just then, Charlene walked through the door.

"Hey, guys," Charlene cheerfully called out as she made her way into the living room. "Uh, did I just interrupt something?" She stopped midway in as I gave her an 'I need help' stare. Byron never looked her way.

"Well," Charlene continued, "I'll just go into the room there and you guys just keep doing whatever it was ya'll were doing."

Just as I heard the bedroom door close, Byron was rising to his feet.

"I better go, then," Byron calmly announced.

"Byron, I'm sorry. I didn't mean for things to turn out like this. I'm so sorry." I was now the one pleading.

As Byron reached the door and I was in tow behind him, he suddenly turned to say, "You will be sorry, Tvoya."
Was that a threat? Nah, it couldn't be.

24

"Forsaking All Others"

After Byron left, the first person I thought of was Margo, my wedding planner. Now that my relationship with Byron was officially over, I could tell her and pray that Byron and I wouldn't lose too much money with canceling so close to our wedding date. In fact, as I was dialing her number, I realized I was still wearing the engagement ring Byron had given me. I wondered why he hadn't asked for it back and why I had completely forgot to give it to him. Now how was I going to return this to him? While, I felt really crummy about breaking it off with him, I thought that giving Byron back his ring in person would not be a good idea. And then the best possible solution came to me. I would ask Margo to return it to him for me. It couldn't hurt to ask.

"Hi Margo, it's Tvoya." I tried my best to sound resolved.

"Hey, gurl," Margo answered, "is something wrong, Tvoya?" Margo knew me well.

"Uh, yes. I mean, no. Everything is well. Yes! Everything is well. I have the Lord on my side and what more can I ask."

"You broke up with Byron, didn't you?" Margo asked. Man, she knew me too well.

"Yeah Margo. I had to. I mean after the word I received on Sunday at church. I knew I had to break it off."

"I knew you would. I was just waiting for your call."

"Oh, Margo. I'm so glad you're not mad at me. I was afraid you would be upset with me…being that it's the last minute and all."

"Tvoya, it comes with the territory. Couples decide all the time to cancel at the last minute. But what's more important is that you listened to God. I was in the house too, when Reverend Pierce-Vertrell gave you that word and I have been keeping it in prayer. I'm just glad you heeded 'what thus saith the Lord.' He should have the final say in all of our decisions."

"Margo, thank you for that. So, what now?"

"Well, just leave everything to me. I'll try to work it where you won't have to lose much money."

"Thank you so much, Margo. God surely knew what he was doing when he had you to be my wedding coordinator."

"Not a problem. I'll get back to you. Ok?"

"Oh, Margo, one more thing. I have a dilemma. I thought you could help me with it." I had almost forgot again about the ring. What was wrong with me?

"Can you do me a favor and return to Byron his ring?"

Margo laughed before responding. "Gurl…I will do no such thing. You hold on to it. Did Byron ask for it back when you broke up with him?"

"Well, no. We kind of both forgot. I guess I dropped so much on him so suddenly he forgot to ask for it back."

"Well, you just hold on to it then. You may need it for leverage against anything that you might owe from the outstanding expenses."

"But Margo, it doesn't seem right just holding on to it. What if Byron asks for it in the meantime?" I reasoned. I didn't want to give Byron an excuse for coming back and trying to convince me I should reconsider my decision.

"I'll call Byron to tell him there may be some expenses incurred due to the canceling of the wedding. And that the ring could pay for it. In the meantime, open up a safe deposit box and keep it there until you hear back from me. Tvoya, you better do this today, just to be on the safe side."

"All right. That's what I'll do." I was beginning to feel better.

"Good. I'll talk with you later. Be well," Margo said and then hung up.

As I was hanging up with Margo, Charlene emerged from the guest bedroom. "You and fiancé seemed to be in the middle of a very serious discussion when I came in. So whatz up?"

"Well, fiancé is no longer that. Byron and I are over. The wedding is off."

"You lying," Charlene sounding sincerely surprised.

"No, it's true. It's over. Done. Finished. Oh, about the gowns, I'll see that everyone gets reimbursed for whatever they have already put out."

"Tvoya, don't worry about it. How are you doing?"

"I'm good. This decision was coming. I couldn't go along with it, knowing God didn't approve." Charlene's glare gave the impression that she didn't have a clue as to what I was talking about.

"What do you mean, God didn't approve?"

"Well, if you would have come to church with me on Sunday, instead of hanging out all Saturday night and part of Sunday, you would have experienced what we call a prophetic word from the Lord. A visiting minister who came to our church to preach, who by the way didn't know me from Adam or Eve, told me that Byron wasn't the man God would have me to marry. Well that's the short of it, anyway."

"And you believe that stuff? You sound like my aunt. She's always prophesying over my life."

"So you do know something about the prophetic word." I was happy to hear Charlene had at least heard of this sort of thing.

"What I do know is….it's just a way for church folk to get in your business and control your life."

"That's not true, Charlene. The prophetic word is God speaking to us through His chosen vessel, what is to come pertaining to what His will is." As I said this I could not believe myself how much I had learned since this past Sunday.

"Whatever. I just hope you know what you're doing," Charlene paused as if she remembered something else. "Oh yeah, I forgot to tell you Royce called yesterday."

"Yesterday? And you're just telling me now?"

"My bad. It just slipped, that all," Charlene said now sounding more like the Charlene I know.

"Don't worry about it," I said feeling drained from my exchange with Byron. And to think I still had to finish my talk with Royce about Jonathan. I wondered how I could also divulge to him that Byron and I would no longer be getting married. I was sure Royce would love to hear that element of my implausible mixed up life. I just hoped he wouldn't try to take the credit for the ending of the relationship. I was sure Royce would now feel that he might now actually have a chance with me. This made me wonder all the more if in all honesty that might very well be true. However intriguing, all of this would have to wait until after I had the chance to tell my mother, Valerie and Priscilla that there would be no wedding. But before them…there was someone else I definitely had to speak with first.

25

"Daddy's Little Girl"

"Hey there, Faye." I tried to sound nonchalant and happy to see her without letting on about the sudden change regarding the plans of the wedding.

"Why, Tvoya? What a pleasant surprise. Please come in," Faye said as she opened the door to let me in. There was never any love lost between my stepmother and me. We just managed to work the formalities well.

"Is Daddy here?" I cut right to the chase. I wanted to be of course cordial, but I didn't want to waste my time there trading small impersonal chitchat with Faye.

"Ah, yes, he's here. How are the final touches for the wedding coming? Are you getting nervous? That day is almost here, you know. If there's anything that I can help you with, Tvoya, please let me know."

"I thought I heard my princess," my father announced as he entered into their living room.

"Hey, Daddy." I ignored Faye's pleas for her involvement as I met my father with a kiss on his cheek.

"What a surprise. Now to what do I owe this unexpected visit?" Hearing what my father said made me feel quite embarrassed. I probably should have called first.

"I'm sorry I didn't call before coming over. But, I needed to talk to you."

"Princess, since when do you need an invitation or an advance notice to come and check out your old man?" He knew I was referring more to how Faye would see my spontaneous drop in than to owing him an apology. "Come on, let's go out back."

I followed my father and Faye followed me. How can I tell her I just want to speak with my dad, alone without her feeling left out?

"Faye, baby, can you get Tvoya and me something to drink?" Oh, my dad was smooth. After she was out of earshot, I asked if I could please speak with him and only him. He smiled, nodded his head and went back into the house. I took a seat at the two-seated table and waited patiently for him to return. When he did, he brought along two tall glasses filled with ice cold sweet tea. My favorite.

"Daddy, I don't mean to be rude about Faye." He stopped me.

"Don't worry about Faye. She went out. She was really on her way out before you even got here. I just had to give her a little reminder, that's all. Don't worry about it."

Yeah, my father and I both knew that Faye was going to find out what our conversation was about, anyway. He told her everything.

"I was wondering when you were going to get around to calling me," he said.

I knew that Faye had told him about the fiasco between me and Byron at Razz. He did call me and left several messages, which I had not returned. He finally got the scoop from my mother, who settled his fears by not telling him the whole story.

"Daddy, I'm really sorry that I haven't returned your calls. But so much has been going on lately that I've haven't had a chance to even catch my breath." He just stared at me, not letting on one way or the other whether he was buying my explanation, so I continued, "I called the wedding off." There, that should put a blink in his stare.

"Well....I'm relieved to hear that," my father said calmly reaching for his sweet tea.

"You are?" It was quite clear I was the one that was shocked. "I thought you were happy I was marrying Byron."

"Tvoya, I was happy, but after I heard what happened to you at Razz, I was furious." I knew my mother didn't tell him everything. And I didn't think Faye could follow enough of what she heard at the shower to piece together the whole story. So how did he know enough to be furious? I decided to say nothing and let him continue.

"Your mother tried to sell me on some bull that I didn't go for, so I went down to Razz and spoke to Kenny myself." I had forgotten that Kenny mentioned to me that my father had been down at the club a few times.

"Oh." I was too mortified to even look at my father. I knew Kenny probably hadn't minced words, giving him an earful as to what happened that night between me, and Byron, and not to mention that it also involved Royce.

"And since you didn't bother to return my calls, I went to get things straight with Byron myself." I couldn't believe what my father was telling me. He went to speak to Byron?

"You spoke to Byron about what happened? Daddy, how could you?"

"How could I? I'm your father. What was I supposed to do? Just let him think that he could get away with man handling you? Oh, no! Not on my watch!" My father's voice was getting louder with every word.

"Oh, so now you're gonna act like my father and protect me?" I was sorry for letting those words get out the moment I said them.

"Tvoya, I have always acted like your father," he said lowering the volume.

Yeah… just a father that wasn't around very much. I dared not utter this truth. This wasn't about whether my father was around much or not. That was beside the point. I wasn't at my father's to split hairs. I felt he needed to be the first to know of my calling the wedding off, since he was footing most of the bill. Which I believed was an act of subliminally relieving the guilt he was in denial of even having in the first place.

"So how did the conversation go with Byron?" I was intrigued to say the least.

"You have to have both parties talking to have a conversation, and since I was the only one talking…and talking loud, I was for sure saying something. Something that he heard loud and clear, too," he said hedging.

"Daddy, please. What did you say to Byron? And when?"

"Never you mind, Princess. It's not important now. I mean, now that you've called off the wedding," my father said smiling.

"Daddy, I do have a right to know what you said to Byron. Did you threaten him? He never even mentioned this to me."

"What I said to Byron is between me and Byron. And no I didn't threaten him. I just put a little insurance to the matter." Insurance? What was my father talking about?

"So, Byron's apology was because of you. Not because I deserved one."

"Well then that should tell you that you did the right thing by breaking it off with him. Princess, you're too good for him. You do deserve better, you know."

My father was right. I did deserve better. But what was better? Was Mr. Better ever going to find me?

"Daddy, about the money…since the wedding's been called off on such short notice, we may have to pay some hefty penalties. I just wanted you to know, you will get back every dime. I promise."

"Princess, I'm not worrying about my money."

"But Daddy, Margo told me to hold on to the ring for this very reason."

"Tvoya, give Byron back his ring!" His voice had now returned to being elevated. And his tone, stern.

"But Daddy…"

"But Daddy, nothin'. Give that man back his ring and be done with it!"

So what was the big deal about keeping the ring? Margo assured me that this was the way to handle the expenses. Why was my father tripping?

Softening, he continued, "When you break off with someone, you want to make it clean. You don't wanna give him any reason to keep coming back. I'm a man, I know these things. Trust me on this, Tvoya."

I said nothing to my fathers' words of wisdom. What did he know anyway?

26

"Forever Hold Your Peace"

While driving home from my mother's hair salon, I had a little time to think and reflect over all the things that had occurred in such a short span of time. I had gotten engaged, Mr. Strickland passed; Royce was back in my life; Elizabeth was diagnosed with cancer; I was no longer engaged, and shortly, I was about to be reintroduced to the child I gave up for adoption so many years ago. Phew! All of this took place in a matter of a few short weeks. And how was I feeling about all of this? Sad? Angry? Disappointed? Hopeful? I wasn't sure. I did know I had to keep my wits about me. I had to remain strong in the midst of this storm.

Facing my father, earlier, had been a quiet walk in the park compared to meeting with my mother, Valerie and Priscilla at the hair salon. My timing left a lot to be desired, since my Aunt Lulu was also at the shop. I tried to set up this impromptu gathering to hit at closing time when all the customers would be gone, but Aunt Lulu had the senses of a pit bull and from the moment I arrived, she perceived precisely that I had a major announcement to make. I was appreciative that on such a short notice, Valerie was able to meet us. Priscilla was helping my mother out at the salon so there was no stretch there.

I arrived just a minute before Valerie did, so no one had to wait long for my dramatic turn of events statement. I could see that Aunt Lulu had made herself very comfortable and wasn't about to leave without the goods, so I proceeded to tell them all the reason for this little soirée.

"The wedding is off! Byron and I are through. Finished. Over!" I said firmly. My tone challenging anyone who would beg for an explanation.

"We get the point, Cuz," Priscilla said, being the first to close their mouth from the shock and utter an identifiable sound.

"I don't believe this!" huffed my mother as if this personally affected and offended her in some way.

"After Marilyn telling me what happened last Sunday in church...I can believe it," said Aunt Lulu as she cut her eyes at her baby sisters' response. "You didn't need that no good so and so no way!"

"As long as you're doing what makes you happy. Life's too short to do anything else," Valerie offered as she embraced me. I felt the draining effect Elizabeth's illness was having on her. I was truly sorry for taking her through my own emotional rollercoaster. Valerie had always been there for me. And at that very moment it hit me that in addition to God wanting me to end my engagement with Byron...He also wanted me to be there now for Valerie.

"All right, all right. So now what, Tvoya? What about all of the expenses? Have you even considered that? And what about your father?" My mother's rifling of these questions told how hurt she was that I was not going to allow her to live her dream of her only child marrying a doctor.

"I've already told Daddy." That oughta shock her even more. "Besides, Margo assured me she'll work on all of that for me. I promise everyone will get back everything they put out to be in this wedding." I then turned to Priscilla. "Even your airfare will be given back to you." Priscilla only nodded.

"So how did Dr. Love take it?" Aunt Lulu interjected.

"Well, he wasn't exactly thrilled about it. I guess he took it the best way he could. I'm sure that once he's had time to reflect on the way our relationship was going, he'll see that it wasn't right. Maybe in the near future, we can be friends," I answered hoping I wasn't trivializing it too much.

"T, did you give back the ring?" my cousin asked.

"No, Margo advised me not to."

"That's right gurl, you keep that ring for all your trouble," Aunt Lulu cut in once again.

I looked over at my mother who was busying herself by straightening up her station. She made no further remarks.

Picking up on that maybe my mother and I needed some time alone, Valerie announced she had to get going. I'm sure she thought this would lead the others to follow. Not. Everyone just waved her off as if her presence wouldn't be missed anyway.

"I'll walk you out," I offered. Furthermore, I needed some air. Once we were no longer in earshot, Valerie commented.

"Your mother is so mad, she could eat nails."

"Yeah, but she'll get over it." I laughed at her commentary of this observation.

"Wow, gurl, I thought Byron was the one."

"Yeah, I thought so too."

"Freshmeat, I'm sorry I've haven't been much support..." I put my hand up to stop Valerie. Was she kidding?

"What? Val, what are you talking about? With what you're going through with Elizabeth, I couldn't expect to lean on you. Anyway, I've been leaning on you most of my life. It's time for you now to lean on me. How is Elizabeth?

I've been wanting to come by or call but I didn't want to intrude." I admitted.

"Well, it's been rough. She'll be staying at my house throughout….I mean…she wants to, um, go here, where she was raised," Valerie continued, "she just told me this morning she's ready to talk to you about meeting Jonathan." My heart leaped at the mention of his name.

"Umm…when should I come by?" I asked sheepishly.

"Tomorrow would be good. You've had enough for one day," Valerie said. See, always thinking of me.

"Ok, I'll come tomorrow." I smiled weakly.

Valerie and I hugged just before she got into her car. I stood frozen as I watched her drive off down the street.

27

"Ours for Eternity"

I entered my condo to the sound of blaring music coming from the guest bedroom Charlene was occupying, only she was no where to be found. Note to self...I must inform her that if she intends on staying here, there were definite rules she will have to abide by. I shuttered at the thought that now that I was no longer getting married, Charlene's stay could wind up being indefinite. It wouldn't have mattered before, but I was no longer moving out and the roommate thing was getting old. After I turned off the radio, I decided to make myself a good healthy salad.

Ah....to be alone... finally. My mind immediately went to Byron. I hoped he hadn't taken our breakup too hard. It was clear he had a problem with alcohol. I just hoped he wasn't somewhere getting wasted. I wondered if I should call him. Or maybe, I could call his mother. But wait. What if she didn't yet know about the break up? I'm sure he would hate for his mother to find out by my telling her. No, that was his responsibility. Besides, I didn't want to talk to her about it anyway. She would probably try to talk me into getting back together with him. I felt bad for Byron. But not bad enough. I was certain I had done the right thing. Besides, God was on my side.

The next person I thought of was my mother. I felt sorry for her, too. But this was my life. Not hers. I was sorry she didn't get a second chance with my father. I was sorry that what she had with Mr. Strickland was gone forever. But again, I reasoned, this was my life. Mine. In the past, I sacrificed a lot of my future for my mother. I had wanted to go off to college and experience campus life, like so many of my friends. While I did learn that this type of decision-making stemmed from my being a co-dependent to my mother's alcoholism, I now had to accept my part. I had to be accountable and responsible for the chartering of my own destiny. I could no longer allow my mother to live her life through me. She had no right to try to live her life through me. She would just have to get used to me, her only daughter, not being married to a doctor after all. It hit me that at this point there was a strong possibility her daughter may be single for the rest of her life. And if that was to be God's will....then it was well.

Charlene must have met the mailperson at the door for there was a pile that awaited my immediate attention. I rifled through it and found there was a pick up slip for a certified letter. The addressor was a law firm, Jackson, Nelson and McCoy. I checked the time and saw that the post office around the corner was still open. My curiosity got the better of me and before I knew it, I was out the door. I stopped for a moment and thought that this could be from Byron suing me for his ring. No, this was too soon, I reasoned; knowing the mentality and the ways of a heavy drinker, Byron was probably somewhere licking his wounds, nursing a drink.

Once I had the letter in my hot little hands, I couldn't wait to get home. I opened it right in the post office. It was a request for my presence to be at the reading of the final will and testament of Mr. John Strickland. Why was I invited to attend the reading of Mr. Strickland's will? Had Mr.

Strickland left something for me? Nah! This was so surreal. I guessed that it was time to return Royce's call. But I soon found out my calling him would not be necessary since I found him climbing the steps to my home when I pulled up. The idling sound of my car got his attention and garnered a wide grin from him that made me quietly flush. It was amazing to me how after all these years I was still very attracted to Royce Strickland. He trotted down the steps to meet me. Although I gave him a suspect eyebrow lift of intrigue that said, 'what are you doing at my door, unannounced', it wasn't my sentiment at all. I was really very happy to see Royce.

"Well, hello Tvoya," Royce said as he held his hand out to help me from my car.

"Well, hello yourself." I grinned returning the greeting.

"Hey, I'm sorry about showing up all unannounced and everything. But, I had to see you...."

"Yeah, we never did finish our conversation," I said cutting him off, "plus, there's been so much that has happened since." I paused to reflect on just how much had changed. "I should be the one who's sorry. I've not yet returned your calls."

"Listen, Tvoya. That's not a problem. But can we talk now?" Royce pleaded.

"Sure, come on in."

We entered my place and good, I found that Charlene was still out. Maybe, I should call her and tell her to stay out a while, since Royce and I had so much we needed to talk about. But I figured if I did that, he might get the wrong idea that I would want him to stay the night. So I decided against calling Charlene. If it were meant to be for Royce and I to have an uninterrupted conversation, then it would be.

"Can I get you anything to drink, eat?" I offered.

"No. I'm good. Tvoya, I need to apologize to you for

something."

"Oh?! And, that is?"

"For not being there for you when you were pregnant."
Wow. Royce got straight to the point.

"Royce, I believe now you never knew about the pregnancy. But what I don't understand is…let me back up. I wrote you several letters about it, but you never answered them. And the letters were never sent back to me."

"I know what happened to the letters, Tvoya."

"You do? I mean, how can you know what happened to the letters, but not about the pregnancy?"

"Tvoya, let me explain." Royce's voice conveyed a strong overtone of solemnity; I dared not continue my probe.

"While I was going through some of my father's important papers trying to find his insurance policy, I stumbled upon two things that seemed strange to me, one, a certificate for a trust fund that was unfamiliar to me. It is in the name of a Jonathan Scott."

I froze at the mention of his name, and for Royce to be mentioning it, to boot.

"I didn't know the name so it didn't matter too much to me, but that it noted the names Gary and Elizabeth Scott as the guardians to the fund and my father the executor."

I dared not speak. I allowed Royce to continue.

"I recognized those names belonging to Valerie's sister and brother in-law, so I kinda slicked Lamar into telling me that Jonathan was their son. But, I'm still not sure of its relevance. Anyway, the other were cancelled checks that were made out to my ex-wife."

"Your ex-wife?" was all that I could manage to say. Now how was she involved, I thought.

"Well, at the time she wasn't my wife. You and I had just split and Gina and I had just moved in together," Royce explained, "so I went back out West to probe her about 'em.

First, she wouldn't tell me anything. Then, when I told her my dad had just died and I needed to know what this was all about, she reconsidered and told me about the letters."

"The letters? Are you telling me Royce that your ex-wife knew about the letters I sent to you." I was getting annoyed and anxious to be finding out that Royce's ex-wife knew about my letters to him all those years ago.

"My father was paying her to not give me the letters and to send them to him instead."

I could not believe what I was hearing. Mr. Strickland and Royce's ex-wife knew I was pregnant with Royce's child? And they conspired to keep this information from him. I felt as though the wind had been knocked out of me. I needed some air. I was literally suffocating.

"When the first letter came," Royce continued, "Gina admitted she opened it and read it. After finding out that you were writing to me to tell me that you were pregnant, she immediately got on the horn to my father to tell him about them," Royce apologetically relayed. He paused to allow me time to angrily respond, interject, or just weigh in on the matter. I just couldn't. My mouth just hung open like a fish out of water gasping for air, hoping someone will throw it back into familiar surroundings. Royce quickly realized I wasn't ready to give a comment, so he treaded lightly as he continued.

"My father instructed her to send him the letter. She did the same with the subsequent ones and he compensated her accordingly. She claims she never knew what became of your pregnancy only that my father promised her he would take care of everything."

This was becoming way too much to take. "Your father promised her he would take care of everything? Everything, Royce? WHAT EVERYTHING?!" I was now shouting to the top of my lungs.

196

"Tvoya, I'm sorry. I'm sorry that my father manipulated this situation."

"SITUATION? This wasn't just a situation, Royce. This is a baby we're talking about. A baby that I gave up for adoption because I thought you didn't want it or me for that matter."

"You gave the baby up for adoption?" Royce cautiously asked.

Through the tears and yelling I realized that Royce didn't know everything. He was trying to piece together a puzzle that had just as much to do with his life as well as it had to do with mine. Yelling at him was not going to help either of us. He was trying to find the truth and as this was unfolding, I was finding there was so much of the truth that I didn't know as well. We both needed to keep level heads to come to terms with all of it.

"Yes, Royce. Valerie's sister, Elizabeth and Gary adopted our son."

As I spoke Royce's expression changed and now he was the one who couldn't speak. "When you didn't answer any of my letters, I was beside myself. I didn't know which way to turn. My mother was no help. She stayed drunk 24/7. I couldn't tell my father until much later. So the only people I had to lean on were Valerie and her family. Abortion was certainly out of the question, but I knew I couldn't bring my baby into the nightmare of my mother's drinking. So after many months of soul searching and relying heavily on Valerie's sister, Elizabeth....I asked her and Gary to adopt our son. They had been having problems having a child of their own. Elizabeth had 3 miscarriages, and they had given up hope of her ever bringing a baby to full term. I lived with them down in South Carolina for the last two months of my pregnancy. "

"So, this Jonathan...um.. that's named in the trust fund. ..

is my son? Our son?"

"Yes, Royce. Jonathan Scott is our son."

28

"For Better Or Worse"

he dawn came in finding Royce and me, filling each other in and catching one another up to speed on what had been transpiring in our lives for the past 13 years. Royce wasn't particularly stunned about finding out how his ex-wife misled him. However, he was very upset to say the least at finding out about his father's involvement. As was I too, since Mr. Strickland had been such a respected man in our community for most of my life. To now find out that he knew about Jonathan and his whereabouts, undeniably put a new perspective on the legacy of Mr. John Strickland. It was now stained. And to think I gave Jonathan his name because Mr. Strickland was his grandfather, the man I respected so. But how did Mr. Strickland know about Jonathan? Where he was and who he was with? No doubt, my mother was the co-conspirator. This new-found revelation was best kept a secret and not audibly questioned in Royce's presence. Instead, I told Royce how I received a letter from his father's lawyers asking me to attend the reading of his will. Royce wasn't very surprised about this, but he was puzzled to hear now I had no intention of going.

"No, Royce. Please don't try to talk me into going. I've already got too much to deal with," I reasoned.

"Tvoya, everything is out in the open now. Going will probably shed some light on why my father chose to do what he did."

"Royce! Are you defending him? What he did was no small thing…he kept us from each other and from our son all of these years."

"No, I'm not defending him. But I'm sure he had his reasons for not telling me…"

"Not telling you? Royce, your father even knew your son had been adopted and by whom, and he still didn't tell you anything about it."

"I know, I know. He probably was thinking about protecting me."

"Protecting you?"

"Yeah, he probably thought that first you had an abortion. You said you'd left the neighborhood for a few months. Maybe when you came back with no baby he thought you had gotten rid of it."

"Oh, you are so in denial."

"And maybe it wasn't until sometime later he found out our son was actually adopted, but by that time it was too late to do anything about it."

"Too late?! Royce, he still could've told you then."

"Listen, you're trying to make my father out to be the bad guy here. He wasn't all bad, Tvoya. He did convince your mother to stop drinking."

"Oh, so that's it! You're gonna just rationalize this, and I'm suppose to just be grateful that he paid for my mother's rehab? And that makes it ok he kept you from finding out about your son? Royce, really!"

"He did more than pay for your mother's rehab."

"Ok, I know, he also set her up in her hair salon and believe me Royce I am grateful to your father for all of that."

"Tvoya, he came to your mother's rescue when she

allowed one of her boyfriends to rob her blind. Yeah, Tvoya, I know it wasn't cool…him keeping my son…"

"What?! One of my mother's boyfriend's did what?" I didn't let Royce finish his statement. I knew my face displayed a despairing glare of unadulterated confusion for Royce answered with a dumbfounded, "Oh."

"Oh, what? What did you just say, Royce, about my mother and what boyfriend?"

"I'm sorry Tvoya."

"Will you stop telling me how sorry you are and just tell me what the hell you're talking about?"

"Tvoya, I thought you knew what happened to make your mother decide that she had to stop drinking."

"Royce, just tell me what you know." I was exhausted with this ping pong pleading.

"My father mentioned to me in a conversation we once had that Yvonne went out drinking one night and brought a man home whom she didn't know. I don't remember all of the details, but my father said that after she passed out, this man called some friends over and they took all of the furniture and other things out of the house. When your mother came to and found her house bare, she called my father. He tracked down the guys…took care of them, if you know what I mean, and got all of her things returned."

"Oh, this is crazy! You're trying to make your father out to be some kind of superman."

"Tvoya, you need to talk to Yvonne about this. I'm sorry I thought you knew about all this."

"I guess we're both finding out a whole lot we didn't know."

"Are you sure I can't convince you to go to the reading of my father's will? We all need closure on this."

"I don't need closure. Maybe you do. I mean since you just found out about Jonathan and all. I, on the other hand always

knew I had a son. But you can bet now I will be going."
Won't my mother sure be surprised. No wonder she didn't
want me getting too close to Royce again.

"Besides..." I decided not to verbalize my thought of
reasoning. There was something Royce still did not know. He
did not know yet that Elizabeth was dying and that she asked
that I meet with Jonathan. I wasn't sure if this was the right
time to tell him this. I was just getting adjusted to all of this as
well.

"Tvoya? You were saying?" Royce asked trying to bring
me back to the present.

"Oh! Nothing. Look at the time. The sun is coming up. You
better go. I have a busy day ahead of me and I do need to
catch a couple hours of sleep."

"Wow! Is it 5:34 in the morning already? I'm surprised we
weren't interrupted by what's his name? Oh yeah, Dr.
Feelgood," Royce said hinting that Byron's name did not
come up the entire night.

"Well, that wouldn't have happened. Byron and I are no
longer engaged." There, another true confession revealed.

"What?! Did I just hear you right?"

"You heard right."

"Thank you, Lord. My prayers have been answered,"
Royce said with his eyes elevated upward.

"Whatever, Royce." I smiled at the thought.

♥   ♥   ♥

It was clear I needed some sleep, but it kept eluding me. I
tossed and turned, playing the whole conversation Royce and
I had over and over in my head. I could not get over the real
reason my mother went into rehab and the fact that Mr.

Strickland knew all along about my pregnancy, the adoption and that Elizabeth and Gary were now Jonathan's parents. I wondered if Mr. Strickland had ever contacted Elizabeth and Gary regarding the trust fund he held for Jonathan. If he had, Elizabeth never mentioned it to me and of course, why would she? She was legally his mother. Yes, I gave birth to him. But I forfeited any further claims to Jonathan's life the moment I signed those adoption papers.

"Are you sure you want to do this?" Valerie said to me as everyone stood motionless in my hospital room. I had just laid eyes on my son for the last time before the nurse took him back to the nursery and out of my life..

"Yes, this is for the best," I said, not looking away from the legal papers Elizabeth and Gary's lawyers had just brought over for me to sign.

"If you need more time...we understand," Elizabeth whispered as she sat at the side of my bed.

"No. It's ok. I'm ready," I declared while fighting back tears that were swiftly swelling in my eyes. I swallowed hard and signed my signature to the legal documents.

"Tvoya, you will not regret this. Gary and I promise to raise Jonathan right. And when the time is appropriate we will tell him about you," Elizabeth said as she cradled me in her arms allowing my tears to flow freely. I knew I was doing the right thing.

It was of no use...I wasn't going to get any sleep. Instead, I got up, took a shower and went for a walk. When I returned it was already 7:00 am. I was wondering if it would be too early to call Valerie's when the phone rang. It was Elizabeth.

"It's not too early for you, is it Freshmeat?" Elizabeth chimed.

"Uh, no. I was just thinking about you, Elizabeth," I said, taken aback that I would hear from her so early.

"So what time are you gonna get your butt over here."

"What time do you want me there?"

"You know I'm dying so don't take all day."

"Elizabeth!" I was stunned by her attitude. But then again this was Elizabeth.

"I'm on my way," I said before I hung up the phone.

29

"Oh! Promise Me"

*A*s I parked my car in front of Valerie's house, I could see Valerie walk from the side gate that led to her backyard. She continued down the driveway as I struggled to retrieve the bag of breakfast goodies I'd picked up from the store on my way over. I wasn't sure what the protocol was for food, when visiting a dying dear friend who was about to prepare one for the meeting of a son, that was given to them to adopt 13 years ago. Were there any books written on that topic? I wondered.

"What ya got there?" Valerie asked as she greeted me with a sisterly hug.

"Oh, just some breakfast stuff. Have you guys eaten yet?" I answered nervously. I guessed I should have asked that before coming over with all of this.

Valerie picked up on it right away. "Tvoya, relax. I can see you're tense."

Tense wasn't the word. Valerie had no idea I had been up all night with Royce discussing his father, my mother, his ex-wife, her sister and brother-in law, her husband and our child. No. This was definitely not the time for bringing her up to speed on all of that. This visit was about Elizabeth and her wishes.

Once we were in Valerie's backyard approaching the enclosed porch that extended from the family room, it struck me in full force how so much had changed. This very backyard had momentous significance in shaping the formative years of my very existence. It once claimed me as its very own private refugee. I would come and sit on the steps that led up to the entrance way after having just run away from witnessing any one of my mothers' drunken tirades. Sometimes, it would be late and I would be afraid to knock on the door, so I would just sit there quietly and listen to the faint sounds of the television or the snores of Valerie's dad fill the night air. I had become a comfortable and frequent visitor before I was found out by my best friend. Valerie had already observed the antics of my mother's drinking (back then, she found it quite comical), and I had confided that there were times I would just leave the house and wander the neighborhood until I thought that my mother had passed out. So Valerie wasn't too surprised to find me out there one night when her mother had sent her downstairs to wake her father to come to bed. Fortunately for me, I was discovered before her father was awakened. Valerie first ushered me swiftly to her bedroom then went back to wake her father. This soon became a routine to the extent where we developed code knocks for me to use to alert Valerie that I once again needed shelter. On these nights she would volunteer the awakening ritual, rescue me from the outside elements, hide me in her bedroom for the night, and some days and no one was the wiser. That is, until Elizabeth caught on to us.

Upon entering the porch, I could see Elizabeth on the far side of the room. The décor was vastly different from what their parents' once was. Valerie took great pains in updating and livening up the old family stead. And thank God for that; Elizabeth certainly needed the uplifting.

"I thought I heard your voice, Freshment."

I smiled weakly as I bent down to give Elizabeth a tight hug.

"Yeah, it's me all right. I brought some breakfast if you want."

"You know me. I'm always down for some food."

"Be careful, Liz. You can't just eat anything," Valerie interrupted.

"God, Valerie, can't I eat what I want before I die," Elizabeth answered cutting her eyes and then fixing them on me. I didn't know if I should defend Elizabeth or Valerie. I indubitably did not want to agree with Elizabeth's declaration of death. Needless to say, I was in fact more than a little uncomfortable with her cavalier references to her own dying. In my humble and probably unwarranted opinion, I believed Elizabeth was too quick at accepting this death sentence, when she didn't have to. Why wasn't she fighting to stay alive?

"What you bring?" Elizabeth's question shook me back to our conversation.

"Whatever," Valerie asserted as she exited the room carrying the bag of food with her.

Elizabeth winked. "She'll be back to feed us." I only half smiled as I sat down across from her.

Elizabeth was lying on a duplicate of the chaise lounge that I owned. Valerie and I shopped for them together and because we had the same taste, could not pass them up. Elizabeth had a shawl covering her legs and another draping her shoulders. She looked so much older than she really was. The granny look that was being sported was to be thanked for that. I wondered if the shawls were more for security than for warmth.

"Well, let me cut straight to the chase. Since my days on this earth are numbered, I thought this is just as good a time as any for you and Jonathan to get reacquainted," Elizabeth said as she shifted to sit more erect.

"Here, let me help you. There," I said rushing to prop the pillows up behind her. I was more than a little lost for words so I kept silent.

"Thanks," she said continuing, "Gary and I talked about this in great length. We have always told him he wasn't our biological son....that he was given to us by someone very special." Elizabeth paused, I smiled, down casting my eyes. I couldn't look at Elizabeth any longer. Still, I said nothing.

"Tvoya, he's gonna need you. I hope you can see that it's time."

Never had I thought there would ever be a time I would be reacquainted with my son. This was not the happily ever after I had envision for him. Giving him up was the hardest thing I ever had to do. And now to be faced with the opportunity to meet him again, under these dire circumstances, was implausibly surreal. Bitter sweet would be putting it mildly. I, Jonathan's biological mother, was getting ready to be reacquainted with him at the expense of losing his real mother, Elizabeth. It just didn't seem fair.

"Elizabeth, how is Jonathan dealing with your situation?" I could not even bring myself to put the label of "dying" on my question.

"A lot better, now. Gary told him first. Then he and I got a chance to talk after he was flown here for a few days. He went back when Mom did. ....Anyway, it was rough. But I have always been straight-forward with him, so I pulled no punches. Hell, that's life, you know? He's strong. He'll survive. Jonathan, you'll come to find out, is very mature for his age."

Valerie entered the room with our food nicely arranged on a serving platter. I watched her as she sat it down on the coffee table that separated Elizabeth from me. She looked as if she wanted to say something but was waiting for the right time. I watched her intently serve Elizabeth. I shook my head no, when it was my turn. I had lost my appetite, and again, my speech. Elizabeth took a small bite from her croissant, washed it down with her juice and intended to continue but it was Valerie who spoke, instead.

"Tell Tvoya the whole story," Valerie said as her and Elizabeth's eyes locked. Elizabeth surrendered expression hinted she would not be contesting Valerie's command.

"Tvoya, this is not my first bout with ovarian cancer. I was diagnosed with it three years ago. Fought it for a year with chemo and was free for two. But now it's back and I am refusing treatment. Walla! This death sentence," Elizabeth announced, almost defiantly.

"There, Valerie, satisfied?"

"So you see, Tvoya, why it's so important to us all that you meet Jonathan," Valerie offered ignoring Elizabeth.

"I understand," I said, not offering my feelings, one way or the other. Maybe because I was in shock. I had no clue any of this had ever taken place. I felt terrible for Elizabeth and betrayed by Valerie for keeping it from me. What was going on in my life? Why was I finding out now so much was being kept from me? All in the name of protecting me? Did I appear that weak to people? I kept hearing a voice in my head say, 'this is not about you.' But my heart was saying something entirely different. In fact, it was slowly breaking.

"I'm really sorry, Elizabeth," I said as I moved to sit next to her while taking her hand in mine.

"Don't be. It is what it is," Elizabeth said, "I'll be set up here in hospice starting next week. Jonathan and Gary will be coming up in the next few days and will be here for the duration. So Tvoya, promise me you will be there for our son."

I had so much to say, so many questions to ask, so much to express. But all I could barely manage was, "I promise."

I had just made a huge promise to Elizabeth that I had no

idea how I was going to keep. I was on the verge of becoming an emotional wreck. And at the same time I felt I had no right to even feeling that way. I didn't stay at Valerie's too long before it was soon time for Elizabeth to get some rest. But I dared not leave without first talking with Valerie. Once we were sure that Elizabeth was sound asleep, we took our conversation to the kitchen.

"Valerie, I didn't know Elizabeth had already had a bout with this thing." I felt guilty this wasn't the time to put Valerie through the drill about not telling me. But I had to know why I was kept in the dark.

"Yeah," she sighed heavily, "we have been down this road before."

"I'm so very sorry."

"No, Tvoya, I'm the one that should be sorry. I apologize for not telling you all about this when we went through this the first time. I should have shared this with you. I don't know…I just didn't want to dump all of my family's woes on to you. You had had enough to deal with over the years. I mean….your mother was just getting over her drinking problem. And I guess because Jonathan was involved…." Valerie's voice trailed off as if she was searching for more reasons to justify her not telling me.

"Valerie, it's fine. It's ok. Please don't do this to yourself. I understand. You really don't need to give me an explanation," I said gently. I was truly embarrassed for even thinking previously that I should be owed one.

"Tvoya, I'm scared. The last time we went through this with Elizabeth, she was a fighter, a warrior….she vowed that this wasn't going to defeat her. Now, this time, it's different, she's different. She's….she's just giving up. She's not even going to fight," Valerie said through sobs of tears. I walked over to my best friend and embraced her.

"Ssssh," I whispered softly. I couldn't say it was going to

be all right. At that point, I didn't have the strength or the faith to back up such a declaration. All I could do was hold Valerie and try as best I could to comfort her. I was at a loss for words.

30

"Holy Matrimony!"

This same loss for words swept over me as I opened the door to my place later that same afternoon to find it in pure shambles. After only moments of taking in an eyeful did it dawn on me that entering would not be the best idea. So I closed the door quietly, being careful not to disturb any intruder who might still be in my place. I then ran down my steps, back into my car and drove off. Where I was going I had no idea. I ended up in front of Mr. Strickland's house and was relieved to see Royce's car parked in the driveway.

"Whoa, where's the fire?" Royce asked as he opened the door just as I reached for the bell. "I could see you get out of your car from the window."

"Royce, someone broke into my place," I said gasping for air.

"What?! Come in, come in." Royce pulled me into his father's house, and closed the door, but not before looking both ways to see if I had been followed.

"Ok, now tell me what's this all about?" Royce said as he handed me an unopened bottled water, while ushering me to a chair.

"I just walked into my place and found it a wreck. Lamps broken on the floor, papers everywhere, curtains torn and off the rods. A pew t mess."

"Did you see anyone?"

"No, I didn't stay long enough to see if anyone was still there. I just had a brief thought that I should jet," I said after taking a long swig of water.

"Good, that was smart, Tvoya. I'm calling the police." Royce took his cell phone out and started dialing as I remembered that I hadn't turned mine on since leaving Valerie's.

"Yes, I'll let you speak with her." Royce turned his phone over to me and I gave the 911 dispatcher all of my pertinent information and the details of what had just transpired. They told me to come to the precinct and that they would send someone over to my place in the meantime. After speaking with them and wondering who could've broken into my home and why, my cell phone rang. I recognized it was Charlene's cell phone number.

"Not now, Charlene," I said aloud while choosing not to answer it.

"Who was that?" Royce asked as we were leaving for the precinct.

"Just Charlene. She'll leave a message. I can call her back later."

"We'll take my car," Royce announced.

As I settled into the front passenger seat, Royce reached for my hand. His stroking made me feel warm and protected.

"Don't worry, Tvoya. It's going to be ok," he whispered gently. I smiled wishing this could be true about everything.

♥　　　♥　　　♥

While we sat at the precinct answering yet another series of interrogating questions, Charlene called my cell phone again. Again, I ignored it. Then I realized I had not even mentioned to the police officer, that Charlene was staying with me.

"Oh, um, Officer, I forgot to mention to you…um…I am currently housing a house guest," I offered.

"Oh?!" he answered. This oversight apparently perturbed my inquisitor.

"I'm sorry I forgot to tell you this. It's just that I've been…." He cut me off with raising his eyebrow and asking me for a name.

"Her name is Charlene Brooks." Man, I hoped that Charlene wasn't involved in this. Just as her name left my lips, my cell phone rang again and again it was her.

"Do you need to answer that, Miss Harrington?" the annoyed officer asked. I looked at Royce who looked over to see who was burning up my cell. He nodded that I should alert the annoyed officer that it was in fact Charlene who was calling.

"It's her calling me now," I said.

The officer held out his hand to me indicating that I should hand my cell phone over to him. I obliged and he answered it.

"Hello, this is Officer Carter. Uh huh, yes this is her cell. She's here at the 205 Precinct. Ma'am slow down and tell me what happened!" Royce and I looked at one another. What on earth could Charlene be talking to this officer about? Of course, Royce and I quietly decided not to say a word.

"Are you all right?" the officer asked her, listened, and said, "Ma'am, sit tight and wait for the patrol car. I'm sending one over right now."

Officer Carter closed my cell phone and politely handed it

back to me. Then he yelled over to the desk behind him.

"Joe, you and Maria go over to Southeast General Hospital. Find a Charlene Brooks, who's at the emergency room waiting with a Dr. Byron Munroe, and get a statement from the two of them."

Royce and I again looked at one another and back to Officer Carter for an explanation of what was going on.

"Miss Harrington, your place wasn't broken into. Apparently, what you walked into was the result of two of your friends fighting in your apartment." Condo, I wanted to say in defense to the downgrade of my humble abode, but decided that would not be a good idea to do, right about now.

"Fighting?!" Royce asked.

"Charlene and Byron had a fight in my condo?" There I got it in anyway.

"Well, that's what Miss Brooks just told me. But of course, that will have to be checked out."

"Officers Smith and Rodriguez are on their way to get their statements. Do you wish to file any charges, Miss Harrington?"

I wish to do this day over. "No, I don't wish to file any charges, Officer Carter. I just want to know what the hell is going on."

♥　　　♥　　　♥

Royce and I arrived at Southeast General Hospital's emergency room and found Charlene talking to Officer Rodriquez. As we approached them, I could hear the officer ask Charlene if she wanted to file charges against Byron.

"Oh, Tvoya, gurl, am I glad to see you," Charlene

announced, neglecting to answer the officer's question.

"Ma'am, will you be pressing any charges?" Officer Rodriquez asked again.

"Uh, no," Charlene answered looking to me.

"Well, then my work here is done," Officer Rodriquez declared.

"Uh, not yet, Officer Rodriguez," Officer Smith interrupted as he appeared at her side, "Dr. Munroe does want to press charges against Miss Brooks."

"What?!" Charlene yelled.

"Calm down, Miss Brooks," said Officer Rodriquez as she looked at each of us, "let's take this conversation outside."

Charlene, Royce and I followed Officer Rodriquez to the outer vestibule of the emergency room while Officer Smith brought up the rear. All the while, I'm wondering where Byron is and why he wants to press charges against Charlene. And then all at once it hits me…why we were at a hospital's emergency room in the first place. Charlene holds a 5th degree Black Belt in Tae Kwon Do. Something other than my lamps must have gotten broken in this fight between her and Byron, and my guess was, it was something on Byron.

"Miss Brooks, Dr. Munroe says you jumped him from behind when a fight ensued between you two, resulting in you subsequently breaking his arm in three places," Officer Smith reported. "Do you care to offer your side?"

"You damn right I do," Charlene spat. "When I came into Tvoya's place, where I'm staying, I found Byron tearing up the place."

Royce and I looked at one another. Charlene continued, "He was yelling something about his ring….you do know he was drunk, right?"

"Yes, we've observed that Dr. Munroe had been

drinking," Officer Smith offered.

"Well, shouldn't y'all be locking him up or something…instead of questioning me?" Charlene complained.

"Miss Brooks, we just want to get to the bottom of what happened," Officer Rodriquez interrupted.

"Me too," I announced suddenly. Hey, after all this was my place that was torn to smithereens.

"Well, like I said, he was just tearing up the place and when I walked in, I must've startled him because then he threw something at me. Thank God, my reflexes are good or I would have caught it upside my head. Anyway, I could see he was drunk and that talking to him wasn't gonna do no good, so I rushed him and wrestled him to the floor. But then he got loose and hit me across my forearm here," Charlene said pointing to the bruise that was increasing in color.

"Did you have that looked at?" I asked.

"Nah, it's nothing," Charlene answered continuing, "that's when I figured I better use what I know…so I did…and then I realized after seeing him yelling, like a schoolgirl in red pumps…." Royce let out a smothered chuckle on Charlene's analogy. I, on the other hand was so thoroughly embarrassed for Byron. I should have just given him back his ring and got back my key, when I broke it off with him.

Charlene continued, "that he was hurt, so after he calmed down and realized he needed my help, I drove him here."

"Ok. Well Miss Brooks, since Mr. Munroe wants to press charges, you will be hearing from his lawyers. You can stop by the precinct and get a copy of the report that will be filed by Officer Rodriquez and myself for your defense," Officer Smith recited as he continued to write in his little notebook.

"And Miss Harrington, are you sure you don't want to file charges?" asked Officer Rodriquez.

"Uh, no," I answered.

"Well, that's all for now, folks. We'll be in touch. Good day," said Officer Smith, leaving Charlene, Royce and me to have our own chit-chat about this whole mess.

No, a good day, this was not.

31

"With This Ring"

"Tvoya, I'm really very sorry about your place, but I'm not sorry I whipped Byron's…"

"Charlene! Where is Byron, now?" I asked cutting her off.

"I don't know. I guess having fixed what damage I made," Charlene said rolling her eyes. "All I know…he's gonna wish he never threatened to press charges against me. That's what I know." Charlene flipped open her cell phone and then walked out of the hospital.

"Wow, this is some wild stuff, huh?" Royce offered.

"Royce, please don't go there, ok?"

"Tvoya, I'm only saying…I'm glad that you cut that loser off."

"Well, I'm going back in to see how that loser is doing."

"I'll wait for you here," Royce resigned.

As I walked back through the corridor that led to the waiting room, I spotted a doctor that looked familiar.

"Tvoya?" The familiar doctor asked.

"Uh, yes, I'm Tvoya." I was right, apparently we did know one another but I couldn't remember from where.

"Hi, I'm Dr. Stephen Healy. Stephen Healy? I'm a friend and colleague of Byron's."

"Oh, yes, I'm sorry. I remember you now."

"Is everything all right? I mean since you're in an emergency room."

"Uh, yes. I mean, no. It's Byron. He's here, but I'm not sure where."

"Really? Well, have a seat here and let me check."

"Thank you." I sat down grateful for Dr. Healy's help. It was a little while before he returned.

"Tvoya, I found Byron. Let me walk you there," Dr. Healy offered.

"Oh, that won't be necessary. I'm sure I can follow your directions."

"Well….let's walk and talk," he said evenly.

"Oh, ok," I answered realizing it would be wise to accept his suggestion.

"Um, Tvoya, when I first found Byron and told him you were looking for him, he said he didn't want to see you."

"I can understand that. You see, Dr. Healy, Byron and I have just broken our engagement very recently."

"Well, that's none of my business. However, I did want to warn you, he does need surgery on his arm, but since he is more than a little inebriated, it's going to have to wait for him to sober up. He's in a lot of pain, so be prepared. He will probably lash out at you," he remarked apologetically.

"Thank you for the warning, Dr. Healy."

"Not a problem. Nonetheless, in spite of everything, he did finally agree to see you." Dr. Healy and I were soon at the section where Byron was waiting for the return of his sobriety.

"He's right over there. Good luck, Tvoya. And I'm sorry to hear of your breakup."

"Don't be," I offered, "I'm not." He smiled while gently touching my elbow as if to safely usher me towards the vicinity of a lunatic. I peeked around the curtain, only to hear Byron scream out, "Get out! Didn't I tell you I didn't want to see her. All I want is my ring!"

I stood frozen as I observed the sad sight of seeing Byron strapped to a chair. Good thing he wasn't at the hospital he worked at. However, that feeling departed quickly as I had to be swift in dodging an oncoming serving tray. Although he was strapped around his arms and torso, his legs were free to cause havoc.

"Don't worry, I'm out!" I yelled over my shoulder as the first rescuers came to see what all the commotion was about and if I needed any help. I told them I was all right but the person behind the curtain did need some help and fast. What Byron really needed was Jesus. How could I have ever thought that Byron was the man I should marry? Thank God, I was allowed to see Byron for who he really was. I had been in some serious denial. Truth be told, Byron more than a few times showed his true self. I was just too caught up in the drama and production of planning a wedding to see it. Moreover, to entertain the possibility of being married and to a doctor at that..., I was trippin' for sure. For real.

"Where's Charlene?" I asked Royce after reuniting with him on the outside of the hospital.

"She said something about checking out a guy named, Crew, who she said will set Byron straight. I told her I could do that for her," Royce playfully announced.

"Royce! You just let her leave like that?"

"What was I supposed to do? Hog tie her?"

"You could have convinced her to stick around, since we have to go back to my place and clean it up!"

"Rough time with Dr. Feelgood, huh?"

"He's not feeling very good right about now. He has to have surgery but they're waiting for him to sober up first." I thought it wouldn't be a good idea to tell Royce of Byron's ranting and raving.

"Wow, Charlene really hooked him up, huh?"

"Yeah, she really did. Did I mention to you Charlene's a 5th degree Black Belt in Tae Kwon Do?"

"Really? And I thought Dr. Feelgood was just a punk."

32

"With The Power Vested In Me"

Royce and I spent half the night putting my place back together. The locksmith had just left before Charlene checked in by phone to inform me that Byron agreed to drop the charges. She had this Crew person to thank for that. I imagined Byron was convinced it would be in his best interest to do so. In addition, Charlene had Crew throw the ring in the deal. She said, it was mine. Free and clear. I wasn't too sure about that. I would have to speak with Byron myself after the dust settled some. Man, Charlene knew some real unsavory characters. She apologized for not being there to help with the cleanup but promised she would send some money my way for damage expenses. She reasoned in addition to this debt, she had a greater one to pay off that night. I'm so glad I'm saved and now living for the Lord; that way of life is no longer an option for me.

"Royce, I guess this is as best we can do for one night," I said ready to hit the hay. "Thanks for your help, I couldn't have done this by myself."

"No problem. Let's get something to eat. I don't remember you having anything since this whole thing started."

Royce was right. I hadn't had anything to eat all day. As tired as I was and longing for some much needed sleep, I guessed going to bed on an empty stomach wouldn't be the best thing.

"Ok, what you feel like having?"

"Oh, good," Royce said sounding surprise by my consent. "Let's see now, what's open this time a night?"

"Well, there's this new diner on Springfield that's 24 hours."

"Ok, diner food it is then," Royce cheerfully quipped. It was then that it hit me…this is what I used to love best about Royce. He was so easy going, so flexible, so easy to be around.

♥   ♥   ♥

While we waited for our order, I contemplated whether I should tell Royce everything concerning Jonathan. I sensed a conviction that confirmed there were no privileges reserved by me in keeping the full story from him. He never knew about the letters or that I was even pregnant. Be that as it may, he was still Jonathan's biological father, and as much a victim of his father's manipulation as I was.

"Royce, there's something else about the situation about…um…our…um, Jonathan, that I didn't share with you last night," I said as I fiddled with the silverware.

"Go on," Royce hesitantly replied.

"Elizabeth has cancer," I started.

"Elizabeth? I didn't hear you right. Did you say that Elizabeth has cancer?" Royce said rubbing his eyes indicating that maybe his tiredness was getting the best of him.

"She could die." I refused to bring myself to agree with Elizabeth's certainty of her premature death. "It's her second go 'round with this monster. She beat it the first time, but now that it's back… she's refusing therapy."

"Man, I'm really very sorry to hear that," Royce's sentiment was sincere.

"She wants me to be reacquainted with Jonathan," I quickly blurted out before losing my nerve.

"That's great, Tvoya. I mean, it's not great that Elizabeth has cancer…but I mean, we get a chance to meet Jonathan."

"We?"

"Well? Why not?" He could meet both of his natural parents," Royce reasoned.

"But, Royce he's dealing with so much already. To throw you into the mix right now, might…"

"Yeah, I guess you're right. I wasn't thinking," Royce resigned.

"It's all right. I understand. I mean it's normal to want to meet the son you just found out only days ago you had."

"Yeah, but I know what you mean. We have to think about him and of course, Elizabeth."

There he goes again. Making me remember all the things that made me fall in love with him all those years ago.

"Tvoya? Your food is here. Aren't you gonna eat?" Royce announced coercing me once again into joining him.

"Oh, I must've spaced out for a moment."

"So when are you going to meet him?" Royce inquired.

As we ate, I told Royce all that Elizabeth and Valerie had told me about Elizabeth's bout with cancer and how Jonathan was dealing with it. Royce was quiet while I did all the talking. I knew he was disappointed but we both realized that him meeting Jonathan now probably wouldn't be the best idea. How greatly this bothered him was about to be revealed.

"You know Gina and I never had any children together," Royce offered out of the blue.

"Oh," I answered struggling hard to sound as if I really cared. Forgive me Lord.

"We tried, that's for sure. Well, I did anyway," he continued mindlessly. I didn't need to hear this. I wanted badly to scream out. What did he mean about 'he did anyway?' Whatever.

"Tvoya, I'm really very sorry about how things went down with you and me back in the day," Royce expressed while reaching across the table taking my hand into his. Well, I guess his rambling wasn't so mindless after all.

"Besides the fact about my not knowing about the letters and your pregnancy, I had no right lying to you about Gina and leaving you the way that I did."

"Royce," I said trying to stop him. This all wasn't necessary.

"Tvoya, please let me finish," Royce interrupted, "I need to say this and you need to hear it."

"All righty then. Go on," I resigned trying to make light of a conversation that was turning way too heavy. It seemed these days all of my conversations were having that same tone. Too serious.

"I was seeing Gina before we broke up. We were set up by our fathers. They had been frat brothers when they were in college and thought for us to meet and date would be a good match."

"Royce, I know all of this. I knew all along about Gina," I confessed hoping he would realize it would be unnecessary and futile for him to continue.

"But, please Tvoya, I need to tell you these things myself. I need to be straight with you so we can wipe the slate clean and start fresh and new."

Start fresh and new? I was afraid that Royce was moving excessively fast. All of the recent events that were bombarding my life were swiftly overwhelming me. I felt as if I was losing control of my self-empowering destiny. I no longer knew what to expect in the next moment. I was quickly being swept away by the undercurrent of uncertainty; further descending me into the depths of caution. I tried to listen to what Royce was saying with a buoyant ear, but at the same time it was all too much to absorb. This man was pouring out his heart. He told me that his marriage failed and how it left him bitter and untrusting. Sort of like where I was coming from. To hear Royce speak like this, one could easily relate forming a bond of unity simply based on the similitude of us both being wronged. And yet, it felt contrary and strange to be now forming this alliance. In any case, I now had a choice to make. I could become bitter, resentful and hopeless. But what good would that do? Instead I could make a choice at that moment to allow faith to well up in my soul. The God kind of faith that says to stay focused and encouraged. The God kind of faith that says trouble don't last always and not to let the storms knock you over and keep you down.

"Anyway," Royce was saying, "I'm glad to be finding out about Jonathan, period. These days, I'm learning to count my blessings. And I'm grateful to know we have a child together."

It appeared, Royce was way ahead of me in keeping a level head and staying focused on what was important.

There he goes again. Giving me another reminder of why…

33

"From This Day Forward"

Except for the periodic disturbing ring of the telephone, I spent the next forty-eight hours in seclusion. All of what had been going on of late needed to be further examined, sorted, processed, digested and if necessary regurgitated. This time for me was crucial. I needed to stay prayerful and fully connected to the will and way of God. I screened my phone calls to ensure I wouldn't be negatively influenced. Albeit they followed in a steady stream, ranging from urgent to the 'I just called to say hi.' My mother, of course, leading the fold. Hers starting with urgent to finally surrendering with, 'I just called to say I love you and please call me when you feel up to it.' Needless to say, her calls went unanswered. I just wasn't ready to speak with her. I was disappointed by what I learned from Royce as to the real reason why she went into rehab, and I firmly believed she was aware that Mr. Strickland knew about Jonathan. She was probably calling to have confirmed, whether or not what she was hearing in her beauty shop about what went down regarding Byron and Charlene was true. I learned through speaking briefly with Priscilla, one of Mommy's customers reported that a family member of theirs was in the emergency room at the time this unfortunate fiasco occurred. I was already the talk of the town, certainly since the incident at Razz. So I knew the deal.

It appeared my life was virtually a never-ending saga from a soap opera for sure. I was intrigued that none of my mother's messages mentioned Elizabeth, Jonathan or even Royce. She was treading lightly, and I guess it was fair that I appreciate the non-intrusion. Royce's approach however was quite the opposite. He was being intrusive and didn't care that he was. When we finally spoke, he tried to convince me it would be a good idea for me to mention to Elizabeth that he was aware of Jonathan's paternity and adoption. I maintained the stance that this would only create more stress to Elizabeth. His argument was that Elizabeth would better go on in peace knowing that Jonathan's biological father not only knew about his existence but that he also wanted the chance in meeting him. A truce was formed between the two of us leaving us agreeing to disagree with a clause for him to promise not to go behind my back to Lamar in hopes of making him an ally.

I checked in with Valerie and Elizabeth a couple of times to offer my love and support, assuming Elizabeth would be the only one I would cut this time short for, until Margo's call came in that is. Anyway, Valerie assured me that for now there wasn't very much I could do. She suggested I spend my self-imposed lockdown preparing to meet Jonathan. Definite words of wisdom from my best friend, the sage.

"Hey, Tvoya, it's time to take that ring out of the safe deposit box and sell it." Margo's announcement is the very reason my seclusion was to be only forty-eight hours.

"I can't."

"And why not? Listen, I've already spoken with Byron and he said you can do anything you want with it....well, he had a few choice words for what that could be. Anyway, the truth of the matter is, we've got to settle these bills."

"You spoke with Byron? Margo, how did he seem?" I wanted to be rid of Byron but I did care how he was doing.

"He seemed pissed off. But that doesn't matter."

"It doesn't matter?"

"Look, T, I know what went down. I ran into Charlene last night. Well, really Yvonne told me half of it, and Charlene filled me in on the rest," Margo admitted. "We better get a move on selling that ring before Byron changes his mind."

"Margo, I've got to talk with Byron first."

"You don't have time to talk with Byron. I'm holding back everyone for now as best I can but pretty soon they're gonna be demanding their money."

"I'm giving Byron back his ring."

"You're what?!"

"I have no right keeping the ring. I broke up with him."

"Well, then you better talk to him about him selling the ring and paying off these people."

"No, I'll get the money from Daddy. I should have listened to him in the first place. I'm giving Byron back his ring."

"Ok, let me know when you get the paper from Thomas."

"All right, I'll do that. Um, Margo, what's my mother talking about?"

"Give her a call, Tvoya. She's worried about you."

"Margo, tell me something, what was the real reason behind her going into rehab?"

"What do you mean?" Margo seemed genuinely perplexed as to my sudden switch of gears in this conversation.

"Why did my mother go into rehab, Margo?"

"She went into rehab because she was ready to stop drinking," Margo said in defense to my pressing inquiry.

"But what made her decide it was time?"

"Well, I don't know exactly. She had been counseling

with my father. I guess he convinced her," Margo said. It was apparent Margo didn't know about my mother's night of transgression that Royce spoke of.

"Did my mother ever tell Mr. Strickland about Jonathan?"

"No, definitely not!" Margo said adamantly. "Did Royce tell you that?"

"No," I answered, ashamed I even resorted to asking her.

"Look, Tvoya, give Yvonne a call. It's clear you guys have some issues to clear up. You need to talk to her. She doesn't deserve to be left out."

I knew where Margo was coming from. She was right. It was wrong of me to keep my mother in the dark. In order to move on I had to forgive her regardless of what she's done or did not do. If Royce could forgive his father and move on then so could I. Right?

I wondered if it could be that simple.

♥   ♥   ♥

"Well, hello Sister Tvoya. How are you?" Pastor Underwood greeted me as he stood at the door of his church after Sunday worship services. He was one of the few pastors who still did this. This went against the advisement of his ministerial staff. Their position was that it was too taxing. Margo joked that his position was that since he was single he was looking for a first lady and what better way but to greet each one every Sunday. It worked well for him since seventy-five percent of our church population was made up of women. How many who were actually single, I wasn't sure. But I'm sure Pastor Underwood knew just who the single ones were.

I was ashamed to admit I was one of those members who

scooted out the side doors to avoid the crowd of others who wanted to shake the hand of their pastor. Today, it was different, today, I needed to set up a meeting with Pastor Underwood.

"I'm well, Pastor. Pastor, can I make an appointment to speak with you?"

"Why Sister Tvoya, you know you don't need to make an appointment with me. You're family," he said with much sincerity. "Take a seat in my office and when I'm finished here, we can talk."

It was actually thirty minutes before Pastor Underwood arrived in his office.

"Pastor, I'm amazed that you take the time every Sunday to greet your members."

"You know, Sis', I wouldn't have it any other way. Many ministers don't think it's a good idea. But I'm a people pastor. That's the way it was back in the day, as they say." I laughed at his choice of words.

"The ministers do have a point, Pastor. The congregation is growing. It's got to be taking a lot out of you."

"No, it doesn't really. The Lord gives me the strength for what He wants me to do," he humbly testified. "But we're not here to talk about me. What's on your heart?"

I found it interesting that Pastor would start with asking me what was on my heart. All that I was encountering had everything to do with my heart.

"Pastor, how much time do you have?"

Immediately following Pastor Underwood leading me in prayer, I proceeded to tell him about everything that was going on in my life. He listened patiently and intently, not once interrupting my flow. And looking back, this was a great feat as I was on a roll. I knew I couldn't possibly share all of what I was feeling with everyone. I couldn't tell Elizabeth, that I was apprehensive about meeting Jonathan especially since she and the family was experiencing probably the most traumatic chapter of their lives. I couldn't tell Valerie I had been hurt that she didn't share with me previously that Elizabeth had already gone through this battle with cancer. No, that would be too selfish of me. I couldn't tell Byron I was disappointed he turned out to be something other than what I was expecting or what I had prayed for. I couldn't tell my mother I was angry she was forced into rehab not by her own will in wanting to be a better mother to me but instead by her stupidity in judgment or lack thereof. I couldn't tell my father I still had abandonment issues from him that resurfaced again when Royce left me and I certainly couldn't tell Royce I was falling in love with him…again. Pastor Underwood got an earful for sure. When I was done pouring out all my heart had been holding, I cried and it brought great relief.

"I'm glad you've released all of that weight," Pastor Underwood said as he passed me the tissue box that sat on his desk. "I could see and feel the heaviness as I greeted you earlier." I only nodded my head in agreement with what he had just said. It was true. When I entered the church this morning, I was on overload and all my circuits were about to break. Having had this talk, I felt a great burden lifted.

"There are no quick fixes to all of this, Sister Tvoya. Now that you have gotten it out, leave it now with Jesus. Be patient, and let him take you and get you through it. Trust Him now."

I only nodded as I blew my nose. Pastor Underwood continued, "Let's ask Him to help you embrace everything that's ahead without fear, as you move forward from this day on. Furthermore, let's ask Him to completely heal Sister Elizabeth Scott."

When Pastor Underwood announced that we could ask God for Elizabeth to be healed it was as if a lightening bolt went through my body. With all the anxiety that went with the knowledge of someone declaring that they are going to die, I had no idea I could ask God to heal them on their behalf. This blew me away.

Pastor Underwood, who was sitting next to me took my hand and we proceeded to pray. When we were done, he said, "You know Reverend Pierce-Vertrell will be back next Sunday specifically as a directive from God to conduct a healing service. Bring Sister Elizabeth."

"I will wholeheartedly try, Pastor."

You can best believe that!

34

"My Solemn Pledge"

*I*mmediately following my talk with Pastor Underwood, I was at Valerie's door; unannounced and ready to take on the world. I didn't even think to call ahead by cell phone. I was excited, pumped and overflowing with encouragement. Valerie answered the door certainly taken aback.

"Hi, Tvoya. I didn't know you were coming by," Valerie said as she held the door open for me to enter.

"Hey gurl. Sorry for coming over unannounced. But I had to see Elizabeth and you."

"Well, you sure seem excited about something. What's up?"

Once I entered, I noticed how still and quiet it was.

"Where's Poetry?" I asked concerned that the mood in this house was becoming too grim for a three and a half year old child.

"She's with my mother visiting my Aunt Ursula. Mom came back last night picked up Poetry and left again. They'll be staying with her for a while. Mom's having a hard time dealing with this," Valerie responded as she led me into the living room.

"Is Elizabeth asleep?" I asked hoping I would be able to

speak with her as well.

"She's been sleeping for a while now, so you may be in luck."

"Good, I really need to speak with her."

Valerie's faced shrouded with dismay. "You're not having second thoughts about meeting Jonathan?"

"No. No! Nothing like that." I decided that if I couldn't speak with Elizabeth first, then maybe Valerie would be a good advocate to get the message across to her.

"Valerie, I just left meeting with Pastor Underwood and we went before the Lord in prayer and asked for Elizabeth to be healed.

"Ok?" Valerie's response was infused with great skepticism.

"I know what you're thinking."

"Now, how do you know what I'm thinking?" Valerie defended.

"You don't believe."

"It's not that I don't believe. I just don't want to get excited about something that may not make a difference." Valerie was singing a different tune than before. I thought she wanted and believed that Elizabeth could get well.

"You sound like you've given up hope."

"Well, what hope do we have if Elizabeth is refusing therapy."

"Look Valerie, God is greater than any therapy."

"But." I didn't let Valerie continue. I refused to give up.

"But nothing, Valerie. God is able!" I surprised even myself by how firm I was standing on my conviction. You better preach, sister! Valerie said nothing, but the wringing of her hands told it all. She was doubtful.

"Valerie, I know this sounds strange and far fetched. Nevertheless, I believe God. Pastor Underwood told me to bring Elizabeth to church next Sunday."

"Oh, that's out of the question, Tvoya. Elizabeth doesn't have the strength to attend a church service."

"Please Valerie. Look, we're having a special healing service. Remember I told you about the incredible experience I had when a visiting reverend spoke a prophetic word over my life? Well, she's the one who will be conducting the healing service."

"Tvoya, I know your heart is in the right place, but this is just so unpredictable. What if Elizabeth doesn't get healed? Then what?"

I didn't have an answer for her. I felt as if she had thrown me a curve ball I couldn't catch. What now Lord? Valerie and I sat in total silence. Then she got up from the couch and slowly walked into the kitchen. I could hear the clanging of dishes and then water running in the sink. I wasn't sure if I should go into the kitchen after her and try to convince her once more or if I should just see myself out. What now Lord? I asked, once again. And then I received the answer. It was a small soft whisper that said, "Trust Me."

I walked into the kitchen to ask Valerie if I could stay to help her out around the house, when I found her leaning against the sink sobbing.

"Valerie?" I said softly as I approached her. She quickly snatched a piece of paper towel down from its holder to wipe her eyes, before turning to face me.

"Oh, Tvoya, I want to believe that Elizabeth can get better. I just…"

"It's ok, Valerie. I understand. Listen, God will help you with your unbelief. Let's just try Him. Give the Lord a chance." She nodded signifying her support.

I hugged Valerie and allowed her to cry some more. Knowing Valerie, she was being strong for everyone else and now she needed someone to be strong for her. This was taking its toll. Her home had now been turned into a waiting for death to arrive dwelling. Thank God, things were going to be turning around. Getting Valerie on board was half the battle. The other was to get Elizabeth to the healing service.

A woman unfamiliar to me then entered the kitchen. "Valerie, your sister is awake," she said while nodding a hello my way.

"Ok. Thank you, Morana, I'll go up," Valerie answered as she wiped her eyes again with the same piece of paper towel, holding onto it as if it were a prized possession. The woman turned and started out of the kitchen.

"Wait, Morana, I want you to meet my best friend," Valerie said as she grabbed my hand. The Morana woman turned around holding out her hand as she walked towards us.

"Morana, this is Tvoya," Valerie continued, "Tvoya, Morana, Elizabeth's nurse." I held out my free hand, which happened to be my right, and shook hers. I started to say 'nice to meet you', but caught myself in time. If it were under any other circumstances, it would have been very nice to meet Morana. But she was there solely for the purpose of aiding Elizabeth as she neared the end of her life. Not! The script has been flipped, my dear. Elizabeth shall live and not die!

"Hello Morana." I smiled cordially.

"Tvoya, wait here. Let me go up and tell Elizabeth you're here," Valerie said as she let my hand go.

"No problem." I sat down at the kitchen table and watched Valerie followed by Morana leave the room. It wasn't very long before I could hear Valerie calling out my name, telling me to come on up.

"Ok, I'm coming." My cell phone vibrated. It was my mother. I could only imagine what kind of message she would leave. Not now, Mommy. As I climbed the stairs to reach Elizabeth's bedroom, I silently made a vow to call her the minute I left Valerie's.

"Hey, you," I announced as I walked into the room.

"Hey, yourself," Elizabeth retorted weakly. I moved past Morana, who was busying herself with straightening Elizabeth's blankets, to give Elizabeth a kiss on her forehead. I noticed that she felt rather warm. I looked to Valerie. Our eyes locked and held. She was aware of the fever. I sat in the chair that was placed at the side of Elizabeth's bed. Valerie wasted no time in getting to the reason for my spontaneous visit.

"Tvoya wants you to come to a healing service at her church on next Sunday."

"Oh yeah? A healing service?" Elizabeth allowed a light laugh to escape her frail lips. She looked a lot weaker than she had since my last visit.

"What do you think, Liz?" Valerie said as she pulled her seat closer to Elizabeth's bed. I noticed that Morana had stopped straightening the blankets. She was now standing still at the end of the bed, waiting as we all were for Elizabeth's response.

"You sound like Jonathan," she said closing her eyes.

"Like Jonathan?" Valerie and I asked. Her audibly. Me inwardly.

"Yeah, he has this friend whose family's been taking him to church. He's been asking God for me to be healed. I told you Tvoya, he's very mature."

"That's wonderful, Elizabeth." My exuberance took flight to this new revelation. I was delighted and all the more encouraged by the knowledge that our son Jonathan was being exposed to the things of God.

"Jonathan's been telling you this and you haven't mentioned it?" Valerie asked.

"God had the chance to heal me the first time," Elizabeth said with disdain. Morana smiled and left the room. Valerie and I looked at one another. Valerie's eyes were imploring me to say something. I was relieved she hadn't given up hope.

"Elizabeth, I can't speak for the first time. But I can tell you that He wants to heal you now." Elizabeth closed her eyes and said nothing more. I looked to Valerie. "Is she all right?" I whispered.

"Yeah, she's fine. Let's go." Valerie shrugged as she stood to her feet. I stood as well, then leaned over and whispered in Elizabeth's ear.

"I'm not giving up."

35

"To Be True"

"How can you be so sure God is gonna heal Elizabeth?" My mother debated.

"Mommy, look. What are the chances of Reverend Pierce-Vertrell coming back to our church specifically to do a healing service?" I reasoned. "Even Jonathan has been asking God to heal her."

"Jonathan?" I thought his name might throw her a bit.

I had only been at my mother's house thirty minutes, and we were already arguing. I made a beeline over right from Valerie's. I had been putting her off long enough. After our initial hellos and how are yous, I apologized to her for being so distant of late. She said that she understood. I wasn't too sure she really had since we hadn't yet talked about Mr. Strickland, the will, Jonathan, or her reason for going into rehab. These topics were of a precarious nature. The entering into them had to be done with cautious thoughtfulness. My strategy was to let her first vent about the incident regarding Byron and Charlene; give her opinion on Elizabeth's health; caution me on getting the money from my father; advise me to keep the ring from Byron (for all of *our* trouble) and the list went on. Once I learned that she and her sisters were cooking a collaborative feast and that dinner would be shared by the entire Grant-Harrington household, I knew it would be best to wait before entering into anything serious. I was just so grateful I had hit the jackpot by coming over on this day. Umm breaking bread. What better way to make amends?

"Hey stranger, haven't seen much of you." The voice behind that statement was laced with pure sarcasm. Without even seeing her, I knew that it belonged to Priscilla. I turned from having my back towards her.

"Hey Cuz," I said trying to make light of my scarcity. Priscilla was right. She had not seen very much of me.

"So, to what do we owe this visit?" Priscilla continued to press. I thought my mother would have come to my defense. Instead, she moved from the kitchen to the dining room setting the table in absolute silence. I guess I was on my own here.

"I know you guys haven't seen very much of me lately. I've had a lot on my plate to deal with."

Just as I was sure Priscilla was getting ready to give me the what for, Derrick, Aunt Lulu's son walked into the dining room.

"Hey, T. How you doing?"

"I'm good, Derrick. How 'bout you?"

"Can't complain. You know, it's all good," said Derrick as he air punched toward Priscilla, as she left the room.

"What's with her?" Derrick asked.

"I think she's a little mad at me. She came all the way out here for a wedding, that's not happening and I haven't spent much time with her. I kinda dumped her on Mommy."

"Well you know ole' Pris, she'll get over it. So, yeah, tell me about that…the wedding being called off. And did I hear right about Charlene jacking up Byron…What's up with that?" Derrick asked.

"It's a long story. Too long to go into now that's for

sure." I could hear Aunt Lulu and Uncle Ray arrive. This wasn't the time or place.

"All right. But, I'm gonna hold you to giving me the 411. True dat!"

"Yeah, yeah." I knew Derrick was just talking junk. Derrick couldn't stay around long enough to hear my torrid tale. His current girlfriend, whom he was living with, probably kicked him out for the day, hence him standing in my mother's dining room waiting to be fed.

Soon dinner was served and all the usual suspects were accounted for. During dinner, the conversation was light. To my very pleasant surprise, no one asked me about Byron, Royce or even Jonathan, for that matter. That is, until all the men folk left.

"I'm so glad to hear you came to your senses and broke up with that doctor guy," Aunt Marilyn said, being the first to dive right into the subject.

Let the mission of meddling into my business begin. My unreceptive grin indicated to her I would be not offering any verbal commentary on that subject.

Aunt Marilyn continued, "Anyway, it wasn't the Lord's will."

"Speaking of the Lord's will, Aunt Marilyn, did you hear that Reverend Pierce-Vertrell will be back next Sunday?" This was as good a time as any to segue into another subject.

"No. I didn't hear that. What a blessing that would be."

"She's coming to do a healing service."

"Well, praise the Lord." Aunt Marilyn was overjoyed and shared in my excitement.

"I'm trying to bring Elizabeth."

"Wonderful! Praise Him." Aunt Marilyn was now standing to her feet with her hands raised, reaching to the heavens.

"And Aunt Marilyn that's not all. Elizabeth just told me

earlier that Jonathan suggested this very thing." Up until that moment, everyone else who was left at my mother's was busying herself with the run-of-the-mill chitchat while cleaning up. I didn't think they were paying us much mind. That is until Jonathan's name was mentioned. Then a hush swept through and held its ground.

"Well, look at God!" Aunt Marilyn proclaimed, "I tell you, that boy already knows how to command an audience." I smiled at Aunt Marilyn's choice of words concerning Jonathan.

"When are you supposed to be meeting him, T?" Priscilla asked.

"Sometime this week," I announced looking over my shoulder to see if my mother heard me, while she fiddled in the kitchen. If she had, she made no hint of it.

"How ya feeling about that, chile?" Aunt Marilyn asked.

"I have to admit, at first I was real apprehensive about it. But now I'm ok with it. Yeah, I'm definitely ok with it." I thought of Royce.

"I think it's a good thing…," Aunt Lulu offered as she placed her hand on my shoulder.

"Lulu, mind your own business!" My mother spat, interrupting her, as she entered the dining room.

"Did I hear you right, Yvonne. Did you just tell me to mind my own business?" Aunt Lulu calmly challenged. "Oh, you weren't saying that when you were talking to whoever would listen…when Tvoya was pregnant with the child." What did Aunt Lulu mean by that? Could this mean that Mr. Strickland was included in the 'whoever'?

"Oh, shut up, Lulu!" Mommy yelled.

"Did she just tell me to shut up?" Aunt Lulu was now directing her question to Aunt Marilyn all the while moving closer to my mother.

"Now, both of you stop!" Aunt Marilyn looked to both

my mother and Aunt Lulu.

"Tvoya is the only one this is concerning," Aunt Marilyn reasoned. This scene was like déjà vu, with the exception of Priscilla; we had all had this same conversation in fact, sitting at the same table years ago when I was pregnant with Jonathan. Everyone gave their warranted and unwarranted weigh in on the matter. It was then as it was now…the lines were clearly drawn. Both my aunts were in favor of me having my child. My very own mother suggesting an abortion.

"Aunt Lulu, Uncle Ray is calling you," Priscilla announced when she returned to the dining room. I don't think we had even realized she had left.

"What does that man want? He just went upstairs." Aunt Lulu sucked her teeth and took a breath in. "Don't think I'm even finished with you, Yvonne," she included before she left.

"Whatever," Yvonne retorted. "Tvoya, you and I need to talk. Alone."

Aunt Marilyn grabbed her hand bag. "I guess that's our cue, Pris."

"I'm catching up and hanging out with Derrick anyway, since my other cousin doesn't have anytime to spend with me," Priscilla called over her shoulder as she made her way out the door.

"I'll make it up to you, Pris." I yelled back. I didn't think she heard me since the door closed before I could get it out.

My mother and I were left to the cleanup in the kitchen. Neither one of us said a word until we were thoroughly done. I didn't know if I should start or when she would. The silence was irritating, so I began after we sat down to have a cup of tea.

"Mommy, I've been invited to the reading of Mr. Strickland's will."

"You have? How did that happen?"

"Because of Jonathan."

"Because of Jonathan? I don't get it?"

"Mommy, I know that Mr. Strickland knew about Jonathan."

"What? What are you talking about, Tvoya? John never knew about Jonathan."

"Mommy please, you knew that Mr. Strickland knew about Jonathan."

"Did Royce tell you that?"

"Royce told me his ex-wife intercepted my letters to him and gave them to Mr. Strickland." My mother just looked at me with her mouth hung wide open.

"Royce also told me that he found among his father's papers a certificate for a trust fund in the name of Jonathan Scott. Naming Gary and Elizabeth Scott as guardians of Jonathan and Mr. Strickland, the executor of the trust."

"Oh my God!"

"Mommy, are you telling me you didn't know that Mr. Strickland knew I had a child?"

"No baby, I did not know!" Our eyes met. "You think I told him about Jonathan?"

"You didn't?"

"No! I didn't! John never even told me he knew about your pregnancy!"

"The letters only told him that I was pregnant. Who told him about Elizabeth and Gary adopting Jonathan?"

"How do I know? I cannot believe that that man didn't tell me he knew all along about the child. His grandchild at that!"

"Well, Mommy, you can't be that upset... you withheld this same information from him."

"Yeah, I know that, Tvoya. But what would make him not even tell his own son?"

Good question.

36

"A Dishonorable Estate"

The reception area of the Law offices of Jackson, Nelson and McCoy was filling up quite promptly. Our appearance was granted for 9:00 am sharp. Royce and I, being the first to arrive, walked in at 8:35 am, followed shortly by my mother, whom we offered a ride but were declined. The three of us made nonessential small talk… that is until Gary and Mrs. Franklin arrived. We dutifully expressed our love and concern and offered support to them regarding Elizabeth. We were careful to avoid mentioning our newly found revelation that Mr. Strickland was aware of Jonathan's existence as well as his adoption to Gary and Elizabeth. Knowing what we now knew, Gary's attendance was expected. However, Mrs. Franklin's was suspect. I can only imagine what Gary must have been thinking…we were thinking. In any case, neither Mrs. Franklin nor he attempted to explain their presence.

You would think that after all these years, my mother and Mrs. Franklin would have more to say to one another than just hello. My mother always felt that Mrs. Franklin looked down her nose at her. However, Mrs. Franklin never did have the tolerance for the antics that were created by my mother's drinking problem, which ultimately influenced her position on what the fate of Jonathan should be. So no, there was never any love lost between these two women.

The next to arrive was Mr. Strickland's sister. She was respectfully cordial but distant. Royce told me later, his father and his aunt had been estranged for years. Prior to this, he had only seen her two times in his life; the first, his mother's funeral and the second only recently at his father's. On the way there, I asked Royce about his brother Roger. Roger, unable to make the trip back east gave Royce his power of attorney to receive his entitlement on his behalf.

Mr. McCoy came through the huge honey oak doors into the reception area to greet our assembled group. In doing an account of who was present, it was found we were a group, missing one. Mr. McCoy apologized that we will need to wait for the arrival of this missing person. He then disappeared back behind the honey oak doors from which he came.

"I wonder who it is we're waiting on," Royce whispered in my ear. I could not imagine who this someone might be, but then again, I couldn't have imagined that I myself would be summoned.

I glanced at each person as we waited. All eyes were downcast and lips were pressed together in a pensive state. The mood was very solemn as if we were attending Mr. Strickland's funeral all over again.

A legal assistant then came into the waiting area and escorted our group into an oversized conference room that contained oversized staunch furniture. I guess fitting for a law firm. We were shown to a big conference table that seated twelve. As we all took our seats, the legal assistant shuffled papers and sat them at the head of the table. This belonging to Mr. McCoy, no doubt. The assistant took her seat to the left of the head. Then another ten minutes passed before Mr. McCoy entered bringing with him an attractive model like looking woman.

"Sorry, I'm late," the woman announced as she walked past each of us to take her seat at the end of the table. I looked at my mother to see if she acknowledged knowing this woman. Her shifting told me that she did not. But it was clear her presence made her uncomfortable. Was this a girl friend of Mr. Strickland? Nah! Couldn't be. Too young. As she walked past Royce, she placed a hand on his right shoulder.

"What are you doing here, Gina?" Royce demanded with teeth clinched and straining to keep his voice down. She only smiled while placing her index finger to her lips. Everyone and everything seemed to fall silent at her command. I for one was in total shock. At that very moment, you could have knocked me over with a feather and slugged me with a baseball bat and you would have received the same result...nothing, because I would not have felt a thing.

So, this was Gina...the woman that Royce left me for. She was stunningly beautiful. I couldn't blame him. I would have left me for her, too. Now that Royce and I were getting reacquainted, I needed to see her like I needed a hole in my head. And maybe a hole in my head was what I had, for my head was feeling like it was going to split wide open. And why did my eyes have to meet my mother's? She gave me a look that said, 'here we go again, T.'

♥   ♥   ♥

"May we begin?" Mr. McCoy asked as he opened his briefcase, taking out several sealed letter-sized white envelopes and one legal-sized yellow envelope. He passed them to his assistant who rose from her chair moving quickly, reading the labels assuring each was placed in the hand that it was addressed. While we received our envelopes, Mr. McCoy instructed us not to open until further directed. I noticed Royce received the yellow legal sized envelope in addition to a white envelope. I also noticed that everyone received one except for Royce's ex-wife, Gina.

Mr. McCoy then announced that we were gathered for the legal reading of the last will and testament for the remaining assets and estate of the recently deceased, one John Eldridge Strickland. He noted our presence was requested, as we were all named beneficiaries to the will. We were then instructed by Mr. McCoy to now individually and independently read the contents of our white envelopes. The tearing into the envelopes and ruffling of crisp paper unfolding inhabited the air. As I carefully read mine, I could hear my mother's sniffles. Oh, boy I was afraid of that. As I neared the end of my letter, the sudden movement of Royce pulling away from the table and jumping to his feet startled me. He started pacing the floor with his arms tightly folded across his chest. Everyone else stopped reading theirs as well to observe Royce's reaction.

"Mr. Strickland, are you all right?" Mr. McCoy asked Royce. Royce only nodded as he shoved both hands into his pockets continuing his pacing. Then he sat back down again this time hunched over, both elbows on the table with his head in his hands rubbing his temples. I reached over and rubbed his back a little, but Royce did not acknowledge me. I, in turn, retracted my hand and thought it best to finish reading my letter. Then, I carefully placed it back in the envelope and waited with neatly folded hands for what was to come next.

I observed one by one, each finishing, folding and filing their letter neatly back into its envelope. When we were done, all eyes were on Mr. McCoy. He began to read, the details of the entitlements. The short and sweet of it began with Mr. Strickland's sister, Ida Strickland, whereas he left an antique bureau that once belonged to their parents, a few art portraits, that were passed down in the family and a photo album that belonged to their mother. To Flora Franklin, he left $20,000.00 for being a surrogate grandmother to one, Jonathan Aaron Scott. To Gina Strickland, he satisfied the outstanding debt he owed her deceased father of $50,000.00. To my mother, Yvonne Grant-Harrington he left the title and deed to the property that housed her hair salon, giving her complete ownership to the salon, Locks and Whatknots, whereby she becomes the landlord to the building that consist of two upstairs rentals. In addition, the mortgage to this property had been paid in full. To Gary and Elizabeth Scott, he named them as trustees to the trust fund for Jonathan Eric Scott for college expenses up to an including $250,000.00. To Roger Strickland, he left his accounting business in Queens, New York, cabin cruiser docked in Freeport, Long Island and stocks and bonds totaling $50,000.00. To Royce Strickland, he left his home in Queens, New York and its remaining contents as well as his summer home in South Hampton, Long Island and its contents, and stocks and bonds totaling $50,000.00. In addition, the contents of a safe deposit box and one legal sized yellow envelope. To me, Tvoya Renee Harrington, he left $150,000.00 for bringing his grandson, Jonathan Aaron Scott into the world. Then we were done.

Mr. McCoy thanked us all for attending and wished us well in our future. As we were leaving the room, Royce took me to the side and asked if it would be all right if I rode home with Yvonne. "Tvoya, I need to speak with Gina. It could take awhile. Can I call you later?" Royce asked hurriedly.

"Uh, sure. No problem." I prayed he wouldn't feel the

need to introduce us.

When we were back in the reception area, the only ones there were Gary and Mrs. Franklin. We hugged. Royce jetted to catch up with Gina. My mother hadn't yet come out.

"Tvoya, I had been wanting to tell you for a long time that I told John about Jonathan," Mrs. Franklin offered.

"Don't worry about it. I just found out recently he even knew about Jonathan and I figured it out when I heard your entitlement," I answered.

"I hope you understand, I had no choice. I couldn't see him not knowing about his grandson."

"Mrs. Franklin, you don't need to explain anything to me. It's not my place."

"Thank you, Tvoya." Mrs. Franklin sounded relieved. "I understand you and Jonathan will be meeting later this week."

"Yes!" I said now taking her hand. "I'm ready."

"Thank you, Tvoya for honoring our request. This is extremely important to us," said Gary.

"It's extremely important to me as well." I hugged them both again.

"Goodbye," we said. I watched them walk out the door. I turned around to look for my mother. She was standing behind me waiting for our conversation to be over.

"Mommy. I need a ride."

"I figured you would, baby."

37

"Love And Marriage"

"*L*et's go get some lunch," my mother suggested as we walked to her car.

"Ok," I said way too fast. I wasn't sure if I wanted to sit down to a meal with my mother where she undoubtedly would want to rehash what took place at the lawyer's office. We didn't say another word to one another until we were seated and ordering from our menus.

"Well, I'm here to celebrate…," my mother was saying to our waiter, in response to his question of what were we drinking.

"Mommy!" I said interrupting her. I was afraid she would exchange her sobriety for her newfound wealth and order an alcoholic drink.

"I'll have a virgin Pina Colada," she said to the waiter. "Satisfied?!" she said to me.

"Well, I was just checking. I figured your guilt would cause you to want to go there."

"My guilt? I have nothing to be feeling guilty about." She paused for a moment to read my expression. "Oh, T, lighten up. We just got paid."

"Mommy, you can just take all of what Mr. Strickland left you and not feel guilty that you never told him about

Jonathan?"

"No harm, no foul. I didn't have to tell him about Jonathan. It's certainly out in the open now that he knew all along about the child. And he never even told me he knew. So no, I do not feel guilty. Not one teeny bit," my mother said, with firm defiance.

"Mommy, I'm sorry I accused you of telling him."

"Don't worry about it. I guess I would have been the obvious choice." She paused to take her plate from the waiter. "So I guess we have Flora to thank for that, huh?"

"But Mommy, I have something else I have to ask you…"

"Shoot."

"Mommy, what's the real reason behind why you went into rehab?" My mother looked as if she was going to choke. She stopped chewing and took a long sip from her virgin Pina Colada. I bet at that point she wished it had at least a little alcohol in it.

"What do you mean the real reason behind why I went into rehab?" Mommy asked, stalling. Why do people do that? When they're about to give you a lie for an answer they repeat the exact same question you just asked.

"Mommy, just answer the question." I was getting tired.

"Well, T, why don't you just tell me what Royce told you?"

"He told me his father told him you went out drinking and brought some man home with you. And after you passed out, he and some friends ripped you off of everything in the house. You then called Mr. Strickland who tracked down the guys and got your stuff back."

"Yeah… and then I went into rehab the very next day," my mother somberly confessed.

"Mommy, how come you didn't tell me about this?"

"Tvoya, baby, I…I couldn't…I just…didn't know how. I was…scared. I was in so much darkness then…"

"Mommy, it's ok." I couldn't allow her to continue. It was bringing her down. "I just wanted to know the truth."

My cell phone rang. It was Royce. "Hello?"

"Hi Tvoya. I'm sorry about earlier. I need to see you. Can we talk?"

"Well, I'm with my mother right now."

"Is that Royce?" my mother asked. I nodded my head yes. "Meet with him."

"Hang on," I said to Royce. "Mommy, are you sure? I mean we're in the middle of something."

"No we're not. We're done here. I'm sure Royce has a lot he wants to tell you," she answered resignedly.

"Uh, Royce? Yeah, we can talk. Where do you want to meet?" he asked where I was and if he could meet with my mother as well.

"Mommy, Royce wants to speak with you, too."

"Tvoya, I don't think…," I mouthed to her that she should. She rescinded.

"Ok, we'll meet you at my mother's in say about thirty minutes."

♥   ♥   ♥

I could not presume to know what Royce would want to say to both my mother and me. It seemed to me that everything there was to say had already been said. Like the saying goes, 'when everything is said and done, there's very little left to say or do'. Maybe he wanted to tell us what transpired in his conversation with Gina as well as what his father said to him in his letter. Well, I guess there was more. Still, he didn't owe me any explanations.

"Tvoya, never tell a man he doesn't owe you an

explanation," my mother said as she pulled into her driveway.

"Oh?"

"You start out telling him that and you'll make it easy for him to disrespect you. If he wants to explain, let him." What did my mother mean by 'start out'? Is that what Royce and I were doing? Starting out? I'll admit, and only to myself, I was surely diggin' on Royce. Once again, I wondered if my mother was subliminally giving me her consent.

"Tvoya, what are you planning to do with your money?"

"I'm not sure if I'm keeping the money."

"Don't be ridiculous, of course you're keeping the money. Now you can give Byron back his ring and you don't have to bother your father with borrowing from him."

So did this mean my mother had finally accepted my break up with Byron?

We were now in the house waiting for Royce.

"So what's keeping him?" my mother asked impatiently.

"It hasn't been thirty minutes yet," I said, glancing at my watch. Just then the doorbell rang. Royce came in and started right away with the apologies. He wouldn't sit down even after it was offered. He apologized for being late. I told him he wasn't. My mother told him he was. He apologized for having to leave me at the lawyer's office. He apologized for Gina's presence at the reading.

"Royce, what did you want to talk to us about?" my mother asked breaking his apologetic cycle.

"I wanted to tell you what my father told me in his letter and about my conversation with Gina." I really didn't want to hear about what was said between him and Gina.

"Go on," I found myself saying, in spite of my insecurity.

"Well, I was taken off guard with her showing up like that. She didn't even come to his funeral. She claims she didn't know he had died until I told her, which was after the fact. Anyway, I had to confront her on what my father revealed to me in his letter." Royce paused. My mother and I only looked at each other, but said nothing. Royce continued now taking a seat next to me on the couch.

"Tvoya, after my father found out you were pregnant, Gina told him that she was also. He was torn between whether to tell me about your pregnancy or allow me the chance to start a family with Gina, who I was planning to marry. He soon noticed that you were gone from the neighborhood. He tried questioning Yvonne about your whereabouts but she wasn't budging. She told my father nothing." Royce paused looking to my mother who smiled in return.

"And... you were saying?" I said, coercing Royce to continue.

"Thinking that you had aborted the baby, my father informed Gina who subsequently told everyone she had had a miscarriage on a weekend that I was here in New York visiting my father. Not long after that, Mrs. Franklin contacted him and told him about Jonathan and that Gary and Elizabeth had adopted him. My father then decided to tell me about my son. But he made the mistake of telling Gina first, who then told her father."

"What does her telling her father have to do with anything?" I interrupted.

"Tvoya, let the man finish his story," my mother exclaimed.

"Remember, I told you that my father and Gina's father were frat brothers? Well, they had also been business partners. They got involved in some illegal activity that my father did not want to spell out to me in his letter. So, to keep Gina happy and me from knowing about my son, her father used this to blackmail him."

"But your marriage ended anyway," I reasoned.

"Yeah, it did. I found out later that Gina was never pregnant and knew all along she could never have any children, nor did she ever want any. We started living our own separate lives. This went on for years. Her doing her thing, me doing mine. She had an affair, was found out and I filed for divorce."

"So how come your father didn't tell you about Jonathan after your divorce?" I asked.

"Good question, Tvoya," my mother added.

"I don't know exactly. He didn't go any further in his explanation. My only guess is timing."

"Timing?" my mother and I responded in unison.

"Well, Gina and I divorced about four years ago. Then her father died only last year and then my father became ill this year. So I'm only figuring that time played a part in why I'm finding out about all of this now."

I wasn't sure if I agreed with Royce's logic pertaining to the aspect of 'timing'; however, I do know that everything is subject to God's timing. Sometimes in our loved ones' attempts to protect us from situations they deem as harmful, they succeed in achieving the very thing they were trying to have us avoid. We become the victims of their victimizations. Ironic as well as moronic. But thanks be to God, He uses all of this to still have His will be done. And that's all that really matters anyway.

38

"I Now Pronounce You...Thankful"

"Tvoya, there's something else I want to share with you," Royce was saying as we were now standing at my front door. I noticed he had with him the legal-sized yellow envelope that was given to him at the lawyer's office.

"Come on in." Royce followed me through the door.

"Wow, this place looks a lot better than when I last saw it."

"Thanks, I've been working hard at it," I announced proudly.

"Has Charlene ever been back to help?"

"Not really. She came through a day or two ago to collect her things. She's now living with that Crew guy."

"Cool. What about Byron?"

"No sightings." Royce only smiled. I made my way into the kitchen to search for something to offer Royce. Then, I hit jackpot. I'd made a chocolate cake only yesterday.

"Cake?" I asked as Royce walked into the kitchen behind

me.

"Only if it's chocolate."

"And you know that it is," I said teasingly. I cut us both a piece and poured us each a tall glass of milk.

"Is this like back in the day or what?" Royce acknowledged.

"Yeah, that's right. Our favorite after school snack," I remembered.

"We were some serious geeks."

"Looks like we still are." We laughed at our assessment of ourselves.

"But seriously," Royce said breaking the fun.

"Aw, do we have to."

"Let me show you what Dad left me in this envelope." He's now 'Dad', what happened to my 'father'?

"Ok, let's give a look see."

He began taking out the contents of the legal-sized yellow envelope.

"They're pictures of Jonathan," Royce said slowly.

"Oh, my God," I said even slower. My eyes became transfixed to the images in the pictures. There were pictures of him at every age. School, sports, Christmas and Easter pictures. Potty, first steps, pony rides, and amusements ride pictures. In the pool and at the beach pictures. Happy pictures, sad pictures. He was absolutely beautiful. He looked like Royce when he smiled. He looked like me when he was serious. I was pulled in and hypnotized by each shot of him. I'd forgotten Royce was sitting across from me. This was my child…my son, I was looking at; looking back at me. He was beautiful. Absolutely beautiful.

"Tvoya, you're crying," Royce was saying.

"This is unbelievable. Where did your father get these?"

"Mrs. Franklin, sent them to him over the years. My dad knew that in death he could be free to have me know about my son."

"Well look at God!" I sniffed, thinking of Aunt Marilyn.

"In all these years, you haven't seen a picture of him?"

"No," I said just above a whisper. Royce didn't challenge my admission, he only looked puzzled.

"I mean, it was the way I wanted it to be. When I gave him to Elizabeth and Gary, I asked that the ties be severed, then and there. Even with my friendship with Valerie, I would only casually ask how Elizabeth and her family were doing. I thought at the time it was for the best, I mean considering…," my voice trailing off, I thought it best to change the course of where this conversation could wind up.

"Tvoya, I know what you were going to say, and I'm sorry you had to make difficult decisions because of the actions of others…myself included."

"Royce, it was very selfish of me the other day to suggest that you not meet Jonathan now. Royce, you're his father. You have to meet him with me."

"Are you sure, it's the right time?"

"Absolutely."

"Thank you, Tvoya."

"Royce, you don't have to thank me. Like I said…you're Jonathan's father."

"No, I wasn't thanking you for that. Thank you, Tvoya for having our son."

I thought of Mr. Strickland's letter to me.

"Dear Tvoya,

Your reading of this letter denotes your agreement in attending the reading of my last will and testament and to that I am grateful. However, I am more and most eternally grateful to you for choosing to give life to my grandson,

Jonathan Aaron Scott. At the very moment, you are reading this, my son Royce, Jonathan's father, is reading another letter written by me, explaining but certainly not excusing my role in why he was kept in the dark, so to speak, from the knowledge of his son. Your mother tells me you are already promised in marriage, but somehow the wisdom of an ailing old man tells me otherwise. If in heaven, I can still hope... I hope you and Royce find each other again. Moreover, if I could enlarge my wish, it would be that the three of you would one day be united.

Eternally yours,
Mr. John E. Strickland"

Thank you Lord, for the revelation of truth and the gift of knowledge.

39

"I Plight Thee My Faith"

My life had flipped upside down in literally one-month's time. On the other hand, maybe the better description would be… that my life had flipped right side up. Yes, up was the direction it was definitely going. And what better way to celebrate than to hang out with my sister girls. I'd invited Valerie, Charlene and Priscilla over to my place that evening to just chill out, relax, spill and dish. Besides, Priscilla was leaving in a few days and I hardly had anytime to spend with her. Not to mention she was thoroughly through with me, and I couldn't blame her. So, I had some serious making up to do. I figured shopping might just do the trick.

Priscilla and I spent the better half of the day in the mall, sending ourselves into a buying frenzy. Priscilla bought so much stuff (and I do mean stuff), that there was no way she would be able to take it all back with her on her flight. This was no bother to her since I was selected to do the honors of sending it to her by air freight. As we shopped, I began to wonder if it would be appropriate for me to buy a gift for Jonathan.

"Well, that could be kind of sticky," offered Priscilla.

"How so?" I asked.

"You have to be careful it won't be taken in the wrong way."

Again, I didn't quite get what my cousin was alluding to. She could tell by my vacant gaze I hadn't a clue as to what she was talking about.

Priscilla continued, "You don't want it to look like you're bribing him into accepting you."

"Oh, I hadn't even thought of it that way."

"But then again, you don't want to just show up after all these years, empty handed either," Priscilla said smiling mischievously, knowing full well she was beginning to annoy the heck out of me.

"Well, since my intention is not to bribe him. I think I will buy him something," I said quite confident he'd accept my intention.

"Ok, so what will that something be?" Priscilla challenged.

"I haven't a clue," I admitted. I'd been so caught up in my life and what I had been experiencing, I hadn't even considered who Jonathan could possibly be. What was he like? What were his likes and dislikes? What made him happy? What made him sad? Was he outgoing or introverted? Did he participate in sports? And if so, which ones? Was he a good student or did he hate school? What were his strengths? Challenges? I didn't know any of this. What I knew for sure was his life was in a crisis. And what gift would suffice? Then the answer came to me. God whispered, "My Word." But maybe he had one already since he did attend church from time to time with his friend's family.

"But does he have a Bible from his biological mother?" asked Priscilla.

♥　　　♥　　　♥

"Do you think he'll like it?" I asked Valerie, who had just arrived after Priscilla and I finally made it back to my place.

I was now presenting to her the gift I had selected for Jonathan. It was a brown leather bound teen study Bible in the New King James version. His name was inscribed in gold letters at the bottom of the book. I took the liberty of writing a message to him on the inside cover page that read:

"It is with great love and sincere care that I give you this gift, The Word Of God. May it bring you Comfort and Solace in times of sorrow. Strength and Fortitude in times of temptation. Unconditional Love and Peace when feeling misunderstood. And Grace and Mercy when undeserved. Always remember you are a blessing!"

Love,
Tvoya

I didn't want to be presumptuous and use the title of 'mother'. Jonathan had a mother, Elizabeth, and in no way did I want to supersede or disrespect her.

"Oh, I'm sure he'll love it." I appreciated Valerie's words of encouragement.

"I hope Elizabeth doesn't think I'm being too forward."

"No. Don't worry about that," Valerie said before her words drifted off.

"What's wrong?" I asked.

"Elizabeth is still refusing to go to the service on Sunday."

"Have you told Jonathan about it?"

"Not me, but Gary did. I told him about it," she answered.

"Well, at least he's on board," I said trying to sound optimistic.

265

"Yeah." Valerie didn't seemed to be convinced this would make much of a difference.

"Don't worry. I feel in my spirit that Elizabeth is going to go."

"I hope you're right," Valerie said, still sounding quite defeated.

"Ain't we here to celebrate?" Priscilla asked as she entered the kitchen.

"Aren't we here to celebrate?" I corrected Priscilla, just to mess with her.

"Ok, Teach. Aren't we here to celebrate?" Priscilla surrendered.

"Yeah, what are we celebrating with? I'm hungry," Valerie chimed in sounding more upbeat.

"I thought we'd order some Chinese food, but I want to wait for Charlene," I said simultaneously to the sound of the doorbell ringing.

"I hope that's her now,' Priscilla said as she went to answer the door.

"Is there a party over here?" Charlene sang as she danced into the living room.

"Hey, gurl," I yelled from the kitchen, "take a look at this menu, so we can eat." I made my way into the living room to give Charlene the menu.

"So, Charlene, is it true you kicked Byron's butt?" Priscilla asked. Now why did my cousin have to go there. This was old news anyway.

"Priscilla, we're not here to talk about Byron. Tvoya has moved on," Valerie interjected to save me, but it didn't help. Priscilla was being relentless in her attempt at getting on my nerves.

"Yeah, she's moved on all right," Priscilla added, taking the menu from Charlene.

"Y'all stop bothering me," I whined.

"She's moved on with Royce." Priscilla grinned.

"Priscilla!" I yelled.

"So, it's you and Royce now, huh?" Charlene was asking. "I'm not surprised. Y'all should've seen how he took care of Tvoya the night Byron showed his…"

"Charlene! I shouted. "There's no me and Royce," I said, snatching the menu from Priscilla.

"Tvoya, tell them about the money you inherited from his father," Priscilla announced, not letting up.

"I didn't even tell you about the money," I said shooting an angry look at Priscilla. Her departure could not come sooner.

"What money?" Charlene asked. No doubt she would be needing a loan.

"Look guys, back off Tvoya." Valerie broke in again to try to steer the conversation away from my love life or lack thereof.

"It's ok, Valerie," I said softly. In all fairness, I was very happy about the direction my life was going. With the exception of Elizabeth's illness, things for me were definitely on the upswing. Even with Elizabeth's illness, it was only temporary for the promise of God to arise in that situation was hopeful.

"I'm getting ready to meet Jonathan," I declared with defiance.

"Who's Jonathan?" Charlene asked perplexed, looking from me to Valerie, then to Priscilla. I had forgotten that I hadn't the opportunity to bring her up to speed.

"Tvoya's son," Priscilla proudly offered.

"Wait a minute. Tvoya, you have a son?" Charlene asked again looking between us three musketeers hoping for a clear answer.

I began to disclose the account of how I painfully, but out of great necessity, gave up all parental rights to my son.

Charlene listened intently; all the while, wide-eyed with mouth fully hung open. When I was about to approach the subject of Elizabeth's illness, I caught Valerie shake her head suggesting that I not go there. I rescinded in my eagerness to share everything, secretly wondering why Valerie chose to be so guarded.

"Tvoya, I had no idea. I mean, I remember you were pregnant when you left school. But when you came back you said that you didn't want to talk about it. So I assumed you lost the baby," Charlene reasoned.

"I figured that you thought that. And believe me, that's exactly how I felt about it."

Charlene walked over to me with her arms outstretched beckoning me a hug. The atypical solace I was receiving lately from Charlene was overwhelming. Contrary to what others would believe, Charlene was becoming a woman of substance.

"Let me show you guys something," I said as I walked toward my bedroom to retrieve the large-size yellow envelope Royce left with me. When I returned, the Chinese food delivery guy was at the door. Valerie was already paying him. I objected, she held her stance and I lost the battle, both noting by eye contact that neither of our other dinner guests offered to share the bill. But then again, I did invite them. We ate as they each begged me not to withhold the contents much longer. I couldn't take the chance of getting food on these precious pictures of my son.

When we were done, the presentation was made. Tah Dah! I proceeded to spread out all the pictures onto the coffee table as we all got down on our knees to explore the life and times of Jonathan Aaron Scott.

"Gurl, where did you get these?" Valerie asked in amazement.

"Your mother sent them to Mr. Strickland over the years.

He left them to Royce with a letter explaining why he didn't tell Royce about Jonathan. Incredible, huh?"

"Yeah, so why didn't Mr. Strickland tell Royce about his son?" Valerie asked intrigued.

"Long story, gurl," I said unable to look away from the collage of prints. This had to be the hundredth time I viewed them. I sat up literally all night the night before looking at each image as if for the first time. Valerie caught my drift that I cared not to go into the saga of the how, what and why Mr. Strickland chose not to inform Royce of his son. Instead, Jonathan's life began to unfold as Valerie took to narrating his story through these pictures. We were told of what occurred at each birthday party, sports event or regular pastime in his life. I again became weepy, for this time I was getting to know my son. Sharing Jonathan through these pictures, although only temporary, was more than I could ever fathom experiencing. It was beautiful! He was beautiful! Absolutely Beautiful!!

40

"Today, With My Whole Heart"

On the morning I was to meet Jonathan, the ring of my doorbell abruptly awakened me. I wondered who it could be so early since, I wasn't expecting anyone until around noon when Royce was due to pick me up. I scrambled out of bed, grabbed my robe just in time to see the florist deliveryman walking back down my front steps.

"Wait!" I yelled as I struggled to get my robe on. He turned and announced that I almost missed receiving the beautiful bouquet of red velvet roses he was struggling to keep from falling. There had to have been at least three dozen roses in the arrangement. It was magnificent.

"Let me go inside to get you a tip," I said now myself struggling with the enormous arrangement.

"That's already been taken care of," the deliveryman yelled over his shoulders as he got back into his truck.

Whom could these be from? I thought as I fished through the beautiful red roses to find the card. It read:

"*My Dear Tvoya,*

I cannot thank you enough for allowing me the

opportunity of meeting our son. This is the only way I know how...for now that is.

Love always,
Royce"

He remembered that my favorite flower was the red velvet rose. It had been a very long time since I had even received this find of flower. The selection was reserved. I wasn't sure why, or for whom. Nevertheless, it was. I now realized that not even Byron was aware it was my favorite. There was nothing and no one to blame but my subconscious mind. Repressed desires hidden due to the result of past hurts and disappointments tend to lay dormant until unexpectedly awakened. A case such as this was welcomed and pleasing. I wore a lingering smile as I prepared for the most incredible day of my life.

♥   ♥   ♥

"Are you sure you're ready for this?" my mother was saying as I tried my best not to let her dampen my mood. She had made an unexpected visit to my place on her way to the salon.

"I've never been more sure of anything in my life," I answered, determined my mother would not be getting under my skin today. Not today, Yvonne. "You want breakfast?"

"What? My daughter's gonna make me breakfast? Now that's a switch." My mother laughed and then suddenly stopped when she turned and took in an eyeful of the magnificent arrangement that was sent to me by Royce.

271

"Oh?! And who are these from?" my mother sarcastically asked. She undoubtedly knew whom they were from.

"Mommy, please!"

"Tvoya, be careful."

"Careful of what?"

"I just don't want to see you get hurt again by Royce. And I don't want you to glamorize your meeting Jonathan."

"Mommy, don't worry. It's all in God's hands."

"I'm sure God wouldn't want you to be stupid," my mother insisted.

"Mommy are you staying for breakfast or not?" I silently prayed she wouldn't be staying and that she'd be leaving very soon.

"Tvoya, I'm just concerned with all the changes that's been going on in your life, you may be too optimistic and setting yourself up for a great let down."

"Mommy, how can I get let down now? I was already let down by Byron and you didn't warn me about that."

"Tvoya, I still think you oughta give Byron another chance." Had my mother lost her mind for sure this time?

"Give Byron another chance? He has a drinking problem."

"That he can do something about, Tvoya."

"So let me get this straight. I'm supposed to stick it out with Byron even if he hasn't yet admitted that he has a problem. I don't think so. Besides, I've tried to call him. He won't take any of my calls or call me back. And I haven't been calling him to get back with him. I've been trying to give him back his ring."

"Tvoya, all I'm saying is...he may need you to help him make that decision. Like John helped me."

"Mommy, I can't. I mean...I'm glad you had someone like Mr. Strickland. But meeting Jonathan and helping him through this thing with Elizabeth is my top priority."

"And Royce?"

"Royce is my second."

♥   ♥   ♥

After my mother left, I stressed over what I should wear. For two hours, I did nothing but try on outfits. Too young, too old, too revealing, too much, too little. I was beginning to doubt I would ever settle on the right one. I even thought that I should make a run to the mall to buy a whole new outfit. It was pitiful. I settled on a baby blue sundress. The weather was still hot and muggy and this dress would help me not to perspire much. It was the third try on of this same dress that it dawned on me that the color resembled the color of the dress that Valerie would have worn in my wedding and then it struck me that this day would have been my wedding day. Irony to the umpteenth power. So this was why my mother chose this day to come over to give me a directive pep talk. The simple fact that it had slipped my mind was proof enough for me that my life was moving in a totally different direction.

"Wow, you look beautiful," Royce admonished as he walked through the door.

"Thank you," I blushed. "And thank you for the beautiful flowers."

"Nah, I wish I could do more to show you how much today means to me," Royce was saying now standing right behind me. He was so close. I could feel his breath on my neck. I turned around and before I could move out of range, he kissed me. I was caught by surprise but I didn't turn away. I couldn't remember ever mentioning to him, my celibacy. Strangely enough, I didn't feel that it was threatened. Deep in my heart I felt that Royce would respect my decision to remain celibate until marriage.

The time had come for us to meet our son. Both Royce and I were eerily quiet on our way over to Valerie's. Even the radio was silent. No one thought to turn it on. When we arrived, Royce turned off the engine and we just sat. It was as if we were either paralyzed or chained to the car seats.

"Maybe we should pray," I said.

"Ok, that would be good. Yeah, prayer is good." I smiled at Royce's nervousness.

"Father God, we thank you and honor you for the privilege of allowing us the opportunity to meet our son, Jonathan. Father, we recognize that you have brought us to this point by your grace and mercy and we don't take it for granted. Lord, help us to help our son adjust to all that he has been confronted with. Help us to be mindful of what is in his best interest and not our own. We ask that he like us and that we like him, although us liking him will not be a prerequisite for us loving him. Also, Father, we thank you for the healing that is on its way to Elizabeth. Give her the faith Lord to have faith in you. Father, we thank you in advance for all that you are doing in this situation. In Jesus' Name. Amen."

"Amen," Royce repeated. "That was nice, Tvoya, real nice."

41

"In The Sight Of God"

Lamar, answered the door. He greeted us and was especially happy to see Royce. Royce had already had his own conversation with Gary, about him meeting Jonathan. It was clear from Lamar's response he wasn't aware.

"Man, am I glad to see you," Lamar expressed. It must have been hell for Lamar not to share any information about Jonathan with Royce.

"Can I get you guys anything?" Lamar offered. We both declined. We were more than a little anxious. Valerie then entered the room and more greetings were exchanged. Where was Jonathan? I wondered. My face showed my puzzlement.

Valerie responded, "Gary and Jonathan are at the store. They should be here any minute."

"And Elizabeth?" I asked.

"She'll be down shortly. Morana is getting her ready."
The four of us sat down, made small talk catching up on each other's lives when Elizabeth's entry into the living room stopped Royce and I cold. She looked even more frail than she had the last time I'd seen her. Her inward illness and attitude was manifesting outwardly. She gave a weak wave, as her nurse, Morana wheeled her closer. Royce and I stood

to our feet as if the queen had just entered the room. I leaned down to give her a soft hug. Royce stood behind me and placed his hand at the small of my back as I straightened up. It was nice to feel his support both emotionally and physically.

"He's the one, Freshmeat," Elizabeth whispered. I only smiled. Royce turned to sit back down acting as if he hadn't heard what Elizabeth said.

Lamar suggested we all go into the family room. I didn't want to be rude and say that all I wanted to do was watch the door for Jonathan, so I conformed and made my way into the family room as well. Just as we settled, I could hear the front door open and voices follow that became clearer as they neared the room. Gary was the first to enter. Then all at once, time, my heart and mind came to a sharp and complete halt. As Gary moved out of view all that stood between me and the young boy who then walked in was an expanse of space that stood as a barrier holding it's ground, prohibiting either of us from coming any closer. He stopped in midstream of completing his sentence and I of taking a breath. Our eyes caught…. held and locked. Someone was saying something but they weren't heard. Finally, my lips found a way to part, allowing sound to make its way through.

"Jonathan?" I said evenly, as I suddenly became aware of my tears softly trickling down my cheeks. He looked to Elizabeth before answering, "Yes, Ma'am?"

"Jon, this is your mother, Tvoya *and* your father, Royce," Gary said placing emphasis on the word 'and'.

Jonathan walked slowly toward me. I wiped my cheeks with my left hand while offering him my right, unsure as to what type of greeting would be appropriate. Jonathan however startled me by giving me a respectful hug. He embraced Royce as well. One could see that Elizabeth and Gary were raising a gentleman. My child, my son was standing right in front of me. However, brief our embrace, it was already engrained in my being for all eternity. Lamar motioned for us all to sit down.

"So, what do you think of our son?" Elizabeth said struggling with her enunciation.

"He's beautiful," I said softly. Jonathan looked embarrassed. I probably shouldn't have said that, but oh, how he was…so beautiful.

I caught Royce's smile. He was thinking the same thing. We grinned at one another as high schoolers would, when sharing a secret.

"Gary…. Elizabeth, would it be ok, if Tvoya and I took Jonathan for a ride?" Royce asked nervously. "That is, of course, if you want to, Jonathan."

Jonathan looked to Elizabeth then to Gary, who both simultaneously nodded their consent.

"Cool," Jonathan answered.

"I'll walk you guys out," Gary offered. Valerie held on to my arm beckoning me to stay behind while Jonathan, Royce, Lamar and Gary left the room.

"It'll be good for him to get out," Valerie said.

"Yeah, I'm depressing everyone," Elizabeth said with a sarcastic chuckle.

"Well, maybe it wouldn't be that way, if you would try to live," Valerie said sounding drained.

"Elizabeth, why won't you agree to come to the service tomorrow?" I probed.

"Let's not go there," Elizabeth said flicking her hand, casting me off, "our son is waiting on you."

"Elizabeth, we're not done with this conversation," I said before turning to look to Valerie who only hunched her shoulders in response. "I'll see you later. We won't keep him long."

I walked out of the room passing Morana on my way. I

felt a chill as we exchanged a muted goodbye. I couldn't put my finger on it, but there was definitely something not right about that woman.

♥   ♥   ♥

Jonathan, Royce, Lamar and Gary were all waiting when once again déjà vu emerged. The scene might have been reminiscent of a past experience if it had not been for the fact that my feelings as well as some of the players had now changed, in more ways than one.

Lamar waved; Gary stuffed both hands into his pants pockets, as Royce's car pulled off. Jonathan rode shotgun, with me riding in the back. Royce offered him free reign of the radio. Jonathan took him up on it, scanning until he found what most teens his age would want to groove to...Rap and Hip-Hop. He might be surprised to learn that I too shared a passion for Hip-Hop. I wasn't sure where our impromptu outing would lead, nevertheless thanks to Royce's quick thinking and consideration, I was sure Jonathan appreciated leaving the house. I watched and listened quietly as the two made small talk, as well as marveled at how easily it was for Royce to get Jonathan to talk. Their conversation wasn't pressing or heavy, clearly designed only for breaking the ice.

Soon we had come to our destination, and I should have known that Royce would bring us here. Oceanfront Park. Again a déjà vu moment. The scene wasn't unlike the last time we were here, still tranquil and serene, perfect for our purpose; to get to know our son and for him to get to know us.

"I bought you something," I said handing Jonathan his

gift, once we had left the car, "I hope you like it."

"Thank you, uh.."

"Tvoya. You can call me Tvoya."

He took the gift, ripped the wrapping that gave way to a box that immediately identified what he was receiving.

"Wow! A Bible. Cool."

"Do you already have one?" I asked.

"Yeah, I do, but not like this one, with my name in gold and all," he answered excitedly.

"Look inside, man. Tvoya wrote you a little message," Royce interjected. We looked on intensely, as he read.

"Cool. I mean thanks," he smiled.

"You're welcome," I answered. We stood against the railing that separated the beach from the boardwalk, neither of us saying anything more in that moment. Jonathan thumbed through his Bible. I continued to watch him as Royce watched me.

"Do you have any questions for us, Jonathan?" Royce asked still watching me.

"Uh, not really. Dad kinda told me everything," Jonathan answered.

"Everything? What did he tell you?" I asked hoping that Royce and I could explain the reasons for our actions concerning the decisions we felt we had to make in the past.

"Maybe we can fill in the blanks...tell you our side of things," Royce offered implying we were on the same page.

"That would be cool," Jonathan answered shrugging his shoulders. Royce and I both began to speak at the same time. We laughed...more at our own nervousness than for any other reason. Jonathan didn't seem amused, and Royce and I quickly regained our composure. This time, I started. Slowly at first, then gaining momentum as the memories began to flood my mind. Royce jumped in from time to time to tell his side of things. It was apparent that it was important to him I wouldn't come off looking like the bad guy to our son. I was glad we decided to do this together after all. It felt right.

When we had completed our say, all was quiet except for the crescendo of the waves crashing against the shore and the periodic squawk of a seagull or two. Royce and I exchanged glances not knowing if we should say something more or just let what we'd just told Jonathan sink in.

"Do you think you can get my moms to go to that healing service tomorrow?" Jonathan politely asked.

There you have it…what did I expect from a thirteen-year-old boy whose mother…, the only mother he has ever known, was literally giving up hope and could possibly die. Our story of the past… the how and the why was the last thing on his mind, or even what he was concerned about. And rightfully so.

When we returned Jonathan to Valerie's house, leaving him there was awkward for me. I know no one expected me to offer any more than what we'd just experienced, but I fought the desire of asking for anything more of him at that point. At our outing, Royce and I did most of the talking and now we had to trust that since God had brought us to this, he would see us through the journey of time it will take really getting to know our son. I didn't get an opportunity to see Elizabeth then, since she was sleeping, to try again to convince her that we all wanted her to give God a try and come to the healing service. I'd hoped what I suggested to Jonathan to put it to prayer would give him some comfort.

Once we were back at my place, Royce suggested we get a bite to eat. But I wasn't very hungry. Instead, I was very tired and needed some alone time. He expressed his disappointment but seem to understand. I was certain Royce was more than a little eager for us to spend time together. He was overjoyed and excited by our meeting with Jonathan and probably wanted to rehash our conversation as well as talk about where this, for us, could lead. In spite of it all, I was still sorting out my feelings concerning Royce. He was definitely saying and doing all the right things. Simply put, I didn't want to jump into anything with Royce right away.

I remembered to turn my cell phone back on once he'd left. It had been off the better half of the day. The voice from the service told me that I had seven messages. Four were from my mother, one from Priscilla, one from my father and one from Byron. I was intrigued by Byron's message, so I returned his call first.

"Hey, Tvoya, I didn't think you were going to return my call."

"That's what you do, Byron. Not me."

"Ok, ok, You're right. That has been my style lately."

"So, Byron, how have you been?"

"Tvoya, do you know what today would have been?" Byron said ignoring my question. My first thought was to ignore his question as well, but I soon thought better of doing that.

"Yes, I realize what today would have been. But Byron, let's not do this. I just called those times to see how you were doing and to tell you I want to give back the ring."

"The ring is a dead issue, it's yours."

The ring wasn't the only thing that was a dead issue.

"Byron…"

"Tvoya, will you please give me another chance? I'm sorry about what I put you through," Byron said sounding more desperate than contrite.

"Byron, me coming back to you is not what you need."

"How you gonna tell me what I need?" Byron said raising his voice. "What I need is you, baby," he continued, now lowering his volume.

"Byron, you need help. You have a drinking problem."

"Tvoya, I went to one of those AA meetings, and they

told me I do not have a drinking problem," he said adamantly.

There it was...the confirmation I needed. I had done the right thing in breaking up with Byron. It had nothing to do with Royce or Jonathan and everything to do with the fact that Byron was in some serious denial. It was time for me to move on. At that very moment I decided to sell the ring and send Byron a check. I was sure he wouldn't turn down money.

"Byron, I've gotta go. You take care of yourself, ok?"

"Tvoya, let me come over so we can talk in person. I know..."

"No. We can't talk. It's over Byron."

"Oh, it's like that? Ok, Tvoya." And then he hung up.

I hated leaving things with Byron this way. But what can one do when someone is in denial of their situation. I was reminded of all the times when family members as well as myself said these same words to my mother. It isn't until one hits rock bottom that they realize they have a problem and it has to be taken care of. The shame part was that in both my mother's and Byron's cases, losing me was not rock bottom for them. Thank God my mother eventually found hers. I wondered what it would take for Byron to find his.

42

"To Love, Faithfully"

Was this the same premise that was paralyzing Elizabeth? Was she too in denial? She certainly wasn't in denial of the possibility of her dying. She was accepting of that. But was that fact? When we're presented with fact, does it out rule faith? That's what Elizabeth was in denial of. Accepting faith. Accepting that having faith in the fact that God could heal her was in itself, denial. It was denying the absolute power of God. My mind was carefully following this train of thought when my land line phone began to ring. I answered, perturbed, I couldn't finish my revelation of reasoning.

"Tvoya? It's Valerie. Have you heard from Jonathan?" I didn't know why Valerie felt it necessary to announce it was her. I would always be able to recognize her voice.

"No. Why? Was he suppose to call me or something?" I was baffled by Valerie's question.

"I don't want to alarm you, but he's not here. He just left and didn't tell anyone where he was going," Valerie answered sounding anguished.

"How long ago did he leave?"

"We're not sure. Last time anyone saw him was about an hour ago when he was talking with Morana in the kitchen."

"What were they talking about? Did he tell her he was going out?"

"I'm not sure what they were talking about but, Morana says she left the kitchen before he did."

"Does Elizabeth know that he's not there?"

"No, she's still asleep."

"All right. Valerie don't worry. Let me call Royce. Maybe Jonathan has contacted him."

"Call me back as soon as you hear anything. Lamar and Gary are out cruising the neighborhood now."

"Good. It's only been dark for about thirty minutes or so. Maybe someone has seen him. Valerie, call me as well when you hear anything."

We hung up. I wondered what would make Jonathan just leave without letting anyone know where he was going. Especially since he didn't know the neighborhood very well.

"Royce, have you heard from Jonathan?" I said trying to keep my voice level and stable; practicing it even before he answered his phone.

"Why? What's happening?" Royce sounded preoccupied.

"I just got a call from Valerie. He just left the house, without telling anyone. No one has seen him for about an hour," I said recognizing my voice had become agitated.

"Calm down, Tvoya. I'm sure he's not lost. He's a thirteen year old boy. He can take care of himself. Maybe he just went for a walk in the neighborhood..." Royce was going on and on about how I shouldn't worry, when my door bell rang.

"Hang on Royce. Someone's at the door." I opened the door and to my surprise stood Jonathan.

"Hey, do you know how many people are wondering where you are? Come in," I said, "how did you get here, anyway? Are you all right?' I bombarded him with a barrage of questions. He only answered with, "Can I talk to you?"

"Sure. Let me just hang up from this call and call your Aunt Valerie to let her know you're here and that you're ok. You are ok?"

"Yeah, I'm cool," he responded.

I assured Royce and Valerie that Jonathan was all right and promised Valerie I would bring him back as soon as I got to the bottom of what his disappearance was all about. It secretly thrilled me to no end that he would seek me out to talk. But his family was very worried about him, and in no uncertain terms, I did let him know that. He understood, but the weight of what was on his mind was far more distressing to him than what he was putting anyone through. He was there because of Elizabeth.

"Ms. Tvoya is my mother going to die?" His question, so pure and innocent could not be answered simply. Instead of answering right away, I offered him a plate of food, leftovers of course, with something to drink, which he politely turned down.

"Jonathan, sit down," I said not sure as to where I was going to begin and certainly not knowing where this conversation would end up.

He sat down on the edge of the couch as if purposely denying himself comfort. I could tell he was awfully uncomfortable. Initially, having him show up at my door unannounced suggested to me because I was his mother, he would seek me out for some comfort. However, I began to realize his sudden appearance had nothing to do with that and everything to do with my giving him a Bible which suggested to him I was the only one he could come to about this.

"Only God knows for sure, when your mother will die. But I believe God wants to heal her and give her a little more time to live."

"But she won't listen to anyone but Ms. Morana,"

Jonathan said putting an emphasis of disdain when he said this name.

"Did you have a talk with Ms. Morana?" I carefully asked. I didn't want to manipulate his judgment of the woman. I already had reservations of my own about her.

"Yeah, she said that my mother was dying and I had better get use to living without her!" he spat.

"Oh, is that what she said?" I was carefully picking my words being cautious of the spirit in which I said them.

"Yeah and she said something else, too."

"What else did she say?"

"She said that you wanted my mother to die so that you can take over and be my mom," he offered. Upon hearing this I felt as if someone had punched me right dead in my chest. My breath caught as if I had forgotten how to breathe. I knew there was something strange about this Morana person. What and who gave her the right to say something like that to Jonathan, and how did she even know about our situation? This was wrong! Very wrong!

"Come on, Jonathan. We're going to Aunt Valerie's to settle this mess for sure!" I was so mad I was shaking. Once we got into the car, I decided to call Royce on my cell. After hearing what Jonathan had just told me and sensing that I was fighting mad, Royce told me to sit tight and not drive over there. He said he would come and get Jonathan and me and we would go together to handle this. He asked that I pass the phone to Jonathan. I only heard 'all rights' and 'oks' repeated by Jonathan answering Royce's requests.

When they were finished talking, Jonathan handed the phone back to me and we waited silently in my car for Royce to arrive. Royce arrived quicker than I'd expected. We all changed seats and with Royce taking the wheel, we were off to get to the bottom of this. When we arrived, Valerie answered the door informing us that Elizabeth was now aware that Jonathan had gone to my house.

"Your parents want to see you now, Jonathan!" Valerie chided as we all walked in.

"Wait, Valerie. I need to see Elizabeth first," I said stepping in front of Jonathan. Valerie looked to Jonathan then to me. Royce then spoke up.

"Val, Elizabeth needs to hear something from Tvoya, before Jonathan gets chastised. I'll explain what's going on while they talk."

"All right. Go on up, T," Valerie resigned.

I walked up the stairs expecting to find Morana also in the room with Elizabeth and Gary since she seemed to have so much input of late into their lives. To the contrary, she wasn't there. Hopefully, I could speak to them both about what Jonathan shared with me, before she would have an opportunity to sway them, as it was becoming apparent this was what she had been doing.

"Guys, Royce and I just brought Jonathan back. But, he's really upset at something your nurse, Morana, said to him," I began swiftly. Not allowing them to ask for Jonathan.

"Oh? And what was that?" Gary asked. I ensued in telling them what Jonathan had told me.

"Well, Freshmeat, that *is* the plan," Elizabeth said weakly managing a touch of sarcasm to seep through.

"Whose plan, Elizabeth?" I pleaded. "Don't you see that this is not God's will? Your son is crying out for help because he wants you to live. He doesn't want me for his mother at your expense. Stop fighting to die and start fighting to live. My God, Elizabeth!"

By this point, my voice had raised to a level, whereby everyone in the house had heard me; and now Valerie was calling up to us, while running up the flight of stairs reaching Elizabeth's doorway.

"Is everything all right up here?" Valerie huffed as she

entered the room.

"Tvoya's just trying to get Elizabeth to see what her giving up is doing to Jonathan," Gary answered, then asked, "Valerie, is Morana downstairs?"

"No, she left a little while before Jonathan got back; said something about running an errand."

"Well, I'm calling the medical service as well as Elizabeth's doctor. I don't want her back here," Gary announced.

"I don't blame you. Royce told me what she said to Jonathan," Valerie admitted.

"What has she been talking to you about?" I asked an exhaustingly looking Elizabeth. I could only imagine the toll all of this was having on her. I felt bad asking her to explain to us what Morana had been filling her head with. But my curiosity was getting the better of me and I wanted to try to undo what hopelessness this woman evidently was attempting to put on Elizabeth.

"She's only been preparing me," Elizabeth said. Her breath sounding very labored.

"Tvoya, let's just let Elizabeth rest. Now that Jonathan is back and he's ok...," Gary was saying as I cut him off.

"But Jonathan is not ok. He needs to know that his mother is going to fight, and she can do that by going to the healing service tomorrow." I could feel I was bordering on being annoying but it didn't matter. Elizabeth had to agree to go before I would even think of leaving that room.

"All right, all right, I'll go. Now will you all go and send Jonathan up," Elizabeth said, more out of desperation to get me off her back than anything else. And for now that was good enough for me.

43

"We Are All Gathered Together, To Witness"

hat if she's changed her mind?" Royce was now asking as he opened the car door for me to get out. Always the gentleman.

"No, I spoke with Valerie earlier this morning. Elizabeth is coming. After she agreed last night to going, I knew she wouldn't bail. If Elizabeth says she's gonna do something, then she's gonna do it."

"Right," Royce answered. We were thinking the same thought...that Elizabeth had agreed to raise our son 13 years ago. And that was an assured promise for sure.

Royce and I entered the church and were met by my mother and her sisters.

"Are they here, yet?" I asked looking around for Elizabeth and the gang.

"No sign of them yet," my mother offered.

"Don't worry, chile," Aunt Marilyn interjected, adding comfort, "I'm sure they're on their way."

"Well, they better come on. The service is getting ready to start," Aunt Lulu announced.

Royce walked out from the atrium back onto the steps to take a look out. He peeked his head in announcing, "Here they are. I'm gonna help them bring Elizabeth up the steps."

My mother rushed to the door and peeked her head out.

"Tvoya, is that him?" She asked her voice shaking. I went to stand next to her.

"Yes, Mommy. That's him. That's Jonathan, your grandson."

Once everyone was in the atrium and Elizabeth was comfortable in her wheelchair, the greetings were exchanged. I took my mother by the hand as I introduced her to her grandson.

"Mommy, this is Jonathan…Jonathan, my mother, Yvonne."

"Hi, Ma'am," Jonathan politely grinned and offered his hand.

"I don't want that hand. You better give me a hug, I'm your grandmother," my mother insisted, pulling him toward her. After their embrace, she started to cry.

"Oh, Yvonne, look at you. You're making that boy all uncomfortable and such," Aunt Marilyn was saying as we all began to file into the sanctuary.

We were then met by Sister Washington, head of the usher board who led us to a section that was reserved just for our crowd. A crowd of eleven. Valerie, Lamar, Elizabeth, Elizabeth's new nurse, Gary, Jonathan, Mommy, Royce, my aunts and me. Upon returning home the night before, I took the liberty of calling Margo so she could arrange for us all to be together as well as to accommodate Elizabeth's frailty. I was glad to see that Gary followed through in getting a new nurse for Elizabeth. Her countenance and demeanor was worlds away from that of Morana's. I thought Valerie was messing with me for sure when she introduced her as "Faith."

"You're kiddin', right?" I asked hesitantly.

"No, that's really her name," Valerie said with a chuckle. "Weird, huh?"

It wasn't weird and definitely no joke. God's sense of humor was right on point. I looked down the aisle at Elizabeth. At first, I thought either my eyes were playing tricks on me or it was wishful thinking, but Elizabeth did appear to be showing signs of improvement already. Somehow, on this Sunday morning she didn't look as frail and tired as she had been looking the last few times I had seen her. There was something different about her. Like an aura of expectancy surrounding her, and I was grateful for its covering.

Shortly after we had settled, the processional of the liturgical dancers, the choir, ministers and Pastor followed the cross down the center aisle of our church. Pastor then took his place behind the pulpit to proclaim, "This is the day that the Lord has made. Let us rejoice and be glad in it." The choir singing all the while slowed the tempo from, "We've Come This Far By Faith", into "His Eye Is On The Sparrow" and at that moment, I knew that nothing in my life would be the same ever again. God was revealing himself in such a way that I wanted to just take off running around the sanctuary, like I've seen so many in the past do, but never understood why, until then.

Several times during the service, I would take peeks down our row to see how Elizabeth was faring. Royce and I headed the row, while Elizabeth and Jonathan were at the end, the four of us serving as bookends with everyone else in the middle. I wasn't quite sure how we ended up this way, since I had wanted to sit closer to Elizabeth but she had to be on the end due to her wheelchair. Nevertheless, they were at church and I wasn't going to complain.

Soon it was time to hear the preached Word of God, delivered by none other than the Reverend Sapphire Pierce-Vertrell. Her message this time was executed much differently than the last time she came to speak at our church. This time her method was in the aspect of teaching. The topic was of course healing and Reverend Pierce-Vertrell prefaced it with how important it was for God's people to understand and accept that it was definitely God's desire for his people to be healed and be made whole. We were taught from the text in the Bible of the woman with the issue of blood and how she knew how important it was for her to get to Jesus. We were taken on a journey that began with what God desires to do for us, to how we need to add our faith ending up with our being made whole.

"We have not 'cause we ask not," Rev. Pierce-Vertrell was saying, "I implore you to ask God for your healing, believing that you will be healed because that is His desire." That was the altar call and the response was overwhelming. I glanced down the aisle to see if Elizabeth had taken her cue, but my eyesight was blocked by Jonathan who along with Gary was already in position assisting her down the aisle. I looked to Royce who took my hand in his and held it tightly. We smiled. Tears stung my eyes as Royce and I stood to our feet to get a better look. In spite of the altar being filled, we could still see Elizabeth. There were so many people waiting to be ministered to, that when Rev. Pierce-Vertrell was finally in front of Elizabeth, she only laid her hand briefly on her forehead and continued on to the next person. That was it?! No prophetic word, no slaying in the spirit? I wondered if Elizabeth was disappointed. I certainly was. I thought that Elizabeth was cheated until I saw her face as Jonathan wheeled her back up the aisle. Elizabeth had been touched by the power of God. I dropped Royce's hand and excused my way to the end of the aisle to await Elizabeth's return. When she arrived, I knelt down to embrace her. She reached up and grabbed my face with both her hands and declared, "I'm healed, Tvoya! I am healed!"

44

"As Long As We All Shall Live"

*J*onathan, Royce and I stood outside Valerie's house waiting for Gary to bring the last of Elizabeth's things out to the car. It had been three weeks since our experience at the healing service, and as we waited, I reflected on what we all had gone through and how so very much had changed.

As instructed by Rev. Pierce-Vertrell just before the benediction, Elizabeth went to the doctor the very next day. A variety of tests was run at Elizabeth's request that gave testimony to the glory of God that Elizabeth had in fact been healed. Thoroughly and completely. The cancer was gone. Even the naysayers with their false viewpoints were silenced and given a new perspective on the ability and will of God. He is a healer, and He is able.

Since the healing service, Valerie's whole family has given their lives to the Lord, and even my mother's faith has been renewed. She no longer doubts the Lord's will and ability to see all of his children be made whole.

"Hey, Freshmeat, take good care of our boy now," Elizabeth yelled out to me as she walked down the driveway.

I looked to Jonathan before responding, "I will, I promise." He smiled at us both before calling out to Royce asking him what happened to the burger he had promised him earlier. Elizabeth and I laughed.

"Are you sure you're ready for him staying with you? He'll probably eat you out of house and home," Elizabeth teased.

"I'm looking forward to it," I replied, not really knowing full well what I was signing myself up for. But willingly and without the right of making a fuss, I was embarking on the most rewarding journey of my life.

It was agreed upon by Elizabeth, Gary, and myself with Royce's blessing and Jonathan's consent that he stay with me for awhile. Since I am an educator in the community's school district, it would be easy to enroll Jonathan before the school term began. We all felt that before the real teenage years set in, and short of Jonathan going to college, this would be the best time for me and him to bond. Of course, Royce would be close by and definitely ingratiated into his life as well. While Elizabeth teased that with Jonathan's staying with me would allow for her and Gary to take a second honeymoon, I knew better. She would be missing him, tremendously. Nevertheless, we all realized this change would be a good one for Jonathan.

Valerie, Lamar and Poetry were now making their way down the driveway. "Well, I guess this is it, Sis," Valerie said as she embraced Elizabeth.

"Yeah, we're 'bout ready to roll. But first I want to thank you all again," Elizabeth said, "I know that I wasn't easy to deal with while I was dwelling in my illness." She then turned to me, "And Tvoya, I can't thank you enough for believing for me, when I didn't have sense enough to believe God for myself." Elizabeth and I then embraced one another tightly and cried.

Everyone stood in line to give Elizabeth one last hug.
Then it was Jonathan's turn. "Be good, Mom," he said. We
all laughed that he would say this to her and not the other
way around as Elizabeth gently swatted his behind. All the
goodbyes were said and Elizabeth and Gary got on their way.

"Let's go get that burger," Royce said as he air punched at
Jonathan then gently pulling him in by yoking his arm
around Jonathan's neck. We in turn said our goodbyes to
Valerie, Lamar and Poetry.

As I sat in the back seat watching and listening to Royce
and Jonathan, I silently began to thank God for all that He
had brought me to and through. There were certainly new
challenges awaiting me, and definitely, there were things that
still needed to be resolved between my mother, father,
Royce, Jonathan and me. Things that I wasn't quite fully
confident of. However, I was confident in the God I serve
and in the fact that all things were put together by Him, for
my good.

EPILOGUE

"And My Beloved is Mine"

(Two Years Later)

"Tvoya, she's so beautiful," Royce was saying as he kissed my forehead. I smiled weakly. I felt as if I could sleep for days, and not fully knowing what would be entailed in the days to come, I should have.

"Is mother ready to bond with baby?" The nurse said carrying in our bundle of joy.

I was still groggy from delivering by cesarean section but I was ready to be introduced to Amanda Joy Strickland. The nurse placed her in my arms while Royce moved to sit on the opposite side of me. I looked down at little Amanda and marveled at how Royce was so right. She was so very beautiful.

"Can we come in?" Elizabeth's knock preceded her question. Royce waved the gang in. My mother, Elizabeth, Gary, Valerie, Lamar, Poetry and Jonathan all filed in.

"Elizabeth!" I remarked surprised to see her and Gary. They had been traveling on and off for the past two years, thanks to my inheritance. Our temporary arrangement concerning Jonathan became more permanent, due to Royce and I getting married a year ago. I was able to be married in my own church with my own pastor presiding. Without my beliefs or wishes compromised, the ceremony was simple but so very beautiful. Jonathan was Royce's best man, Valerie my matron of honor, void Charlene and Priscilla who were in attendance but not part of the wedding party. Elizabeth and Gary could not be there due to their extensive travel itinerary. They were missed, but it was understood for our plans were made quickly and without the fanfare of a big wedding.

"When Valerie told me the baby was due any day, Gary and I cut our trip short and came right to New York," Elizabeth said as she hugged Royce making her way over to me. "It was bad enough we missed the wedding. We surely weren't going to miss the arrival of Miss Amanda Joy," Elizabeth added as she warmly smiled down at me and the baby.

"Hey, Jon, come and meet your sister," Royce said getting up to put his arm around Jonathan's shoulder. Jonathan kissed me on the cheek before beaming down at his sister.

As everyone made small talk and goggled over Amanda Joy, I thought back to how we had all came to this place in our lives. Hindsight is truly 20-20 vision, but having faith in God gives us a glimpse of what hope can bring. Trusting God is better than going through life blindly, having only our own instincts to follow. I've learned that on our own, we don't have a clue or much of a chance.

My mother is learning this also, as she recently entered a new relationship. Nice guy, too. I wish them well. She has a newfound respect for Royce and has expressed remorse over her part in my having to give Jonathan up for adoption. She's also working at being more than just civil with my father and Faye.

Jonathan and I have had our share of the 'getting to know you' ups and downs. He's a very intelligent boy who appreciates the guidance of God. What a blessing that is! Royce is crazy about him and he returns the opinion. Jonathan told me just the other day that he's doubly blessed.

True that!

Royce and I…well, neither of us were very surprised by our flourished romance. And no one else was either for that matter. I realized I'd never stop loving him in the first place. I've since forgiven Mr. Strickland for his part in keeping us from one another. But as Royce from time to time reminds me… 'no weapon formed against us shall prosper'.

"Mama T, she's so tiny." Jonathan's remark of his sister quickly brought me back to the present.

"Here, hold her," I said as I motioned to Royce to make the transfer. Royce carefully took Amanda as Jonathan sat on the side of my bed. When he was settled, Royce placed her in his arms. Then Royce stood behind him to keep them steady.

"Oh, what a beautiful picture," my mother said tearing up.

"Who has a camera?" Valerie asked looking to Lamar.

"I do!" Elizabeth offered passing the camera to Gary to take the picture. "Courtesy of our recent trip."

"Say cheese!" Gary called out. I looked to Jonathan, then to Royce. The three of us thinking the same thing turned to the camera and said, "Jesus!"

Amen!

About The Author

Pamela R. Jeffers gives all the glory and honor to her Lord & Savior, Jesus Christ. She is the Editor In Chief of CQ Christian Quarterly Magazine and the CEO of her own publishing company, Harvest Time Inner-vations LLC. Ms. Jeffers resides in Somerset, New Jersey with her husband and two daughters.

Because we are charged by the Great Commission to go and make disciples of all nations, we are committed to ensuring that we include "The Prayer of Salvation" on all our publications. If you want to be saved and have Jesus be the Lord of your life say this little prayer and you will be saved.

"Father God, I humbly come to you acknowledging that I am a sinner and I now repent of my sins. Lord Jesus, come into my heart and forgive me of my sins. Wash me in your blood and make me clean. Baptize me with your Holy Spirit and teach me how to honor you and give glory to your name. I receive you by faith as my Lord and Savior and I thank you for receiving me. In Jesus Name, Amen."

If you said this prayer, you are saved and we welcome you to the Kingdom of God. Please find a good Bible believing church where you can be taught the Word of God. We would love for you to share your experience. Please send us a testimony to *harvesttimeinnv@gmail.com*